WEAVERS

For information contact :

John Walker

https://www.walkerwritesnovels.com

Cover design by Kenji Uchima or @mkuchima

ISBN: 9798664399738

First Edition: Month 2020

10 9 8 7 6 5 4 3 2 1

WEAVERS

Weavers Book One

John Walker

SIGN UP FOR THE MONTHLY NEWSLETTER

TO RECEIVE SPECIAL OFFERS, GIVEAWAYS, DISCOUNTS, BONUS CONTENT AND MORE:

WWW.WALKERWRITESNOVELS.COM

Prologue

THE CHAIN LINK FENCE rattled as the two girls hopped onto it and launched themselves over. Their heavy boots hitting the dry grass. They took off across the lawn, their dark clothes keeping them like shadows as they made their way toward the auditorium.

The dry Texas summer air was broken as a cool breeze washed over them. Magdalena stopped and closed her eyes, feeling the relief from the heat. Her long black hair hung loose and rustled around her in the breeze.

"Imagine doing this all the time. Feeling this," she said to her friend who stood a couple of feet ahead of her, unaware at Magdalena's sudden stop.

Her friend sighed and walked back; Tanya waved her hand in sarcastic circles as if in awe.

"Oh yes, let me blow air, how exciting," she said in a hushed tone. Then she closed her hands and grew serious, her black gloves stretched across her fist.

"Now fire, THAT is exciting." She grinned, fixing her knitted cap back over her hair as the wind jostled it out of place. She had black hair like Magdalena but chose to color it with deep magenta stripes and pulled back into a bun to keep it under her hat.

Magdalena shook her head sympathetically at her friend.

"I wish it was that simple, Tanya. But air is freedom, and I could use some of that."

Tanya continued toward the building, not wanting to wade into Magdalena's sob story. Not waiting to see if she was being followed, she coyly looked back at Magdalena over her shoulder and whispered,

"Well Maggie, only one way to find out."

The girls crossed into the shadow of the large auditorium. It was built a couple of years ago as Rockwell's center for political meetings, the occasional county play, and to host the yearly Attunement Ceremony.

It took on a more traditional neoclassical design to pay homage to old-school political buildings like in Washington, D.C. It contrasted with the surrounding buildings of brick most establishments and homes in Texas employed. It was seen as a thing of pride for the city. They were quickly growing, and it was even rumored that it would hold the Attunement of multiple cities next year.

Magdalena flashed her light into the dark hallways through the glass doors. A click issued from the lock as Tanya pulled back two pieces of metal and opened the door smiling broadly. Gesturing with her hand and a mock bow for Magdalena to enter first.

Magdalena shook her head and walked in. "I can't believe you actually picked the lock."

Tanya brushed off her shoulders vainly, but admitted, "It really wasn't that big a deal. Places like these don't hold anything important to securely lock it down. Plus, it's Rockwell, not exactly a hub for dangerous activity."

Magdalena's light flashed over plaques and trophy cases. They showed the history of Rockwell, transferred from any of the schools and town halls after the creation of the auditorium. Sports accolades and trophies in cases, notable people like politicians and leaders had their pictures hung on the walls. Normally this was all there was to see, but now banners and signs were placed all along the halls. That weekend it would host the Attunement, where kids going into their freshman year of High School would come and learn what their true affinity was.

Tanya stopped suddenly and grabbed Magdalena's arm with the flashlight and pulled it down. Magdalena was about to object but followed Tanya's eyes far down a branching hallway and saw a light on. It looked to be the janitorial closet. Shadows were cast as someone inside moved.

"Should we go?" Magdalena whispered.

Tanya grew a playful grin. "It's just a janitor. We'll be in and out before they know we're here," she continued confidently.

The girls swung open the doors and looked out across the seating in the auditorium. Tanya strolled in, and Magdalena had to grab the door she dramatically left swinging to make sure it didn't slam. Sighing, she went to stand next to Tanya and waved her flashlight throughout the auditorium. Magdalena's light finally rested on the stage, and at its center was a long table with four large bowls placed on top.

Tanya gave her a wicked grin and sprinted down the steps, jumping up to the stage. Magdalena followed hesitantly, growing nervous as if she only now realized what she was about to do.

By the time she reached the stage, Tanya was already lighting a fire within a bowl that contained wood. She then grabbed a bottle of water from beneath the table and poured it into an empty bowl. The other two didn't need any modifying. One contained small stones and dirt. The last bowl was rigged with small fans planted in it to create a current of air that rotated around the bowl, small bits of glitter and baby feathers were inside. Tanya turned it on, spinning its contents around, but they remained within. Magdalena's eyes rested on this one the longest.

Kids growing up could do little bursts of all four of the elements, but it wasn't until this moment they could learn what they could truly excel at and train to use their element effectively.

Magdalena began to say, "Who should–"

"I'll go first!" Tanya interrupted.

Magdalena stood back as Tanya paced in front of the table, rubbing her hands together in glee. Weavers controlled the elements by infusing their own essence into the natural energies of the elements. It's almost completely inherent and doesn't require too much focus especially after a few months of practice, but the strongest way to test the connection is blood.

Tanya pulled out a pocketknife and flipped it open. With dramatic flair she took off her glove and drew a thin line across her hand. She walked over to the bowl swirling with glitter and small feathers. She made a sound of disgust,

"Might as well get this over with." She let the blood drop down into the bowl, closed her eyes, and held her hand open.

Nothing happened as the blood slowly streaked along the sides. Tanya snapped her eyes opened and giggled moving on.

"Pft, you probably didn't even try that hard," Magdalena said under her breath, rolling her eyes.

Tanya did the same with the bowl of water, her blood dripped down into it, but only made ripples and then settled again.

Tanya then came to the burning wood in the third bowl. She squeezed her blood in and held out her hand. A breath later and fire leaped out of the bowl and spun around her hand.

Magdalena started forward as Tanya let out a screech. At first Magdalena thought it was of fear or pain, but then she saw Tanya balancing the fire in her hands, the flame igniting her reflective eyes with an orange glow.

"I knew it," she whispered to herself. She stepped away from the table still staring at the fire.

Without a word Magdalena stepped up and took her turn. She cut her own hand, wincing as the blood trailed down her arm. She did earth, water, and fire first. Her heart lightened and hope spread through her. She knew it was ridiculous to be nervous now, but she couldn't be sure until she was sure.

She went to the air bowl and dropped in her blood, held out her hand and was still. A breath passed, then two, three, a whole minute later. To Magdalena it felt like an eternity, but nothing happened.

Tanya finally pulled her eyes away from her fire realizing what happened. Her brow furrowed.

"That can't be right, I've known you for years, I've seen you Weave. Try harder," she encouraged.

Magdalena gulped looking down at the air bowl as her blood simply made slow laps around, streaking into Tanya's. She stepped back so she was centered in front of all the bowls. She closed her eyes and focused. She pushed herself to feel the elements, to link with them. Something began to stir within her, she began to tingle.

This must be it, she thought. She pushed with all her might, to ignite that spark inside. The room seemed to fill with energy, Tanya's hair stood up on end, and a scent of ozone spread.

A flash and crack of light struck out in front of Magdalena. Lightning exploded the Attunement table; pieces of it and the stage flew out into the seating.

Magdalena's eyes widened, quickly pulling back her hand to her chest as if she was harmed. Then she looked down out her hands as electricity trailed along her arm tracing her veins.

Tanya's ball of fire dropped from her hand disappearing in a puff, now seeming very dwarfed by what Magdalena just did.

"Maggie...you-...you're an Anoma-"

"DON'T SAY IT!" she cried before Tanya could finish the words. Fear spread through her like the lightning she just created.

Terror was in her eyes, and she managed to meet Tanya's whose were more akin to excitement, awe, and yes, even a little fear.

Magdalena's phone vibrated, her hands shaking she pulled it out of her pocket and looked at the image of a sweet smiling boy looking at the camera. *Matty*, was scrolled along the top.

Her stomach plummeted, her fear crescendoed, and an arc of electricity flashed down her hand cracking and frying her phone. She yelped and dropped it, staring down at the broken black screen, with nothing but her fearful eyes looking back up at her.

Without a word she ran from the stage and out the emergency exit into the accusing moonlight. Tanya moved to follow, but at the door looked back at the stage. The lightning had started fires that licked across the stage and seating. She looked down at her hands realizing what power she now had.

With a last glint of fire in her eyes she walked out, the door slamming behind her, leaving the building to burn.

Weeks Later - Brazil

A figure looked down upon the famous layered city. He stood with his hands behind his back, clothes flapping in the wind. The large statue of Christ the Redeemer towered above him watching over the city.

The figure looked up and smiled. "What does your watchfulness do here, god?" he drolled.

He turned back to the rising cinders and smoke as the city burned. Lava flowed unnaturally through the city streets. The figure was too far away to hear the screams, but he could imagine.

He felt a wrong was being righted, that every person snuffed out worked to balance the scales.

He dug into his pocket as his phone vibrated. Pulling it out and looking at the message:

Possible Target Located - Houston, Texas. United States

He hummed in thought, his eyes washing over the destruction of the city below. Someone approached from behind.

"Sir," the arrival announced himself.

"Yes?" Replied the figure.

"Most of the groups are pulling out now, but the Anomaly won't make it out. Not without help. He's too far in, and Elemental Marines have arrived."

The figure began walking away from the new arrival and the city.

"I have a new matter to attend to. Leave him."

"Wh-what?" The other managed to choke out. "But shouldn't we-" he was cut off as a burst of energy flew from the figure, almost knocking him off the cliff.

The figure barely turned but emanated annoyance and impatience.

"I said, *Leave Him.*"

The other gulped and simply nodded.

The figure crouched low. Without another order or look, he lept into the air. Wind currents caught and carried him into the sky, disappearing into the night.

Chapter 1

One Year Later

VIN HEARD HIS MOM'S muffled call through his bathroom door. He ran one last hand through his quaffed, purposely messy hair and opened the door heading downstairs. He reached the bottom step just as one more, "VINCENZO!" echoed throughout the house. Vin clapped his hands over his ears in pretend pain.

"I'm here mother. Deaf, but I'm here," he smirked. His mother didn't return the smile but traded it for a death glare.

"I'm quite aware you're deaf. Hence, me yelling for you for the past thirty minutes. AND your cold pancakes," she lectured while stabbing her spatula toward the table.

Vin sat happily, quickly pouring syrup across the puffy cakes. "Sorry, I was just making sure I looked...ok. For today."

His dad finally looked up from his tablet, "Well I'll be. Is that my Vincent wearing a tie?" He smiled proudly.

"Yes dad, it's not that big of a deal," Vin responded, now chopping into his pancakes, turning red.

"Non e vero," his mother said, dropping her English to switch to her native Italian. "You look very handsome," she complimented while trying to pat down his hair in vain.

Her own brown thick hair pulled back matched Vin's. She was quite aware how hard it was to tame. Vin decided to accept and work with it rather than against it.

"Oh yes Vinny, very handsome," came the sarcastic voice of his older sister. Who, to Vin, unfortunately decided to join the family in the kitchen. She smiled, teasing her brother while heading to the fridge to grab more orange juice.

"You know, Juliette, you don't have to go," Vin replied, glaring. She didn't take the bait, throwing back her head in a laugh. Her long box-of-bleach locks fell back to cascade down her back, her bubblegum pink lips smirked with humor.

"Please, and miss you flunk out at the Attunement? Wouldn't dream of it."

Vin grumbled as she walked out of the room, "Anywhere with you is more like a nightmare."

With a flick of Juliette's finger, a pebble sized bit of dirt flew from the potted plant sitting on the table and smacked right into Vin's forehead.

His mother quickly placed a firm hand on his shoulder, giving him a look that deterred him from reciprocating the blow. Vin huffed and returned to his pancakes. His mother pulled a tiny stream of water from the sink faucet and gently rubbed Vin's forehead, washing off the dirt smudge.

"Don't let her get to you. You know perfectly well you're going to be attuned." Vin sighed at the encouragement, swatting away her hand.

"There's always the possibility I won't. My Weaving could just...fade." He tried to be confident, but the fear for every person of age always came.

His dad just scoffed, "Don't be silly Vincent, your mother and I are both Weavers. Our parents were first generation Weavers. It's not going to skip you." He smiled, a little smug in Vin's opinion.

"Your father's right, Vin. Our bloodline is quite strong. Though," she paused giving a quick glance to her husband, "I wouldn't mind if we evened things out here and got another Water Weaver." She walked to the large window over the kitchen sink to stare into the backyard. "It would be nice to get some help with the garden."

Vin snorted as he took his dish to the sink to rinse and dry.

"You pegged me, mom. That was my whole goal. To attune to the most appropriate element to help with chores." His mom didn't appreciate the sass and made a quick motion with her hand, flinging the water into his face before retreating to the table to sit next to her husband.

Vin patted his face with a towel. *Well, I know where Juliette gets it from*, he thought to himself.

He took a moment to stare out the window. Ivy creeped around the edges of it, creating a perfect portrait style picture to his mother's garden. She grew lots of things. Italians were nothing without spices, and his mother grew theirs fresh. Vines of tomatoes stood out from the green as bright red bulbs, purple eggplants perpendicular to the tomatoes ran down the lengths of the yard with lots of other vegetables.

She loved the garden; it made her think of home. Her parents had a large farmland in Italy. She never experienced it because they moved shortly after World War II. Many things changed after the War. People still speculate, but it was pretty obvious that after the bomb decimated Japan the world changed, and people with it. They could start controlling the elements at their whim: fire, earth, water, and air were manipulated with the simplest of motions.

Not everyone could do it. The strange ability to combine human energy into elemental energy. Weaving, as it is called. Now 70 years later people are still figuring it out.

"Mom," Vin started, turning from her garden. "Why didn't grandma and grandpa ever just rebuild their farm? Especially once they developed Weaving?"

His mother glanced up at a portrait hanging on a wall above another potted plant. It was yellowed with age and made her smile.

"There was a lot of fear after the war. I think it was too much to start over for them, at least there. America was very appealing." She looked over at her husband, he smiled at her as they grasped hands. "I'm glad they did in the end."

Vin pretended to be sickened but left the kitchen smiling.

The traffic to downtown Rockwell was terrible. Vin sat bored in the back seat of his parent's SUV. Every couple of minutes catching his reflection in the glass. His white button up, black tie, and wild brown hair. He would always straighten his tie whenever he saw it.

"If you don't stop fidgeting with your tie, I'm going to choke you with it," Juliette said coolly, not raising her head from her phone.

Vin scowled and looked back to the passing vehicles. It was especially busy today, this year, because Rockwell was hosting most of the neighboring cities. Any child entering their freshman year of high school who displayed competent ability to Weave was taking their own Attunement all across America. There would be some who had shown the ability to Weave when they were younger, but it being so weak they were tested separately.

You didn't want to gather hundreds of people just for some nervous kid to stand there as nothing happened until they were overcome with a sensation that led them to puking all over the stage.

Its why Vin should have known to be more confident. He always displayed a strong affinity to the elements, but it never works to tell a teenager not to worry about peer pressure or failing in front of one's peers.

They made a quick stop to pick up Vin's grandfather, which to Vin's dismay forced him to sit even closer to his sister.

Finally, they arrived, pulling into the parking for Rockwell's Football Stadium. Vin got out and stretched, eyeing the building across the street. Scaffolding and work crews littered the large building that was previously Rockwell's Auditorium. It had been a whole year almost to the day that it caught fire and nearly burned down.

Vin went around to the other side of the vehicle, helping his Grandfather out by holding out his arm. Juliette came up behind them, handing him his cane and giving him a quick peck on the cheek.

"Grazie, Bambini," he said to them in Italian. He took a moment to stretch himself, his old bones creaking. He sighed and exhaled with his face turned toward the sun and his arms outstretched.

"I never get tired of that summer heat," he said absently.

Out of nowhere Vin was practically tackled to the ground. Two strong arms, though, kept him up right. He was embraced in a large hug that when finally pulling away left Vin faced with his best friend's bright smile.

"Hola, mi amigo," Matt said simply, but his infectious grin was still plastered upon his face.

"Matty," Vin shook his head but eventually succumbed and adopted a matching smile. "Ciao, mi amico," Vin finally returned.

Matt turned to follow where Vin was looking before he one-man bulldozed him. He gave the remains of the auditorium a once over. Rockwell tried very hard to get it repaired within the year. It took everything the mayor and city council had to keep today from being given to a different city. When they realized it just wouldn't be done, they relocated the Attunement to the football stadium, the only other place big enough.

Matt lingered a little longer on the cross that skimmed the sidewalk in front of the auditorium. A small shrine to Eduardo Pineda, the unfortunate janitor who was trapped in the building last year. He noted fresh flowers surrounded the memorial, most likely left there after the one-year anniversary that recently took place.

"Good Morning, Mr. DeLuca," Matt said to Vin's Grandfather, though Vin didn't think his smile quite reached his eyes this time.

"Little troublemaker," Mr. DeLuca teased. Shaking his cane at Matt as he continued, "Don't think I don't know it was you that put my crap under my mattress. It took the nurses a whole week to find that! It reeked for a whole week!" Matt's eyes twinkled mischievously. He had ordered a spy pack, one of those themed monthly subscriptions. He was more curious than serious, but it had come with a little tab that when peeled would create an offensively strong odor. It was supposed to act as a distraction device, said the spy instructions, but Matt preferred it for its pranking capabilities.

Vin insisted it would have been a waste of money. Now, Matt didn't let him forget it.

"Sir? I don't know what you're talking about," Matt said, playing dumb.

"I may be old, but I can still torch your behind!" Mr. DeLuca berated, holding up a finger as a flame sparked to life.

Matt immediately jumped behind Vin for cover. Vin couldn't help but note the loss of spark in his grandfather. He used to be an extremely powerful Fire Weaver. Even when joking he'd light up his whole arm.

"Now Dad," came the voice of Vin's father who finally joined them. "Kids will be kids, remember?"

"Well, he sure won't grow into an adult if I have anything to say about it, Giovanni." The old man grumbled, but gave a playful wink to Vin, who did his best to contain his smirk.

Vin's mother came up next to his father, wrapping her arm around his. "Go on guys, before we have to tell Matt's parents why he won't be attending the Attunement." She smiled sweetly. "Look for us in the stands."

"Come on, you won't believe some of the stuff here," Matt said, pulling on Vin and escaping from the old Fire Weaver into the crowd.

Chapter 2

V IN AND MATT MANEUVERED through the crowds. It wasn't just families of Weavers that were here. They saw city officials, military recruiters, even foreign dignitaries. The last ones interested Vin the most. He thought it was interesting that people from other countries would visit for Weaver ceremonies.

He looked to Matt, wearing similar clothes to himself. Black slacks and a white button up, though his fitted slightly tighter at his chest and biceps.

"I knew you were working out this summer. I didn't realize how much you bulked up," Vin said, flicking his friend on the arm.

Matt smiled smugly, rubbing his arm. "I might as well get started; Earth Weavers are notorious for strength work outs. I really doubt I'll end up with anything else with both my mom and dad being Earth Weavers."

Vin didn't respond at first, looking out into the crowd, not focusing on anything in particular. Matt took this as a moment in need of encouragement, elbowing Vin.

"You should have bulked up with me. There's a fifty-fifty shot you'll be like me!"

This got a chuckle out of Vin. "If there was a chance I'd end up like you, I think I'd dread this even more than I already do. If that's even possible."

Matt snorted a laugh. "If only you could be so lucky."

As they walked by a group Vin and Matt recognized, Matt's hand shot out and snatched something out of one of the other students' hands. The kid looked bewildered for a moment until he saw Matt and Vin walking away.

"Mateo! Ass! Give that back!" he called. Mateo kept walking and opened the booklet with absolutely no intention of giving back.

"Bite me, Aaron. You owe me since you broke my bike," Matt replied over his shoulder.

"That was like the third-grade, dude!" Aaron tried, but Matt and Vin were already swallowed by the crowd. Vin shook his head,

"You know, these are being passed out everywhere," he offered. Matt just gave him a look of incredulity. Ignoring Vin's attempt at reason, he shoved the page he was reading into his hands, pointing at the two columns.

"See. Even if you are a Water Weaver, a lot of our classes would still line up," Matt said.

Vin looked through both columns. The whole booklet was information on their future. Depending on your attunement, it reflected which classes and courses you would get. Each element afforded different fighting styles or life courses. Earth and Water had more classes geared toward nature, plant life, and such. Fire, being clearly the most dangerous of the four elements, had classes on control. It was also one of the most useful elements to assist with natural disasters. Though they are uncommon, disasters involving fire were usually the most detrimental, so their Weavers were important.

Vin turned to the page regarding Disaster Relief. This was the most common use of Weavers, what every one of them were trained for. If one didn't have the slightest idea of what they wanted to do, it was straight to Disaster Relief. Vin skimmed the pages; it showed a nice handy picture in case anyone didn't know what a tornado or volcano looked like. It listed which element helped with that disaster. Air was on all of them. They could be used for every occasion. Forest fire? Suffocate the fire. Volcano? Route the gases and clouds safely. Earthquake? Provide sight from above and get stranded people out of tough situations.

Vin flipped back to the page with the classes. Air was stuffed, learning protocol for all disasters, leadership classes since they were expected to give orders, strategy for both natural and human disasters, like war and criminals. This drew him to the page on the military. Enlisting was already being promoted and any Weaver is useful.

Vin began to stay a bit farther away from the men in uniform now. Letting out a breath, he sighed as if weighed down by all the decisions he would have to make. Some being forced onto him.

"Dang, we're only 15 years old, and I feel like we're already being shipped off to battle nations and hurricanes!" Vin worried, but Matt kept his optimism.

"I wouldn't worry about it unless you're an Air Weaver. They get drafted for Relief all the time. There's never enough of them. My dad feels like he's always requesting one."

Matt's dad was a police officer, on the force for all of Matt's life.

"Speaking of which," Vin returned, "how is he? Any better?"

Matt just shook his head, losing some of the pep in his step. "No, this past year he's been so weird. I thought maybe he was getting in trouble, but the other officers and higher ups are always trying to get us to go out to functions and stuff like we used to. But my dad always makes up excuses not to go. It just hasn't been the same since..." He didn't have to say, Vin knew exactly what happened a year ago.

Vin stopped Matt, turning to face him. Matt wouldn't meet his eyes at first. "Look man, I know it's been a year since she ran away, but I don't think-" He was cut off as someone called Matt's name. Matt looked over Vin's shoulder to see his mom and dad. His dad was uncharacteristically not wearing his uniform. Even off duty officers wore them to events like this. His mother smiled sweetly and waved at Vin.

"Hello Vin," she said in her Mexican accent. Vin returned the wave.

Then Matt took Vin's hands off his shoulders. "Thanks Vin. I know, buddy. I'll see you out there." He walked away. Vin calling after him,

"Good...luck?" What else does one say to a heartbroken friend who lost a family member a year ago and now has to pretend they're happy? He thought about Magdalena for a moment. He missed her. She was a lot nicer than his sister most of the time.

He took a look at the booklet again, soldiers staring up at him saluting from the pages. He scoffed and tossed it into the garbage. Giving the area a look around, families and attendees were starting to head inside. He watched military men, politicians, tribesmen all shuffle by him to take their seats. He thought they were interesting; he's heard of rituals in other countries. They were more primal, really connecting to the elements to find their attunement. Theirs similar but definitely not as archaic. Vin imagined him dancing in circles in the dirt, his sister's gaudy oversized gold bracelets dangling from his wrists and arms as he chanted. Covering himself in paint that he just bought from the nearest Hobby Lobby.

It took him a moment to realize someone was standing nearby, also watching the crowd. He was bald with markings on his face, he seemed humble and wore long robes. He looked like a monk, someone from very far away mountain peaks. The man looked over at Vin and held his gaze. It didn't seem unkind, but Vin stood a little straighter, like he was being analyzed. After an awkward second, Vin raised his hand to give a little wave. The monk returned it with a curt nod.

"Your people are heading in. You're not joining them?" he asked Vin. His voice was soft and stern, but Vin breathed with relief that he spoke English. Vin ended up walking a little closer.

"I will be, I'm just…nervous." The monk just went back to looking at the crowds, nodding like he understood, which Vin seriously doubted.

"How does this all work where you come from?" Vin asked, trying to distract his nerves.

The monk thought for a moment then replied calmly. "We don't have this," he said, gesturing to the crowds around. "The elements are more…sacred to us, and personal." This comment made Vin blush, it was a pretty broad generalization about him and his culture. He thought about the booklet, the classes, and the expectations and admitted he couldn't fault the monk.

He continued, "We don't have these ceremonies of Attunement, we just let the elements find us. Instead of hunting them."

Vin tilted his head in thought. "The elements find you?"

The monk nodded then lifted his hand as a spark of fire wrapped around and then concentrated in his hand.

"Your people know the basic definition. Human energy, Weaving into

Elemental energy. But you don't give this thought. These energies can be felt, like airwaves, they ebb and flow like a living thing. It's not just fire, rock, water, and wind. That's like pointing at someone and just saying, person. The elements are deeper than this, layered. You can't just look at what's in front of you. You have to see all the details, all the smallest parts."

Vin didn't completely comprehend what he was saying. But truthfully, he didn't really think that the man expected Vin to.

"I appreciate…and respect you trying to tell me." He looked down, slightly ashamed, "I wish I could understand." This got a reaction out of the monk momentarily before smoothing out his features again.

"Well, that is the first step. Most do not care to listen to the elements. You do that and my words will not have been in vain." He gave Vin another look then gestured toward the stadium.

"Go on then, it's your time to listen to the elements." Vin could tell their conversation was done, and he was late. Not looking back, he dashed into the stadium to take his place with the rest of the students, nervously waiting to find their future.

Chapter 3

"VINCENZO DELUCA," Vin offered to the bored looking man in the lab coat behind the check-in booth. He held out his hand for an ID, and Vin provided it. After a couple of seconds, the man handed Vin a white cylinder about the size of a syringe. It might as well have been.

Vin nodded, smiled, and said thanks. The man gave no indication he heard it and just called, "Next."

Vin walked off to follow the line of other students.

Couldn't they get someone a bit more cheerful? This is one of the most exciting times of our lives and this robot is giving us the key to our future.

Vin chided himself after this thought. That was a bit dramatic, but the sentiment stood. He continued to follow along with the line. There was no specific spot he needed to be in. There were far too many people for them to care to organize or alphabetize.

The speakers throughout the stadium and in halls reverberated with the voice of Rockwell's mayor. He gave the guests a greeting, almost made a joke about the heat but decided to steer clear as if not mentioning it would magically make the high temperature go away. He then, with great vigor, announced the Attunement Ceremony would begin.

It took Vin about ten minutes before he even left the hallways and entered onto the field. A massive crowd greeted him, stands almost completely filled except for one section which was color coded for the student Weavers to separate into after they attuned.

The large stage stood directly in the middle of the field. It was set up with the normal attunement tables, times four this year to account for the large number of participants.

Vin's phone vibrated in his pocket and he checked it. A text from Matt just came in. It told him to look toward the front of the line. Vin obliged, tracing his eyes along the students until he saw his best friend and his messy black curls, which were already starting to slick with sweat.

He nodded to Matt, who returned with a wink and smile, sticking his tongue out the side of his mouth. Which reminded Vin of an energetic puppy.

When it was Matt's turn, he slicked back his hair from his face and strode up to one of the tables. The earth bowl was first, which Vin was sure Matt would be fine with. Most likely he would have skipped right to it anyway.

He pulled out the white cylindrical cartridge, held it out over the rocks, and clicked. A large drop of blood plopped on and into the bowl. Matt closed his eyes, held out his hand, and to no one's surprise that knew Matt, a stream of dirt and rocks swirled out and curled around his arm. He smiled, shot Vin another wink, and with an unnecessary flourish sent the earth back to its bowl.

He hopped off the stage after depositing his blood cartridge into a biohazard box, whooping and pumping his fist as he sat in the stands with the other attuned Earth Weavers.

Though now that distraction was over, Vin grew nervous again.

Vin assumed that when he got on the stage he'd be overwhelmed by the cacophony of noise. He was surprised to feel as if the world went completely silent and still, holding its breath for Vin's precious minute.

He made his way to one of the tables, pulled out his blood cartridge and clicked it over the first bowl. The blood splatted on the earth and dribbled down into its crevices and soaked the dirt. His attention lingered a little too long on the mix of blood already in the bowl. He's had his share of scraped elbows and cuts, but the mix of his nerves and this stressful ceremony made him queasy. He stood back, held up his hand, and before he closed his eyes caught a group of bald men and women in the crowd. Vin didn't see the monk that he talked to outside, but his words now reverberated through him.

Closing his eyes, he tried to feel the element, pictured the waves like ones he would see across the pavement on the hottest of summer days. Nothing special came to him, and he realized he was standing there too long, the earth not budging. More students moved around him to and from the other tables and his stomach continued its descent into evacuation territory. Nervously he moved onto fire, dropping his blood into the open flame, it sizzled on contact. Trying again to feel the elements, for them to speak to him. He succeeded at nothing but feeling foolish.

He just had to get through air and then he'd be attuned to water, like his mother. He dropped his blood into the vortex of the air bowl. Vin thought it would be nice to attune to water. He felt more akin to it, the flow, the beautiful movements. His mother always looked so peaceful when Weaving water and working in the garden wouldn't be so bad, he thought.

In the middle of him imagining working with water, he felt something, and his eyes snapped open. His hand still hanging over the bowl of air. Closing his eyes again he felt the energy from the air, like a pulse or heartbeat. He urged his focus into it, and for the first time felt the word everyone had casually thrown around all his life. He Weaved and pulled on the air, opening his eyes again as a flood of feathers launched out of the bowl. Vin guiding them around him, the current sweeping the feathers around his arm, along his body, up and over his hand.

He's moved elements before, all children did that possess the potential to Weave. But he'd never *felt* it like this before. He hadn't realized he was smiling, and then he felt a bit self-conscious as if he was showing off. But none of this compared to his realization as he recalled the booklet. The classes, the expectations, the next four years he had imagined suddenly were utterly different.

He caught Matt's eyes in the stand, a mix of awe and a hint of disappointment. It hit him all at once, Vin dropped the connection and the feathers floated off on the uncontrolled breezes. He was an Air Weaver.

Chapter 4

3 Years and 3 Months later

VIN SHOOK HIS TOWEL over his hair. It wasn't wet, but he always did this after he dry-gelled it. He pulled the towel away to see the stylish quaffed hair he wore often, patting down any stray hairs on the sides. It wasn't as long as he used to wear it before his Attunement. He discovered very quickly after training that long hair was annoying to deal with while Air Weaving. He now had shaved sides and back with the top just long enough to style.

He grabbed his backpack and went to his computer. An image of campus pictures he was looking at last night winked out to black as he locked his computer. Heading downstairs he found his mom and dad sitting on the couch watching the news. He gave it a quick glance; it showed aerial shots of damage to a west coast city. The news caster attributing it to the work of Anomalies.

Vin went to the kitchen and grabbed a protein bar, shoving it in his bag. Then he thought for a moment and grabbed one more. Heading back to the living room, he kneeled by the front door to put his shoes on.

His dad was shaking his head as a different report came on. The weather reported a tropical storm heading for Louisiana.

"It's bad enough we have these hurricanes popping up, but now we have to deal with these Anomalies going crazy and destroying cities," he sighed. His dad looked tired, bags under his eyes. Vin wasn't even sure why he was up. He worked a late shift last night and assumed he'd be sleeping.

Vin's mother patted her husband's hand like comforting a child. "Louisiana's pretty close. You don't think they'd draft Vincenzo, do you?"

His father shook his head. "I wouldn't worry about it, Noemi. He's still new, and it's not that close." This made Vin scoff. Having finished tying his shoes, he plopped down in one of the armchairs.

"That didn't stop them from sending me off to Florida my sophomore year," Vin stated, recalling the time he was drafted. He was still so new at the time he almost got whipped away by the winds he and the other Weavers were creating. They had to have an Earth Weaver lock him into the ground.

"I almost got blown into the storm," Vin finished.

"And what a loss we would have suffered," Juliette added as she came in, still in her pajamas. Vin returned her comment with a mocking face. If he was surprised his father was up, his sister being awake might have meant hell was freezing over.

"I see you're still working hard at getting out of the house. I'm sure you'll find a good college eventually. Even Satan needs education, you know," Vin teased. Juliette returned the face and flicked her finger. A rock flew from one of the planters. Vin didn't have to move, the rock reflecting harmlessly from his face, a brief shield of air blocking it. The rock bounced off Vin's shield, hitting another vase in the room. The sound of glass cracking drew everyone's attention to the vase. His mother's eyes widened.

"Vincenzo!" she immediately scolded. Vin's mouth dropped.

"Me?" Vin stood appalled. Throwing his arms to his sisters retreating form as she left for the kitchen. "SHE started it."

"Don't give me that Vincenzo, you know better." She wagged her finger at him. Vin was left at a loss for words. Starting one sentence just to lose it and try another. In the middle of Vin looking like a guppy with his mouth fighting to defend him, as his air did, a knock at the door broke their silence but not the tension.

Saved by the bell...sort of, he thought, swinging the door open. Matt stood on the other side, looking in with a goofy grin.

"Hi Mr. and Mrs. DeLuca."

Vin snatched up his backpack he put by the door and walked out.

"Gotta go, bye," he quickly gave his parents before rushing out.

"Hey! You need to fix this!" His mother called to him.

"Get your daughter, I hear she's not that busy," Vin responded, shutting the door.

"Brutta Faccia!" she yelled in Italian through the door.

Matt looked between Vin and his house confused. "What was that about? What'd she say?"

Vin waved a passive hand at him as if it was nothing. "Just that I'm a wonderful, amazing son." This caused Matt to smirk as they got in Vin's car. Matt was dressed in a tight dri-fit workout shirt and black shorts. He was lightly covered in sweat from his run over. He no longer had to wipe his hair out of his eyes as he's had it cropped short in a Caesar style for at least a year now.

He had grown a lot thicker over the years too from all the weight training Earth Weavers performed. In contrast to Vin who may not have been as muscular and big as Matt but far leaner and toned. Air Weavers preferred to be light in order to lift themselves.

"I think you need a refresher on Italian," Matt responded to Vin's lie. Which sparked a thoughtful hmm from Vin.

"That's a great idea for an elective, speaking of which." He pulled out pages he had printed and handed them to Matt.

"You still haven't told me what you'd want to take." He started the engine on his Dodge Durango and pulled out from his house. Vin spent a good deal of the summer researching colleges. Though Matt constantly brought it up and expressed how excited he was for them to find one, he didn't particularly participate in the search.

Their summer was a pretty good return to form for them. Their first three years of high school pulled them in many directions, none of them together. Vin was happy to have Matt around again going into their senior year. He just wishes he put the work in to match his excitement at college aspects.

"I'm ready to schedule the tours," Vin continued. "But I need some kind of opinion from you." Matt gave the papers a halfhearted look then dumped them in his own bag.

"This is what you trained for, Vinny. Why else spend three years in Advanced Strategy," he said those words in a robotic tone, "if not to use it to plan our future."

"Our future is going to get a little less plural if you don't start pulling your weight," Vin snapped back.

Matt didn't lose his composure as he started to flex. "Sounds like someone is jealous of the weight I can pull around."

"Ridicolo" Vin mumbled, adopting his mother's way of insulting people in Italian.

Matt changed the subject. "Your dad was up. I thought he worked late nights now?" he asked while gazing out the window. The brief fields of Rockwell's back roads breezed by.

"He is, I think the stress doesn't help him sleep. That and I think he misses us. We're pretty much up and gone by time he's awake."

Matt made a noise of agreement but didn't add anything new. Vin looked over at his friend, trying to determine his uncommon silence. At an empty four-way intersection, he used that silence to send a quick text to his dad. In hindsight he wished he would have taken more notice as to why his dad may have been up. He wished him a good morning and told him that he loved him and to get some sleep.

"You know he's still looking for a partner," Vin said after finishing the text and locking his phone, pulling away from the stop sign. "I think if he had someone familiar it wouldn't be so bad. They can both complain about their unruly sons."

Matt broke his silence, smiling. "I think you mean bragging about the excellence that is their prodigious offspring."

Vin gave an earnest chuckle. "Or that," Vin agreed. But Matt didn't give a real answer. Vin's father worked as a Roadway Restoration Worker, which was an obnoxious way of saying he fixed Weavers' mistakes. Earth and Fire Weavers could work together to heat stone and concrete, then mold it. They usually worked streets and buildings, anything damaged by Weavers. Matt and Earth Weavers were the typical offenders. With a flick of their fingers they could turn paved roads to broken heaps of asphalt.

Vin gave Matt a couple more seconds in hopes of an answer, but it was clear this conversation was done to death. It had been three years since his father inexplicably left the force. Just a few months into their Freshman year. Since then he's always had jobs, but Matt was concerned his new work wasn't fulfilling. Bad things followed those who are unfulfilled in life.

Vin braced Matt's shoulder, who looked over. Vin gave a comforting, knowing smile to go along with his firm grip. Matt simply nodded appreciatively as if to say I know. They had almost a decade and a half of expert nonverbal communication.

Chapter 5

V IN BEGAN TO SLOW as they passed the blinking yellow light indicating the school zone. Rockwell High loomed on the approaching hill. It was a large, brick building with recently added wings that added a modern touch to it. Lots of glass windows around the building provided a view of the practice turf fields, track course, and the lake sparkling in the dawn. There was also a baseball diamond next to the overflow parking lot across the street from the main school buildings.

Matt inspected the main parking lot from the passenger side. It looked full and so did most of the overflow.

"I'd say just head for the overflow. No point in wasting hours combing the main lot," Matt suggested. Vin agreed and pulled into the overflow lot;

he could see farther down by the baseball entrance a large crowd was gathering. They parked on the farther end and got out.

Matt stripped out of his workout shirt. His long necklace fell back against his chest as he grabbed a graphic tee, stretching it over his torso covering the rock pendant. It was two cartoon characters speaking to one another. One representing an Earth Weaver telling the other *Of course, I'm Shook* while his body looked like it was quivering.

Matt threw his gym bag back in the Durango and then looked sheepishly as he asked, "Hey, Vin do you have-" Vin tossed him a stick of spray deodorant before he could even finish. Matt saluted him before spraying it on. When handing the deodorant back, Vin traded it for his second protein bar. Matt's eyes immediately lit up.

"You're too good to me." He said lovingly.

"Tell me about it."

They began making their way toward the crosswalk, which was toward the entrance of the baseball diamond and the large group of students. Matt nodded to the crowd as they walked.

"I'm betting Joey Grace is trying to put his whole fist in his mouth again."

Vin raised an eyebrow, judging that they were a little too old for such bets. Vin was often seen as the serious type, but Matt had a way to break through all of that. Vin smirked and replied,

"Definitely Madison Weber eating fire again." Matt's eyes brightened with the memory.

"That was so cool. I didn't know she'd be returning so soon. I thought she was still in Houston getting treated."

Vin's postured slackened. "Oh crap, I think you're right." Matt returned with a winning smile.

They reached the perimeter of the crowd. The group had gathered to watch a boy, thicker in build with bouncy blond hair. Students were throwing objects as he blasted them out of the air with impactful blasts of air. The trees closest to them were already completely stripped of its leaves, branches snapped and broken lay on the ground.

"That's Gregory Sikes," Vin said to Matt.

Matt quirked his head trying to think of the name. "Didn't he fail out of most of the Air classes?" Vin nodded his response,

"Yes, but it was the more-" he paused trying to think of a kind word "-skill-based classes. Strategy, Leadership, Aerodynamics, stuff like that. He was never a 'bad' Weaver," he finished, throwing quick air quotes with his fingers.

"Well, he's even better now," came a new voice. Vin and Matt recognized him.

"What's up, Blake? How was your summer?" Matt greeted their friend. They exchanged handshakes. Vin noticed Blake's girlfriend next to him and waved, but she didn't return the greeting.

"Decent, worked most of the time. Didn't take any trip to the Himalayas, that's for sure," Blake responded. Matt raised an eyebrow in question.

Vin caught on. "You're not saying he took his Pilgrimage over the Summer, are you?" Blake just nodded, looking back to Gregory as someone threw up their lunch sack and he blew it into pieces of chips, sandwiches bits, and, unfortunately for one girl standing in front, chocolate pudding.

Vin shook his head in mild disbelief. The Pilgrimage was a rite of passage. After some seniors graduated high school, they would travel to the Himalayas. They are supposed to be following their elemental roots, they train with the monks there, help open a better understanding of their power. It's still rare. No one Vin knew but his uncle actually performed it, and they haven't seen him in years since he moved to Asia.

Vin didn't really think, of all people, Gregory would have made the Pilgrimage successfully.

The group roared as he blasted an earth ball a Weaver created into dirt particles. A large cloud puffed and settled over the group. The crowds, after the pudding accident, decided to have taken a couple of steps back before this.

Gregory shouted out, his hands still lifted in excitement, punching the air, "Who wants to challenge me?"

Blake's girlfriend let out a groan. "This is pathetic, I'm out of here." She left without waiting to see if Blake was following.

He relented though, adding, "Yeah, I got to work after school. I can't afford to be caught in this and risk detention. Later guys." He waved, then ran to catch up.

Vin and Matt returned their attention to the center. A kid half offered to fight, most likely peer pressured. Vin thought he was maybe a Fire Weaver, a sophomore. He couldn't confirm it because he didn't make a single punch before Gregory slammed him back toward the ground. He laughed, and other students snickered.

Vin looked more shocked and annoyed. He had to admit that was a crazy strong hit. Gregory was lucky he didn't knock the kid out. The challenger now slowly got to his feet but dashed into the safety of the crowd.

"Anyone else?" Gregory bellowed.

"Do it, Vin!" Matt said in his ear, giving him a firm shove. Vin planted his feet, looking back at him incredulously.

"What? Why? I don't want to fight him."

"Oh, come ON! You're the best match for him. I've seen you fight, you're great." Matt gave him another shove. Vin continued to push back.

"I haven't trained for fighting, you know that. Its logic, and strategy, and-"

"And leadership, blah blah blah." He grabbed him by his backpack and pulled Vin close. "Listen man, that Air Weaver is giving you all a bad name! It's your duty to stop this travesty."

Vin would have rolled his eyes at this, but too quickly Matt pulled off his backpack and pushed him clear in the center of the circle.

Gregory let out a chuckle. "Vincent. I should have known it was you," he mocked, looking around the parking lot, his hands covering his eyes to shade the sun and standing on his toes.

"I didn't see your high horse pull in." He lost the mocking impression and smiled greedily. He would enjoy beating Vin. Vin looked around. The crowd was hungry for it, their eyes were ready to eat up a fight. He locked eyes with Gregory, his challenger waiting for Vin's retort. He sighed and gave none, instead planting his feet and launching himself forward.

Vin was fast, he knew this. He also had great endurance. His training told him it was better to attack fast; one of two things would happen. Firstly, the obvious outcome would be to tire the opponent out, outlast them, whittle them down. With an opponent this dangerous it was more likely you'd get hit by an attack you couldn't shake.

This is where the second and more likely outcome would happen for Vin. Vin would attack wildly, making his opponent assume how he will act. Vin meanwhile would be testing to see how Gregory controlled his element. He needed to see where Gregory was strong and, more importantly, where his weaknesses lay.

Vin started with a leg sweep, his energy pulsing out, grabbing the air and Weaving it toward Gregory. Gregory jumped over. If he had not, it would have taken his legs out easily. This was a common and effective start to a fight, in the air they had a less defensive position. Vin didn't even wait to see how Gregory would react, he already knew, sending multiple open palmed thrusts to Gregory's predictable location.

Gregory crossed his arms over his chest and flung out his attack. It was more powerful than Vin's, decimating the blasts. Gregory's strike wasn't meant to hit Vin, simply block his own shots, but it still had enough energy to follow through and reach Vin. Vin put up a simple shield of air that stopped Gregory's diminished attack.

His real counterattack was already performed. Vin had reached out with his senses, feeling for the focus of his opponents' power, but he needed more information. Gregory and Vin traded a few more blows, Vin having to use his agility to dodge around them rather than block like Gregory was doing. Each one of Gregory's blasts allowed Vin to learn about the nature of his ability.

For instance, Vin was able to put together where most of the elemental strength came from in his attacks.

Gregory formed a large air blast, a little bit bigger than a beach ball, and launched it. Vin closed his eyes, his hands reached out, palms open like he was going to catch it. He sensed the energy coming toward him, his focus on the elemental properties revealed that the strongest collection of the elemental power was along the outside of the orb. The center and tail of the attack was the weakest.

Vin's eyes snapped open, using his energy to guide the blast up as he side-stepped it, letting it fly harmlessly into the air. Vin then did something he wasn't comfortable with, but he needed to put on display. He chuckled, goading Gregory.

"Come on now, I thought you were supposed to be powerful? Those the best you got, you'll never hit me with those puny sized air blasts, Greg." Vin felt stupid and childish but luckily it worked. Gregory's face grew red, he started motioning with his arms, grabbing mass amounts of elemental energy, Weaving another blast. It was getting so massive he had to start holding it over his head. Vin had to admit he was impressed, but it wouldn't matter how big it was, he knew the weakness.

Gregory yelled out as he launched his attack, a Smart car sized orb of turbulent air flew at him. The crowd behind Vin already panicked and fled as Gregory had gathered it.

"Nowhere to run from this," he yelled.

Vin then did something none of them expected, he ran toward it. He went forward with both hands out and to his sides gathering energy and skidded to a stop, one foot in front of the other. With the momentum gathered, he swung his arms forward. They met, creating a loud clap, while Vin using control to create a focused beam of air that shot forward. It penetrated the center of Gregory's blast where the energy was weakest. Vin then flipped forward, following up his attack. The center ripped open and Vin sailed through the middle as the powerful energy soared around and past him. As his flip came around, he thrust out his feet, continuing to use the momentum to send a compact but powerful gust right at Gregory. He was so caught off guard that he took the strike full force in the chest. He was launched straight back, hitting the wooden planks that served as the fence for the baseball field, then fell to the ground groaning.

Vin landed crouched on his feet from the flip, using an air current to keep him from falling on his back. He stood, the crowd around him silent for a moment. The first noise was from the Fire Weaving sophomore, who busted out laughing. The rest of the crowd joined in, laughing or hooting. They clapped Vin on his back, complimenting him as he made his way back to Matt who still stood at the back of the crowd. He held out Vin's backpack dangling on a single finger, his other arm tucked beneath his elbow and a smug smile plastered on his face.

Vin just shook his head trying to hold back his own smile.

"Told you so," Matt said proudly.

Chapter 6

V IN WATCHED MATT bump shoulders with an Earth Weaver and high five another as they entered the halls. This was how first day of school went. There was always an energy in the air, excitement at seeing friends you didn't get to over the summer. For seniors, Vin thought it was at an all-time high. Most have completed their major testing and didn't have to take too many classes, so they got off periods or could leave early. Although, there were the seniors on the opposite side of that spectrum who took even more classes to make up for any last-minute college qualifications or to get ahead.

Matt flung himself against the locker next to Vin, looking at him expectantly while Vin put in his combo and began shuffling his books in and out for what he needed. Vin allowed a quick glance, then without looking, sighed.

"Can I help you, Mateo?" This earned a look of exasperation from

Matt. Leading to him slapping Vin on the shoulder.

"Don't be coy, that was amazing! You beat an 'Awakened Weaver'!" He put in air quotes because there wasn't a better term for someone who completed their Pilgrimage. Vin quickly flashed through the fight in his head, Gregory's fighting style, and more importantly his elemental control.

"He didn't complete his pilgrimage. He must be lying," Vin said simply, shutting his locker and pushing Matt toward his own.

"How can you tell?" Matt asked, then nodded to some more of his friends from the football team that passed by. Matt didn't notice Vin attempting not to look uncomfortable.

"He had no control. I've never fought an Awakened, but I feel like they should have better manipulation. He's just really good at gathering it, and then flailing it around like a cyclops tossing stones."

Matt looked incredulous with a fake sense of offense. "What's wrong with tossing stones?"

Vin rolled his eyes, but Matt continued offering a wry smile. Vin patted Matt on the head.

"Nothing when you do it, Matty. You're doing great!" Vin added, like talking to a small child about their refrigerator drawing.

Vin had spent most of his freshman and sophomore years trying to relate to Matt what the monk had told him that day at his attunement. The feeling of the elements, to really connect to the ethereal force of it. But Matt would zone out and punch a rock into the horizon to show he had all the connection he needed.

Matt finally relented. "So I guess I'm ready to hear it then, wise master. How do you know he has bad manipulation?" he asked as they got to Matt's locker. He gave it a quick sideways glance before saying, "You know I didn't bring anything with me."

Vin, not missing a beat, immediately set off toward their home room.

"I know, I just hoped you'd have grown into a responsible young adult," Vin replied. Matt's face spread with glee.

"Your optimisms cute, Vin," Matt chastised. Vin simply gave him a smile that was genuinely cute. Matt hated it. With Vin's fluffy hair, broad face, and round features, he pulled off adorable quite well. He was the guy that always got the girls, and grandmothers, to ooh and aah at his winning smile. Matt was tempted to squeeze Vin's cheeks in a grandmother's death grip, but Vin continued his explanation.

"During a fight, my strategy is to see where and how they move their elemental energy. Imagine, let's say, a hollow ball made of clay. Like we used to make back in elementary school. Imagine using the clay to make a ball. You're pushing it and molding it. Unless it's perfect, there will be sides that are thicker than others." He motioned forming an orb with his hands as he continued.

"Weaving is like that. We gather the elemental energy and move it. But it's not always evenly distributed. So, I usually test where they are moving the energy. Gregory's never changed. He had no control, so I found his weak spot and attacked there."

Vin looked at Matt as he finished. His eyes had gone a little squinted as he thought about what Vin had said, looking at his hands like he was visualizing the clay ball. He eventually just shrugged and gave up.

"That's crazy, Vin. I didn't know you do that. I don't mess with all that when I Weave. I don't think about it, I just toss my rocks."

Vin shook his head wondering why he was surprised. "It's not about thinking, Matt, its feeling."

Entering their homeroom, Vin went straight to a window seat that overlooked a long hill that rolled to the street. Across the street was their practice football field and track. Matt got lost soon after entering the door, catching up with some of his baseball friends. Vin would have liked to join a team, but Air Weavers were notoriously prevented from doing so. It was too hard to make sure they didn't use their abilities, whereas water, earth, and fire were obvious. You could physically feel and see those three elements. There would be too much debate to Air Weavers if they played.

Although, in Vin's sophomore year there was a quarterback a couple of cities over that would wet his hands and could control the flow of the ball after he threw it. Even though it was scummy, Vin was still impressed by his control.

They sat in Mr. Baxter's English class for homeroom. Vin had him later in the day, but they always gathered here before first period to take attendance, hear announcements, and recite the Pledge of Allegiance.

Someone took the seat next to Vin, and he looked over to see Natalie Banks. Vin was pretty sure she had a crush on him since middle school. He gave her a small smile, one that you use for passing hello's when you don't intend to stop and have a conversation. She was about to say something when a bag dropped onto her desk. Natalie jumped and they both looked up to see Matt standing over her.

"Oh, hey Natalie? Nice summer?" he asked. She opened her mouth to respond, but Matt continued as if she answered already, "That's super. But wait is that-" He sniffed dramatically, looking around like he caught the whiff of something pungent. "Is that a new perfume? What is it? *Desperation* by Dior?" He stared with a raised eyebrow and a knowing smile.

Natalie reddened and scowled at Matt before getting up and leaving. Matt immediately plopped in her vacant spot. He took out his phone started flipping through it without purpose, though Vin could tell he was waiting for a reaction. Vin just stared incredulously before finally commenting.

"Where did you get that bag...that's not yours."

Matt shrugged and answered like it was obvious, "It's Omar's."

Vin mentally face-palmed. "You took his bag just to bring it over here and slam it down. Didn't you?" Vin asked. He only received a sly smile for an answer.

Vin chuckled, "You're so dramatic."

Homeroom began with their Pledge of Allegiance, then they all sat to suffer the cringey morning news. They tried to make it fun and whacky, but most of the jokes fell flat. Vin thought the two anchors had enough chemistry though and their audience is possibly the most judgmental group you could ask for, so Vin gave a spirited smile at their attempted humor.

Afterwards Mr. Baxter took attendance and gave some start of the semester announcements. Two particularly pertained to all the senior students.

"Don't forget now that you're all mature adults on the precipice of your future, we now allow you around fire." The class let out a mutual giggle before Mr. Baxter continued, "That's right, the Senior Bonfire will again be hosted this December. A plus one is allowed, but don't get crazy."

"Next item: Senior. Project." Mr. Baxter enunciated. "You will find a subject, you will study it, master it, and regurgitate it to us," he continued. Vin tried to not imagine momma birds feeding their young as Mr. Baxter passed out sheets to the students.

"It can be anything. Compel us, teach us, and more importantly teach yourselves. College is going to have many broad open assignments. Those brave enough to eventually get to your Master's will find this experience particularly useful."

Vin gave a passing glance to Matt who was already at work doodling all over his sheet. His bold and dynamic ink drawings stood out on the plain white page.

Vin looked back over his page. It was about as vague as Mr. Baxter had explained. Pick any subject, write a paper or presentation describing your goal, and create an interesting way to relay the topic. Vin's concentration was broken as Matt's finger shot into view tapping excitedly at the bottom. Vin's eyes followed it down to where he pointed. It seemed Matt actually read some of it between his illustrations to notice one of the options stated the project could be in groups of five students or less. He looked up at Matt who was mouthing, *Group Project,* and gave two thumbs up.

The bell rang and they got up, Matt tossing his "borrowed" bag back to Omar who nearly didn't register the projectile and was almost struck in the face.

"I'm off to Physics. Why I had to get it first thing in the morning, I don't know. Someone hates me in the faculty, I think," Matt complained.

"Probably the receptionist. You did play that prank on her freshman year. I hear she has a good memory," Vin responded dryly, showing his clear lack of concern for Matt's current predicament.

Matt thought about the event. He rigged all her pens to explode so anytime she tried to use one she got ink everywhere. "Ha, Ms Kirkpatrick, that was a good one." His humor left his face. "You don't think a receptionist can affect class schedules, do you?"

Vin simply shrugged. "Who knows? But we're still on for the movie after school?" he asked, holding out a fist to Matt.

He nodded, bumping fists. "For sure, absolutely. See you at lunch, bud."

Chapter 7

V IN'S FEET LANDED lightly from his release of the
rings. It was lost amongst the harder footfalls of his fellow
gymnasts. He rolled his shoulder and began massaging his
neck as he went for his gym bag, fishing out a bottle of
water. He watched a gymnast, Callie Baker, perform her vault. Almost a
flawless Yurchenko double full but stumbled on the landing and ended up
in the foam pit a couple of feet behind the mats.

Callie was good for a non-Weaver. It was something even Vin
struggled with when he first started training freshman year. Now it was
something he could do with a quarter of her run speed and no springboard
needed.

That's just how it was for Air Weavers, they excelled at acrobatics
and aerials. There were two other Weavers with him in the gym, but they
were practicing floor techniques, and Vin was just wasting time until Matt

caught up with him.

He pulled his phone out of his bag and checked the time, just reaching 2:50pm. School normally lasted until 3:45pm, but Vin's last class was out at two and Matt's at three.

Vin stretched his tank top down to tuck it into his shorts as he made his way toward the vault.

"Callie, you taking a break?" he called to her as she struggled to get out of the pit, tossing red and blue foamed cubes out of her way. She responded by giving him a thumbs up and calling, "Go for it!"

Vin had long ago stopped commenting or encouraging other gymnasts. He once thought it would be comforting but realized when you told someone, *Good Job,* or, *You almost had it,* while you could easily knock down any obstacle they had, it just came off as patronizing.

Vin stepped on to the mat, took a quick breath, and ran at the vault. He started halfway closer than where he was supposed to, and went down on two hands, twisting his body into a handspring. All the while wrapping air around him so that when his two feet hit the board on launch, the air boosted his release. He soared far above the vault table, not needing it, completing a triple Arabian layout. His body stayed completely straight as he rotated three times in the air before landing back on the mat.

It was flawless, it was perfect, and no one cared. Not even Vin was impressed anymore with what he could do in the gymnasium. When he first started, however, Vin loved it. The more he progressed meant the higher he could go, the more maneuvers he could perform, and Vin loved the feel of it. Gymnastics was one of the best ways to Air Weave. The act of rotating was a natural way to collect and move the element. Building up the power came easier and faster.

"You done showing off?" A familiar voice called to him. Vin looked over to where Matt was standing, Vin's gym bag over his shoulder.

Vin crossed the springy floors of the gymnasium to Matt, performing a quick forward tuck. Flashing a smile as to say, *now I am.* Matt threw a towel to him when he got close enough.

"How was Computer Science?" Vin asked.

"Computer Applications," Matt corrected, "and it was pretty simple. Just a matter of tying the ODBC to the database and then pulling the individual data needed for analysis via a query or SQL."

Vin raised an eyebrow, "Right, simple." He wrapped the towel around his head and scrubbed at the sweat, "Now who's showing off?" he mumbled.

"Alright, let's get going," Matt said as Vin wiped the sweat from his face and arms.

"I have to change first," Vin responded.

"Nonsense Vinny, you look cute in your little shorts."

Vin tried to suppress going red. He was too old to be made fun of for his clothing, but he was still a teenager and they were nothing if not self-conscious.

"It's for-" Vin started, but Matt cut him off. Moving his hand like it was a talking mouth as he mockingly retorted,

"Wind resistance, blah blah. Whatever, you can't fool me." He nodded to a girl doing a routine on the balance beam. "I know it's really just to impress Judith. I'm sure it's working."

"Hey Judith!" he called to her. "Looking good!" Which made her promptly lose her balance and fall hard on the mat below. She looked around for who called her, seeing Matt waving enthusiastically and Vin quickly covering his face from embarrassment. She replied with a harsh middle finger and a glare.

"Sweet girl," Matt said turning toward the exit and handing Vin his keys.

Vin and Matt crossed the small grassy patch of land separating the parking lot from the theater. It was located at the Harbor, a recently constructed shopping center right on the lake. Vin had changed into a pair of khaki shorts and t-shirt regardless of what Matt had commented.

They walked along the outside of the building. On their left were displays of glass cases with coming soon movies. On their right was an open circular seating area cut out to drop lower into the ground. A grand fountain in the middle sprayed clear water into the air, catching the light. Rainbows shimmered in and out of view. The fountain leaked out and dropped lower, creating a waterfall and river that flowed into a lake that sparkled like sapphire diamonds in the summer sun.

It was fairly empty with most still in school, but there were some older couples out enjoying the soft breeze and view. Two water weavers were tossing an orb of water back and forth before occasionally launching it into the air, exploding to release another wave of rainbows and a cool mist to coat the area.

"Edmund Brooks!" Matt yelled squeakily, pointing at one of the movie posters they passed. He fanned himself with his hands pretending he was about to pass out.

Vin looked over to the poster he referred to. Edmund Brooks, one of the most famous actors in Hollywood right now. He was brilliantly handsome, charming, and had an accent to make any woman, or Matt, swoon. You wouldn't find him as anything but the leading man.

"Another Agent Gemstone movie? Already? Wasn't there one just last year?" Vin groaned. The series was famous, and in Vin's opinion notorious, for cheesy spy movies where each entry had a new bodacious leading lady named after different a stone. She would mysteriously be nonexistent for the next entry. According to the poster, a beautiful caramel skinned woman would have the honor of playing Viveca Tigerseye.

Vin shook his head as they continued. They bought tickets for a new animated movie about a group of African animals who got lost on their way to a zoo in Asia and ended up in Antarctica to live with Eskimos and dancing penguins.

The premise for the movies always seemed ridiculous, but Matt and Vin had seen every single one since they were little and refused to skip now. Especially considering the gap their friendship created since freshman year when their attunement split their classes.

"You know I'm looking forward to senior year," Matt contemplated while they waited for the concession worker to load their bucket full of popcorn.

"Now that most of our elemental classes are out of the way, we have more free time to…" He trailed off as he hesitated to say what he was really thinking.

Vin decided to help him out by offering, "Watch movies?" Matt nodded in agreement. Social norms dictated that teenage men couldn't admit they missed one another.

They made their way down the halls, drinks and popcorn bucket in hand, a good majority of it already having ended up in Matt's black hole of a mouth or a trail along the floor. They just passed an auditorium that's film had ended and recognized the guy standing outside, looking at a sheet of paper.

"Hey Blake," Vin said. Blake snapped his head up in surprise.

"Oh, hey guys," he returned.

Matt, with a mouth half full of popcorn, commented, "Aren't you supposed to be, y'know, inside the theater cleaning it? You letting the others clean it for you?" He elbowed Blake in a playful manner like he was onto his plan and liked it.

Blake just shook his head. "Credit watchers. Can't start cleaning until everyone's out." He looked down as annoyance flicked across his face. "And it's just me."

"Well, I'm sure it's not that busy with everyone in school. You have help tonight?" Vin asked. But Blake just continued to shake his head.

"Nope, you don't need anyone else when I can just throw a bucket of water down, collect the trash, and clean up spills in one go." He wasn't even looking at them anymore as he continued. "Over and over, forty rows, 16 theaters, all night." He left that comment hanging in the air to generate tension.

"That's not fair," Matt finally added, taking a break from the popcorn.

"Yeah," Vin added. "This isn't a specified Weaver job, they shouldn't be able to make you work more just because you can Weave."

Blake let out humorless laugh. "Yeah, it's called discrimination." He stood up straighter as a couple came out of the theater giggling, not paying attention to any of them.

"I swear, if I have to clean up another condom…" he grumbled to himself. Matt and Vin exchanged horrified glances at each other. But Blake waved his goodbye and went inside, saying more to himself than them, "Just long enough to get money for tuition."

Vin looked over at Matt who just shrugged and walked to their auditorium.

"Ok, I don't think the elephant could have NOT broken through the ice while it danced," Matt commented as they walked down the steps of the auditorium, the credits scrolling along the big screen. He carried with him his third bucket of refilled popcorn, though he seemed to have lost interest in it half an hour ago.

"THAT'S where your suspension disbelief ends? Not that a lion probably couldn't survive the artic temperatures or how a giraffe's hoof wouldn't slip all over the ice?" Vin replied with his own skepticism. They knew it was illogical to argue the logic of a cartoon kids movie, but it became a tradition to critique them none-the-less.

Blake stood at the bottom of the stairs which staunched their current argument. He looked eager, which Vin thought odd considering how their last conversation ended.

"I promise, I didn't make a mess," Matt immediately said, holding his free hand up in mock surrender.

Blake laughed, "I trust you. But I was thinking about what we were talking about earlier."

"I promise we cleaned up the condom too," Matt interjected, earning himself a deep elbow in the ribs from Vin. Popcorn falling out of his bucket as Matt hitched forward, the air leaving his lungs.

Blake just gave them a raised eyebrow but chose not to comment. Vin made a deft motion with his hand as a current collected the fallen food and dumped it into Blakes waiting trash can.

"You were saying?" Vin asked.

"Right. There's a rally happening at the end of September for Weaver's rights. It's in Dallas, so it's not crazy far. I was thinking you guys would want to go?" Blake asked, the hope impossible to miss in his eyes.

Matt and Vin exchanged a look.

"A rally?" Vin asked, "I didn't think things were that bad for Weavers." Blakes hope was replaced with irritation.

"That's because it's Rockwell. It's a privileged city, hidden behind fancy new grocery stores and nice paved roads and beautiful houses. Just watch the news! This needs to happen, and you should want to be a part of it." Blake began to grow defensive.

Matt finally shrugged. "I mean, sure dude. Why not? As long as

Ashleigh drives. Her Escalade is SO nice."

If it was possible, Blake looked even more defeated. They now realized what he was thinking about when they first saw him before the movie.

"We broke up. She was…tired of Weavers. And dealing with *us*," he said the last word like vinegar on his tongue.

Vin's eyebrows shot up in concern, but when he looked at Matt, he seemed to have suddenly thought his stale popcorn was interesting again and shoved it in his mouth. Giving Vin a look like, *Can't talk, mouth full*, forcing Vin to make the next move.

"Sorry to hear that. But we're in, for sure. We'll go," Vin said, adding an attempt at a comforting smile. Blake returned it and lightened up again.

"Great to hear! We can even make it our Senior Project! We can be a group," Blake added. Vin and Matt refused to look at each other this time, afraid the discomfort would be obvious, but alarm bells went off in their heads.

Vin, as usual, covered for them. "That sounds like a great idea! But we already got one and my-" he had to hesitate for just a second to think of an excuse, "-dad would never forgive me if we didn't do it. It's been a passion project of his for a while."

Blake just nodded like he understood.

"That's too bad. But that's cool. Maddie Gieler, Rosie Stems, and I are probably gonna group up to do it."

Matt's face brightened up so fast, the excitement came on a little too strong. "That's great!" he exclaimed, slapping Blake on the shoulder. Walking past him, tossing the popcorn in the trash, and calling back, "See ya at school, man!"

Vin gave another small smile and pat him on the same shoulder with less intensity. "Try to have a good night," he said before following Matt.

They swung open the side door to the theater, and Matt ran out, dropping to his knees in the grass as if he hadn't been free for years. But after the interactions with Blake, Vin understood the relief to leave. He took a second to enjoy the night air as the breeze rushed by, kissing their skin with the soft relief of water from the lake.

Matt used the earth to bump his knees, bouncing back onto his feet, and began to stroll toward the car.

"THAT was one of the most uncomfortable interactions I've had in my entire life," Matt mused.

"Pretty much, almost as awkward as last year when we did No-Shave November and by the end you barely had enough whiskers for it to be considered facial hair."

Matt shot Vin a glare and then slapped a hand to his heart as if he were wounded.

"It's not my fault you're part bear!" he said defensively.

"Whatever," Vin ignored. "We should head to Hestle Park this weekend."

Matt spread his arms and legs, walking like a large creature. "Does the bear want to visit his natural habitat?"

"Shut it, whiskers," Vin said, grabbing at Matt's hairless face. Which evolved into a lighthearted slapping fight until they reached Vin's Durango.

Chapter 8

THE FIRST WEEK OF school crawled by at a snail's pace. The initial energy of seeing everyone quickly dissipated, leaving a slow introduction to all the classes and their expectations. Cutting summer cold turkey was so painful that as soon as Vin pulled up to park their first weekend, Matt launched himself out of the vehicle and began jumping around. Vin followed with less enthusiasm. They both wore tank tops and gym shorts, but Matt exuded 'sun's out guns out' energy as he snapped open his sunglasses, placed them on his face, and began strutting down the path.

"Matt, you're being extra weird today," Vin commented. This seemed to only encourage his behavior as he gave a runway turn and began walking backwards as he replied.

"It's the weekend! And it's a nice day!"

He wasn't wrong, thought Vin. The summer heat was taking a break, leaving clear blue skies, warm rays, and cool breezes.

"Ooh frisbee!" Matt noticed, pointing to a tree they were walking under. Sure enough, a pale blue disc sat on its branches. Hestle Park was massive, broken up into three different parts with woods, a river, and a frisbee golf course snaking through it. It was common to find wayward frisbees lost throughout the park. Matt's father's entire collection was found frisbees.

Matt lifted and stomped his left leg facing the tree, Weaving out energy that shook the tree. It trembled and dislodged the frisbee. Two irritated squirrels also fell from its branches.

Matt tossed Vin the frisbee and looked out across the park. They came to the third section of Hestle. It was more for picnicking as it just held a large pond with a fountain and shady trees. Spotting a standing metal pole, a basket and chains wrapped around it, Matt gestured to the sixteenth hole of the course.

"There, I'd say that's a good quarter mile." Matt took a step back, holding his hands forward like an announcer allowing the presenter to take the spotlight.

Vin smiled and stepped forward, his left foot in front of the right, the frisbee held in his left hand. Though it wasn't his dominant, the work he was about to perform needed the dominate for the second part of the throw. He twisted his body to the right and rotated back with a quick snap, releasing the disc. He followed through with his rotation until he was in the same position before he released the disc but now his right arm in front.

Gathering a source of air, he snapped a second rotation as he Weaved the pocket of air after the flying disc. It caught it, shooting it forward and farther, arcing the quarter mile until it crashed directly into the net. It was far enough they couldn't even hear the clang of the chains.

Matt leaned back on his heels, hands on his hips while he whistled with admiration.

"You know, the distance isn't that big of a deal anymore, but it's the aim that's impressive," he commented. Vin bowed dramatically before continuing down the path.

They saw a couple of families under umbrellaed tables. A father and young daughter, she looked to be seven, were by the pond. The father twirled water for the little girl. She giggled as he turned it into funny shapes with it. She reached out and held the water, Weaving it for a moment before it quivered and fell back down. She looked upset until her father drew more water from the pond and began playing again.

Vin smiled at the interaction, thinking about what Blake had said to them. *Was it really that bad for Weavers?*

They walked further along the path until they were completely shaded by a canopy of trees on both sides. They nodded to a jogger who went by, Matt giving his invisible hat a tip in their direction. He grabbed a stick he found along the way and began smacking it on passing trees. In between whacks he finally said,

"Camping! That's what we should do for Spring break. A last hoorah."

Vin thought about it, and to him it did sound nice. He knew of a great spot in Oklahoma he went to as a kid. The camping site was around a river that fed to a waterfall. You could camp at the bottom around the base or higher up along the stream.

"Sounds kind of quiet for spring break. No Cabo, Cancun, Puerto Vallarta?" Vin teased. Matt made a rare shift to being somber and thoughtful.

"Nah, quiet sounds good. Maybe even learn some of the fancy

elemental stuff you're going on about."

"Why wait until then?" Vin spread his arms, motioning around. "There's plenty of elemental energy right here?" Matt scoffed but threw down his stick and turned toward Vin. He put his hands together in front of his chest and bowed deeply.

"Yes sensei, teach me."

Vin wasn't surprised he lost the serious tone as quickly as it came.

"Ok. Well first, as you know, the definition of what we do is taking our own energy source and weaving it into the energy that the elements produce. We aren't taught that though, to really move the energy around."

Matt humored him by nodding like he was following along. "Got it, so what do we do?" he asked.

"We meditate. Close your eyes and feel your energy. Imagine yourself a color, and let it leak from you." Vin had closed his eyes and begun to do so. He felt his ethereal source bleed from him and reach out, touching and mixing with the wind around him.

Vin continued, "Let your color blend with the Earth to create something new. Then your body is the brush." Vin demonstrated by dropping low one foot stretched out as he quickly spun in a three-sixty. The air gathered around him in streaks of his energy. Then he launched himself up using the circle he just created to send him soaring through the trees. Branches shook and dropped their leaves to rain down on Matt.

Vin came back down a second later gracefully landing where he stood before, "If you train yourself to do this, you open yourself up to being able to do more than just throw rocks and blasts of air. You control where the strength goes, where it's weakened."

Matt began nodding with understanding. "Like with Gregory." He started smiling. "Alright, I got this. Stand back!" he warned dramatically, throwing his hands out. Vin didn't humor him and stood in his same spot watching Matt close his eyes.

They stood there together, silent and still as the natural wind breezed through them, ruffling the branches and sending the leaves dancing along the path. Vin closed his eyes again after a moment. He sensed for Matt, but he couldn't feel him connecting to the earth. After about thirty seconds, Matt sighed dramatically and threw his hands up.

"You know what? You're right. Maybe Cancun is better." He turned and continued down the path, admitting defeat. He was still talking, assuming Vin was following, but Vin couldn't hear him anymore. He was distracted, his senses picked something else up.

A strong energy was coming from somewhere deeper in the woods. Vin followed it, the forest floor crunching under his feet until he came to softer ground. Coming to a large cluster of bushes he heard the sounds of water beyond.

His hand reached out and pealed the leaves apart. The sun awaited him on the other side, and immediately he reached his free hand up to shield his eyes. Vin stepped through, seeing the light reflect off the water and a figure stood in the middle of the stream. She looked to be floating above the calming waters, but as Vin blinked the spots from his eyes, he realized the water was just very shallow where she stood. Barely ankle deep she stood, bare feet, her body leaning forward letting her long thick waves of hair cascade down her shoulders. They looked to be the color of caramel in the sunlight and her skin a natural light brown.

She held one hand forward while her other made large slow circles in the air. Below her the water matched her hand motions, a rivulet of water began to funnel up to meet her hand. Soon the whole stream was being pulled toward her. Vin realized what he had followed now, it was her pull on the water. He could sense her caressing the energy all around her. He was beyond impressed, especially if he could feel her from back by the path.

Vin didn't know what to do, so he purposely stepped on some gravel at the bank of the water to make noise. The girl looked up, but never broke concentration. When she saw Vin, she elegantly let the water return to its source and the flow of the stream continued.

"Hi." Vin said simply. She walked toward him. She wore a simple green tank top and dark brown khaki shorts that exposed long tan legs.

"Sorry to interrupt you, I, uh...sensed you from the path." He immediately grew self-conscious as he heard the awkward words come out of his mouth. "Well, your Weaving I mean," he quickly covered and hoped it didn't sound too weird.

She got close enough now he could see her face better. She had large stern lips and a strong nose with a broad chin. Then their eyes met. She had beautiful soft eyes, like fresh soil, and when she smiled, they looked full of life.

"Sensed me?" she asked, looking past Vin, over his shoulder toward the path. Clearly not weirded out, her smile was so infectious Vin returned it as he answered.

"Yeah, I could feel you communicating with the water from down by the path."

"Communicate," she repeated softly, tasting the words on her tongue, and she seemed to enjoy them.

He thought she looked so stoic and proud. He realized now that he recognized her too.

"You go to my school," he stated, not even a question.

She nodded and replied, "Yup, and your Vincent?" He liked the way she said his name.

"Yeah. I'm sorry, but I don't know your name. I don't think we've had any classes together?" He rushed out the last sentence to try to cover the awkwardness.

"We haven't, I only started last year. But don't feel bad, I wouldn't have known if the whole school wasn't talking about you and Gregory fighting."

Vin felt an assumption hang in the air after her comment that left him self-conscious. He avoided her eyes and kicked at the dirt, bashful.

"I don't normally do that," he reassured her. She just shrugged like it didn't matter either way.

Vin walked around her to the river's edge, hoping to change the subject he commented, "It's really nice here. You come out here a lot?"

"I do a fair bit, it's the closest body of water to my house. Usually the emptiest too."

"Oh-" Vin grew warm with embarrassment. But was happy to see that when he turned to look at her, her eyes were wide in shock at the implications of her comment.

"Oh no, not like- I didn't mean you," she struggled to get out.

Vin ended up letting loose a laugh and she did as well, easing the tension they awkwardly built up. They let the laughter fade away as the forest resumed its orchestra of running water, blowing branches, and singing birds. They stood in the comfortable silence absorbing in the forest.

"Ambrosia." She finally spoke a couple of seconds later.

Vin looked to her, "I'm sorry?"

"My name," she smiled, "is Ambrosia, but you can call me Amber."

Vin repeated her name. "Ambrosia," he whispered, letting it settle on his tongue like a new flavor. "That's pretty."

"Thanks," Amber replied, a new gust of wind blew down on them strong enough to take her hair into a fitful dance with it. Vin held out his hand, channeling his power and Weaving a buffer against the wind. He controlled it to be a thin veil so that it didn't stop the cool breeze entirely.

He was sure if anyone had been watching them, they'd feel

uncomfortable. He wouldn't have thought he could have met a stranger and had so much silent eye contact that didn't make himself feel strange. But there was something so settling with her, and to him it felt natural.

Vin opened his mouth to speak, but the woods where Vin had come out of were disturbed. Mumbles could be heard, and the bushes shuffled until Matt's familiar form stepped out. He looked distracted until he finally saw Vin.

"What. The. Hell. Dude?" Matt enunciated as he stomped over to him. "You LITERALLY just disappeared. I thought an axe murderer got you."

Vin looked between him and Amber, which made Matt look over to her.

"Uh…hey," he said passively, waving at her half-heartedly.

Amber crossed her arms, bemused. "Hey." Matt didn't seem to give her a second thought so she continued, "Sorry Vincent, I didn't realize you were on a nice stroll with your mother. I wouldn't have held you so long." Vin couldn't hold back his laugh as he watched Matt's face turn to incredulity.

"Excuse me?" Matt shot back. "Who even are you?" He looked down at her bare feet and judged her overall appearance. "I thought they cleared out all the hobos last year."

Amber humored him with a crooked smile, "Witty." She looked back at Vin and her face smoothed back to a genuine smile.

"It was nice to meet you, Vincent, I should get going," she said, walking back across the river, the water separating around her as she went.

"Nice meeting you too! Maybe I'll see you around!" Vin called after her. She picked up a bag at the edge of the forest, a case with art supplies and a sketch book jostled around inside the canvas. She looked back to give Vin a pleasant nod before she disappeared into the forest.

Matt stood watching Vin for a couple of seconds as he looked after her.

"What in the hell did I just walk in on?" he asked.

Vin finally looked at his friend and just shook his head, wrapping an arm around his neck as they wrestled their way back toward the path. His mind still half on his encounter with Ambrosia.

Chapter 9

MATT CRINKLED UP HIS taco wrapper and threw it into the trash can that looked a lot like the passenger seat floorboard and hopped out of the SUV. Vin gave a quick sigh as he got out of the driver's side, holding up a hand that caught the trash ball he Weaved into his grip. Vin tossed it into their trash barrel and walked up the steps behind Matt who strolled into his house like it was his own.

"Afternoon family!" He greeted Vin's unconscious dad who had fallen asleep while watching tv.

"Tsk, not quite the greeting I expected," he playfully mused. Vin gave him a shove and went to the kitchen to grab them two bottles of water.

Matt as usual didn't bring a change of clothes so he went upstairs to steal from Vin, getting out of his sweaty tank top.

"You know we can't wear the same size anymore," Vin said absently as Matt came back down in a too tight red polo, he sat at the table across from Vin.

"I told you, you need to bulk up some!"

"I'm not going to ruin my form just so you can steal my t-shirts and not look like a baby-GAP model."

"Pft, I still pull this off. And getting muscular isn't 'ruining your form', dip." He said the last part in a mocking tone.

Vin pointed his bottle accusingly at Matt. "Muscle is heavier than fat. I Hulk out like you and I can't float."

Matt just waved his hand at him dismissively as Vin's mother came in from her garden. Dirt sprinkled her nose and spotted her knees and apron. "Good afternoon boys, how was the park?"

Matt raised his hand to her in a grateful example. "Now THAT'S how you greet someone." He looked to Noemi. "Thank you, Mrs. DeLuca, at least someone in this house has manners." Vin and his Mom exchanged the look they always did with Matt's antics. "And the Park was great, thank you for asking," he finished.

"Lovely to hear, Mateo. What were you two talking about?"

"Just how Vin doesn't feel like gracing us with his presence on Earth. He'd rather be up in the clouds."

Vin shook his head. "That's an exaggeration, you're being dramatic."

"Hey, don't look at me. I'm grounded, humble, and realistic. The down-to-earth type you know. My affinity says so," Matt responded smugly.

A new voice came in from the living room. "Don't forget sensible, sturdy, and unmoving," Vin's dad called, having awoken.

"I think you mean stubborn," Vin retorted.

"Dense," Noemi added.

"Barbaric?"

"Barbaric," Vin's mother agreed. "And simple." They laughed. Matt pretended to be hurt.

"I'm wounded. Perhaps I'll join more like-minded individuals," he said as he got up and joined Vin's dad in the living room. They shook hands before he sat in one of the plush armchairs to the right of the sofa. Vin took the one opposite and his mom settled in next to her husband handing him a glass of fresh squeezed juice.

"So how was the first week?" Vin's dad asked in-between sips of the sweet drink. "I haven't had time to check in with you, bud." He looked regretful, but Vin just smiled back.

"It's ok, Dad. I know you're busy. School was fine?" He looked to Matt for confirmation. Matt nodded his head in agreement. "Fine."

Vin's Dad nodded to the tv. "They announced the hurricane is dispersing before hitting the shore so you shouldn't need to worry about possible recruitment."

"Well that's a relief," Vin said, laying back. "Now we just need to figure out what we're doing for our Senior Project."

"Ugh, let's not talk about that yet," Matt groaned.

"The sooner we at least get the subject the better. Especially if Blake asks about it, we need something to cover what we told him."

Vin's mother gave the two a look, not appreciating their dishonesty. "What was so wrong with his idea you didn't want to do it?"

Vin mulled over his response. "It's not really a bad idea. Just kind of…"

"Intense," Matt finished for him. "Plus, Blake was kind of laying all his problems on us, and we're cool and all, but we don't hang out. We're more like…"

"Acquaintances," Vin finished for Matt, and they smiled at each other's synergy.

"Well, can it be anything?" Vin's dad asked.

"Yup, they gave no restrictions. Just have to find a subject and write about it in a compelling fashion."

His dad looked contemplative for a moment. "Well, I'm not saying you have to, but maybe it would be good for you write about your grandpa, and what's going on with people like him."

Vin adopted his father's look of contemplation. "Well, it's not less intense than Blake's idea."

"But it is closer to home," Matt offered. His playful look sobered.

"True," Vin agreed. "I think we'd present something better if our subject meant something to us."

Vin's mothers sweet voice interrupted their back and forth, "You don't have to decide right away. You're going up there to visit him next week, right?" Vin nodded in response.

"Well take your time to visit him and think if it's something you want to pursue."

"Sounds good to me," Matt said.

"Alright, we'll go next week. Ask around about the Fading."

A new report attracted his father's attention. "Speaking of ill news." The report displayed footage from an attack in Seattle. Buildings were broken, the metal bent at impossible angles.

"Another Anomaly attack?" Vin asked. His dad nodded.

"They're too frequent now." His father turned up the volume as they began to interview a doctor. PhD Miran Phlacker from MIT.

"Doctor Phlacker, can you give us more insight into these Anomalies?" The reporter asked.

"Our research determines these individuals to be those born with, or have developed, psychoses prior to the Attunement age. Schizophrenia, postpartum, bipolar. If these are treated, they are manageable in humans. In

Weavers, however, they pose a huge risk. The sooner we catch it the better."

"Thank you for that assessment, Doctor Phlacker," the reporter said in a sickly-sweet smile, as if he was discussing his grocery list rather than the serious concerning story it really was.

"Can you provide any more insight into these disorders and what to look out for?" the reporter continued. The doctor growing momentarily uncomfortable.

"Well, yes. But keep in mind you should see a licensed doctor if you or someone you love sees these symptoms. The most dangerous we usually come across is schizophrenia. It can start in early adulthood. They can believe they are hearing voices or that people mean them harm. It's best to do your research on these or see someone as they are quite complicated. Dissociative Identity Disorder occurs after extreme trauma in young children's lives. Those with bipolar go through extreme mood swings of highs and lows and some have difficulty with communicating."

The doctor went on a bit more discussing additional signs of mental illness and what to look out for. "Oh my, these sound quite dangerous indeed," the reporter summarized like it was some weekly gossip.

The doctor made a face of discomfort. "Well that's not necessarily the case. We are not sure why they seem to exhibit elemental abilities that differ from many Weavers. It would be more correct to say they have the highest potential of risk. Their powers are strong, and their emotions can be unpredictable. Our goal is to help-"

The reporter cut him off, "Thank you so much for that information, Doctor. Unfortunately, we are out of time, but I'm sure we will all be more on guard in these times of terrorism," she said as they switched to another correspondent covering another section of the city.

It took the four a moment to realize Juliette was standing in the entrance to the living room.

"That's some heavy shit," she said eloquently.

Vin's mother gasped, "Juliette! Language!"

Juliette just shrugged, "What? It is! I feel like Magdalena was like that. She was always bouncing all over the place." She turned and left just as suddenly as she came. She didn't see the look on Matt's face at the casual mention of his sister.

"I, uh, should get home," he said awkwardly, getting up and heading for the door.

Vin's mother and father looked worried, but Vin passed them with a hand on his mother's shoulder, giving them a confident nod and walked out with Matt.

"Matty, I'm sorry about Juliette. You know how she is," Vin apologized.

Matt looked irritated but finally said, "Honestly, it's ok. At least someone talks about her. Unlike…" He paused as the heaviness settled between them.

"Your parents still acting like…she's not around?" Vin also couldn't say it. Anger replaced Matt's irritation.

"Existed, Vin. Say it. They act like she never existed." He just shook his head and turned to head down the street.

"Matt, wait! Let me drive you home," Vin offered.

"No, I need the walk, I'll talk to you later." Vin reached out and grabbed Matt by the arm. They stood there for a moment. Vin feeling swallowed by the guilt at not being able to help his friend.

"Matt. Remember that time, must have been seventh grade, Jessica just dumped you, and your sister brought us on top of that building over Buckler Ave?" A smile slipped across Matt's face at the memory.

"Her and her friends would always use that as a backup place to smoke, but she saved it for us on those clear nights. The stars were always amazing, and she always had the foresight to bring those ice pops." A laugh slipped out between the memories.

Vin grew somber, letting Matt go. "She wasn't always bad, Matt. When she was good…damn was she good."

Matt nodded, not daring to turn and face him lest he see the threat of tears in his eyes.

"Thanks Vin, I'll talk to you tomorrow, ok?" Vin nodded, though Matt couldn't see it as he jogged off down the streets. The streetlamps flickered to life as the sun began to drop below the horizon and the dark sky started collecting stars.

Chapter 10

VIN AND MATT WERE out on the bleachers at the Weavers Arena Monday morning before school. It was half the size of a football field, domed, open roof in a circular structure. Each element was presented around the arena. Water lapped around its circumference; the ground was dirt mixed with stones. For those that couldn't conjure their own fire there were receptacle-like tubes sticking out of the walls that could be lit to cause a flame.

A Fire and Earth Weaver were practicing in the middle while others watched or just hung out. Matt was pretending to flip through his history book while Vin wrote an analysis for his book in English.

Vin looked up as Matt passed over a section on World War II. "You know we're only on Chapter 3."

Matt stared at Vin in confusion. "What?" Vin gestured with his pencil at his book.

"You're on like Chapter 20. You finally turning into an over-achiever or something?" Vin teased, Matt shutting his book and stowing it in his bag with a sigh.

"Yeah right, just bored. Look at the way Tony's creating his wall!" He suddenly changed the subject pointing to the Earth Weaver. "Let me go teach him a lesson, he's embarrassing the rest of us."

He hopped over the railing and into the arena berating Tony. Vin chuckled and went back to his paper.

"He's passionate," a voice interrupted his homework. Vin followed it to see Ambrosia. Her long brown hair pulled back into a high ponytail, her warm eyes on him. He returned her smile and scooted over, an unspoken invite for her to take the seat.

She did, and Vin looked back to Matt. "He can be, though I think he just likes the distraction."

They looked at each other for just a moment before Ambrosia flashed another grin, eyes lighting up.

"So, I thought of another one!" she said, referencing a conversation they had the day before. "The Redwoods, in San Francisco. I feel they had to have some help being made."

Vin put the pencil to his chin as he thought. "Maybe, but it could just be natural. Are there bigger trees in the world?"

Ambrosia looked shocked. "Heavens Vin, you need to see them sometimes. They are the biggest trees in the world. I would know, they are in the Sequoia National Forest. My dad used to take us there most summers. He felt it would be a nice olive branch to my grandmother."

"That sounds amazing. My family is usually for beaches and fields. We vacation in Italy a lot, so there aren't too many massive trees where we go. Your dad's not Native American?"

"No, he was almost full American. I mean, I know everyone is mixed in America, but I'm thinking a mix of European. My mom's side is Cherokee."

Vin caught the past tense when she talked about her dad. He paused for a moment to consider asking when he noticed an inquisitive face leaning on his arms from the arena floor. Matt stood with a raised eyebrow. Vin wasn't sure how long he had been standing there.

Matt finally asked, "Soooo, this is a thing now?" He pointed his fingers between Vin and Ambrosia.

They exchanged glances, but Ambrosia left it to Vin to placate his friend. "Kind of. We found each other on Instagram yesterday. Just got to talking."

"Mhmm," Matt responded, not convinced.

"We were talking about what I might do for my Senior Project," Ambrosia added. "I'm thinking about structures or natural locations that could have been influenced by Weaving."

Matt looked confused, hopping over the edge and retaking his seat next to Vin. "What do you mean? How much stuff has been made since the 1940's?"

"Well see, that's what I'm getting at. I'm thinking of stuff before World War II. Like the Pyramids and Stonehenge."

"Huh…that's kinda interesting." Matt bumped his elbow with Vin. "We're just going to learn about old people."

Vin flashed him a glare. "It's not just 'old people', Matt." He looked to Ambrosia as he continued, "We're going to look into the Fading."

"Oh," Ambrosia looked surprised. "I actually don't know too much about that. I've kind of heard about it, but no one in my family has ever been effected."

"Yeah," Vin sighed. "My Grandfather was-" he caught himself on the words, "I mean IS a Fire Weaver. I think most people know the general definition of the Fading. It's a progressive disease that causes elders to lose the ability to Weave. I know it can be helped with therapy and management strategies, but for the most part that help is temporary. We were going to see what my Grandpa knows, maybe get some accounts of people who are affected by it."

"Wow," was all Amber managed. "Losing your Weaving? I can't even imagine."

Matt checked his phone and nudged Vin as it was getting close to first bell. He began gathering his things and Vin followed his lead.

"Maybe you would want to join our project? If you don't want to work by yourself?" Vin offered shyly. Matt's jaw dropped, and Ambrosia looked between the two.

"If you're ok with that, Mateo?" She asked. Matt composed himself and just shrugged.

"As long as it's less work for us. HEY TONY!" The Earth Weaver from the arena jumped as he tried to get by their trio without being noticed. "Make sure you hold your arms firm." He gestured putting his forearms together in front of himself, fists clenched the closed palms facing his body.

"Don't let them break your composure or your rock wall might as well be sand," Matt finished. He earned an awkward bow from the frightened Tony who then ran off before he could be yelled at again.

Matt looked incredulous as he stared after him. "Did...he just bow to me?" he asked. Ambrosia and Vin released the built-up laughter and started to make their way to the school.

"That's cute, he respects you. You must be good," Ambrosia said.

Matt waved away the condescending compliment. "Pft. They're just underclassmen. They're scared of everyone." He let a pause fill their conversation as they walked before smugly adding. "I am pretty good though."

The three had crossed the street from the Weaver Arena and had just entered the school building when an out of breath Blake caught up to them.

"Hey guys!" he said between breaths.

"Blake," Vin and Matt said in a greeting.

"I just had these printed this morning." He handed them each a flyer. In bold letters it declared the March on City Hall in Dallas.

"You guys are still gonna go, right?" The pitiful puppy-dog eyes came back, and Vin and Matt exchanged a quick glance of regret.

"Yeah, of course. We'll see you there," Vin answered.

"Sweet! I heard there's even going to be some professionals there that younger Weavers can talk to. Like about school and stuff."

Vin gave the idea a thought. "Does Weaving affect college that much?"

"Maybe not if you have some other talents, good grades or more importantly money. But I just need to find some good colleges that accept us. I can't handle too much more of this-" He lowered his head, pained, "discrimination."

Matt made a *Here we go again* look. Blake didn't notice, but Vin clapped a hand on his arm.

"Well, it sounds like a great opportunity. Looking forward to it now," he encouraged.

Blake looked happy about that. "Yeah, should be. Anyway, I gotta go pass more of these out. I'll see you later!" He then scampered off like someone just tossed him a ball to catch.

Vin shot Matt an accusatory glare after Blake left. "See, at least *he's* thinking of his future."

Matt just shrugged and looked down reading the flyer. "Dang, all the way in Dallas on a Saturday. That's like a six-hour drive."

"More like four," Vin corrected him.

"A Weavers March? Sounds interesting. It's next month," Ambrosia added.

"You want to go? Shell in for snacks and gas and you can catch a ride with us," Matt announced.

"She doesn't have to pay for gas," Vin chided. Then he looked to her, "But you can definitely ride with us, if you're interested in going."

Ambrosia smiled, "Sounds good. And as much as I'd like to learn about the world and how it was affected by elements, I have plenty of time to travel after school's done. I'd be happy to do the Senior Project with you. When're you guys starting?"

"I was already planning on visiting my grandpa at his retirement home this weekend. We can start then," Vin answered.

"Sounds good." She smiled warmly again, and they lingered on each other longer than Matt would have liked. "I got to go to class, I'll talk to you later."

She turned and left Vin absently waving, her wavy brown curls bouncing as she receded down the hall.

Matt just shook his head and turned the other direction. "Should've taken the gas money."

Chapter 11

DIRT BILLOWED OUT behind Amber's jeep as she rode down the unpaved back roads to her house. The trees came together alongside the rode, draping her in shade that immediately cooled her with a break from the sun. Her home came into view as she rounded the last bend. Dark wood paneling crafted the walls of the modest one story. Amber parked her jeep and hopped out, grabbing her bag from the back seat. She had her hair pulled back into a ponytail while she drove, helping with the wind. She pulled the elastic band out of her hair to release her long curls and headed inside.

As soon as she stepped inside, she turned to a photo of a smiling man with Amber's brown hair. She rose her thumb and forefinger to her head in a bow and then to the photo before continuing into the room. She passed her grandmother watching tv in the living room and gave her a quick kiss on the cheek. Her grandmother let her know she was there with a quick pat on her shoulder but kept her attention on screen.

Amber gave the tv a quick glance. *The Price is Right* played on repeat, and her grandmother never missed an episode. Even if it was the fiftieth time she'd seen it.

The sound of drawers opening, utensils clacking, and aroma of dinner let Amber know her mother was cooking. So Amber stayed clear and went straight to her room. She put her bag in the empty wicker chair and powered up her laptop. She threw herself down on the bed and started playing with a braid of colorful strands she kept next to her bed. Trees just outside her window brushed against the glass.

Amber closed her eyes and imagined herself back amongst the trees. Running along soft dirt paths through an infinite forest. She always came here in her mind, always there to escape. Except this time, she wasn't alone. Through the trees she spotted two green spots of color. They stood out from the leaves but not a contrast, a compliment. She went toward them until a shape filled around the green, dark skin, almost like hers. Fluffy brown hair bleached by the sun. A gentle smile.

She didn't get to imagine running through the forest with him as her door opened and her mother's voice pulled her back to reality.

"You didn't say hi when you got home."

She rolled away from facing her mother and pretended to start digging something out of her backpack. "I'm sorry, Unitsi. I know you don't like to be bothered while you're cooking." It was an attempt at a lie and a terrible one. Her mother taking a seat at her desk.

"Don't give me that, Ambrosia." A silence was left hanging, and if Amber spent too much more time in her backpack her mother would start to think she had Mary Poppins bottomless bag. Thankfully, her mother finally broke the silence. Unfortunately, Amber wished she hadn't.

"What's your Senior Project?" her mother asked.

Amber whipped around, "My wha-" She saw her mother looking at her laptop a reminder on the screen saying **Tell Vincenzo about the Senior Project**.

Crap Amber thought. "Well we pick a subject and study it-" she didn't know how else to further describe it, "and present it," she ended awkwardly. Her mother turned to look at her with a look Amber reserved for her grandmother every time she asked how to work the internet.

"I know *what* it is, Ambrosia. I meant what are you doing for it?" she asked with a hint of annoyance in her voice.

"Oh…" she had to pause to think, the truth would only make things worse. "I don't know yet." *Good lie,* she thought sarcastically.

"Well maybe you could do it about your tribe? The Cherok-"

"Please mother," Amber cut in. "I grew up with Grandma, you think I don't already know about our people? We're supposed to be studying something *new.*"

Her mother chewed on this for a moment, flashing a look back at the reminder still on the screen. "And this Vincenzo? He's helping you?"

"Yeah, him and his - well our friend, Mateo."

"And they're Weavers?"

Amber couldn't control her sigh that escaped her lips. "Yes mother, most Weavers work together in school."

"It doesn't have to be that way, Ambrosia –"

Amber cut her mother off, not in the mood for the same speech again, she never was. "Well it *IS* that way mother."

Her mother shook her head and reached for a small frame that sat on her desk. The same dark skinned, brown haired man stared at them. He held a big pot with a tiny sapling sprouting out, a large grin spread across his face. Her mother picked it up and began wiping the glass as if it wasn't already spotless.

Great, the sympathy attempt again. She thought begrudgingly.

"You don't need to surround yourselves with them. They're dangerous and your fath-"

Amber jumped out of bed, her bag falling off the chair abandoned.

"I *AM* one of them, Mother! And so was Dad! Now if you don't mind, I really should get to researching, you know, my project." She pointed at the computer screen as if her mother needed reminding. With a sigh of her own, her mother obliged and returned the photo to its spot. She made the same gesture as Amber had when she entered the home and got up and walked to the door.

Without turning back, she said, "Dinner will be ready in about fifteen."

Amber went to shut her door then fell into her desk chair, her hands on her head and the mess of curls fell in front of her. She looked between the break of brown waves to the photo of her father on her desk. She saw herself back in her forest but this time a great flame was approaching her, consuming the woods as it came. She squeezed her eyes shut, trying to run away. She hated when she couldn't control this part, but two beautiful green eyes stood out among the leaves, and then her phone vibrated.

She swept her hair back and picked up her phone. A smile spread across her lips as she read the text ID.

Chapter 12

VIN TEXTED AMBER the address to his house and told her to meet them Saturday morning at 9am. After that they texted late into the night. Matt ended up joining and a group chat commenced.

So Vin, I was doing some digging after our super engaging talks with Blake. – Matt

Digging? Is that an Earth Weaver pun? – Amber

Shush, New Girl. – Matt

Peace, children, what're you talking about, Matt? – Vin

I'm talking about the hobo from the woods coming into our lives and sassing me! – Matt

… - Vin

No I mean what did you dig up? – Vin

Dingus – Amber

I'm going to ignore that. – Matt

For once… - Vin

ANYWAY! – Matt

I thought it was interesting because there happened to be an article that JUST interviewed Edmund Brooks. He was talking about how unhappy he is because his co-star ended up being paid more than him. The movie studio SAID it wasn't because he was a Weaver. But Edmund claims that not to be the case. – Matt

Really? – Vin

That's crazy…I wonder if that's gonna happen a lot now. Like when you learn something that you never knew and all of sudden it's all over the place and you're just thinking, 'how did I not see this?' – Vin

:(- Amber

That's kinda awful. I don't really get on social media that much so it's definitely something I'm not aware of. – Amber

Eh, they're probably just paying him less because he's washed up and Agent Gemstone movies are getting stale. – Matt

Wow! That's really sensitive of you to say. – Amber

Thank you! I pride myself on being a paragon of sensitivity. – Matt

Matt…I know you're fluent in sarcasm. Stop being an idiot – Vin

You know…I'm not liking this dynamic that's forming -__- – Matt

It was just after one when Vin had just about enough of the two arguing about which Agent Gemstone movie was the best, Vin having resigned to say all of them were terrible and wished them a good night. He went to his computer. About fifteen tabs were opened for different schools and apartments in their areas. He put about half of them in a bookmarked folder and climbed into bed. His curtains billowed gently from the constant wind that flowed through his open window. A soft orange glow colored his room from the streetlight outside.

He reached his hands in the air and started Weaving the current around his room. There wasn't a lot he could control in his life over the past couple of years. This was something he could. He kept creating patterns, calming his mind until his eyelids grew too heavy and sleep took him.

Amber's knock came at 8:45 in the morning.

"You must be Ambrosia!" Noemi said as she opened the door.

Amber smiled her greeting. "Nice to meet you, Mrs. DeLuca." She walked in at the wave of Noemi's hand. She took in the living room, giving it a chance to settle. She had to admit her heart beat a little faster at the idea of being in Vin's house.

"Anything to drink or eat, dear?" Noemi asked, shuffling off to the kitchen.

"I'm good, thank you! I already ate before I came over," she called to Vin's mother. Though she had lied, she was too nervous to eat that morning. She slowly made her way around the room, landing on a photo frame with a collage of photos. She immediately pointed out a younger Vin, big hair, big cheeks, and pretty green eyes. She gave an unreserved smile and hid it well as she turned to the couch and Matt, who relaxed on it with his drawing pad rested on his knee.

She took a seat next to him and continued to examine the room. Every glance around let her in a little bit more on Vin and his family. Plants hung on suspended pots in the corners of the room, more on end tables and parts of their entertainment stand. She could see past art projects Vin and his sister did when they were younger. Inevitably to the chagrin of the creators they stuck around, though their quality was lacking.

Amber enjoyed the large painting on one of the walls that looked like a scene from an Italian street, painted with bright warm colors, a simple shot of a restaurant and corner. She got goose bumps being in such a warm home, their love radiated from every knickknack and family photo.

"New girl," Matt greeted her. Not looking up from his pad.

"Old man," Amber replied, leaning back into the cushion of the sofa and putting on her best attempt at confidence.

Her comment got Matt to look up at her, an eyebrow raised. He liked her way of turning a phrase. He relented giving her a smirk,

"Our fearless leader is helping his dad in the garage. He should be out in a bit."

Amber nodded and continued to let her eyes wander. She finally couldn't resist and examined Matt and what he was drawing. She was immediately drawn in, unlike her soft watercolors, he used deep and bold markers that leapt off the page.

"That's…" She didn't know how best to describe it. It wasn't something you'd see in a museum, more like blown up on the side of buildings, like graffiti. "Really cool."

Matt smiled earnestly. "Thanks," he said, holding it up so she could see it. Amber held out a hand, requesting a better look. Matt obliged letting her take it.

Her eyes ran down the page, every dynamic line twisting and sending her off to a new place to explore.

"You do art too, right? Vin told me," Matt asked.

She nodded silently, still taking in his art. It was a pale, white face. Red strokes painted lines around it, arched and bold eyebrows accented the eyes which were missing. She realized it wasn't a face at all.

"It's a mask," she stated, more than a question.

"Yup, it's called a Kabuki mask. My sisters friend had them in her house. When I first saw them, I thought they were the coolest thing."

Amber moved a hand to the corner of the page. "May I?" she asked. Matt nodded and she began flipping through his sketch book. Each as bold as the next. Deep purples with silver and trimmed with gold created a masquerade mask. Some were more delicate, a sleek black one that would just cover the eyes but had an extravagant peacock feathers.

"You like masks," she commented.

Matt shrugged. "I seem to be good with them," he laughed. Amber handed him back the sketch book, and they fell into a comfortable discussion of the supplies they use and inspirations they have.

"I didn't expect you to drive a Durango," Amber said as she climbed into Vin's back seat later that morning. Matt was already in the passenger seat plugging in his playlist.

"What did you expect me to drive?" Vin asked as he started his SUV and backed out of his driveway.

"I don't know something…cooler."

"Ouch," Vin playfully threw back. Matt let out a chuckle.

"What about me?" Matt asked.

Amber thought about it, added a hmm and a finger on her chin. "Definitely something sophisticated. Perhaps a tricycle? Or a very, very small car that fits many people?"

Vin burst out laughing while Matt gasped in shocked offense.

"Are you suggesting I'm a-" he pretended to get choked up on the word, "a clown?"

Amber shrugged and leaned against the car door. "If the 16-inch large red shoe fits." A grin splayed across her lips.

Ten minutes later Vin pulled into Rising Sun Retirement Center. The three entered and Vin went to the front desk while Amber and Matt hung back. Amber looked around with a frown on her face.

"It's not very…lively in here," She commented to Matt.

He responded with a laugh. "Well I mean they are old."

Amber scoffed at him and smacked his arm. "I meant the building, not the people."

Matt watched an older gentleman across the lobby on a walker making his way across the hall, slowly. *If he's lucky, he'll make it down the hall by Christmas*, Matt thought.

"Yeah sure, whatever you say."

"Tell Vin I'll be back in a bit." She immediately turned and left out the door.

"Wait, what?" Matt tried after her, but she was already gone. His mouth was still hanging open, confused, when Vin finally came back with visitor passes for them.

"Where's Amber?" he asked.

"One of the geezers said he lost his teeth in his pants and asked her to find them. I've never seen someone run so fast, not even you after we ding-dong ditched Mr. Mahjin's house. Guess she just doesn't have the stomach for this. We'll probably never see her again." He faked a sympathetic shrug.

Vin gave one of his 'cut the bullshit' looks, and Matt relented.

"Ok, you're right. That's unrealistic. What actually happened was one of the gentlemen, strapping fellow, swooned her into becoming his 7th wife and you just missed them driving off into the sunset. Guess she wanted someone more mature. Sorry bud, maybe next time."

Vin hit him on the arm, shaking his head as he turned down one of the branching halls and pulled out his phone to text Amber.

They got to his grandfather's door, but his room was empty.

"Uh oh," Matt said. "Grandpa's missing too. Maybe he was the charming old man that Amber ran off with."

Vin ignored his comment, he couldn't think of enough comebacks to counter Matt. He didn't think it was worth the air, and by now he thought himself an expert on how to use air.

"The receptionist said he's in therapy right now. We're just dropping off our bags." Vin let his slide off his arm onto the sofa pressed up against the wall while he read the text he received from Amber.

"She wants us to grab any of the empty planters, vases, or dead flowers and bring them out to the courtyard?" he read out loud to Matt, looking at him confused.

"Don't look at me, you invited her."

Fifteen minutes later Vin and Matt stood out in the middle of the Center that acted as an outdoor courtyard for the residents to get some fresh air. They were surrounded by every pot or vase they could find, which made them look they had arranged, at best, a funeral for sad plants or, at worst, some strange ritual. They didn't have to bear the strange looks for too long as Amber finally returned, a large bag swung over her shoulder with words *Rose's Flower Emporium.*

"Alright," Matt started, "we've officially made the workers and old people concerned enough that we probably have five minutes until they call the local psych ward to make sure they aren't missing three strange pot stealing teenagers. What exactly are we doing?"

Amber smiled as she dropped the bag down with a solid smack that gave the appearance it was far heavier than she let on. "We are going to brighten the place up!"

She began to dig through her supplies, pulling out small bags of seed and sacks of soil. "Help me plant these. Any dirt that looks too old or unfertile replace it." She gestured to the walls along the courtyard. "Check those trees and bushes too. They are looking a little worse for wear."

"How the hell am I supposed to know if dirt looks too old or unfertile?" Matt complained. Amber stopped what she was doing to turn and face him. Matt took a step back from her glare that made Matt feel like he just asked if Santa Clause was real.

"You don't know? You're an Earth Weaver and YOU don't know?" she chastised. Matt looked to Vin who shrugged in agreement with Amber.

"She has a point," he said.

Matt threw his hands up in surrender. "Alright, alright, stop judging me."

Vin began to immediately start helping, not wanting to incur Amber's wrath. Matt remained unconvinced,

"This is all well and good, but are we going to come back all the time to make sure they grow? Plus, summer's almost over, won't it make it harder to grow?"

Amber set to work replotting potential plants that didn't need to be trashed and placing them in new soil. "We don't need to come back or wait. We're going to grow them today."

Vin even stopped his work so both him and Matt could look at her skeptically. "Ok, so apparently the psych ward IS missing a patient. What're you talking about?" Matt asked.

Amber stopped in her annoyance to look at Matt before pointing at him then back at herself. "Me. And you. Are going to grow these plants."

The three stood in the courtyard, hands dirty and rough, faces smudged with soil, admiring their work. All the planters contained new seeds and soil was switched out of the worst spots. They even planted new seeds around the lining of the courtyard to accompany the current bushes and trees that resided there.

Matt opened his mouth slightly, a question on his tongue, but Amber put up a finger silencing him.

"Just work with me here. Close your eyes." She did so, not waiting to see if he followed suit. Matt looked to Vin who just waved his hands at him mouthing go on. He sighed and closed his eyes.

Amber started to raise her arms as she spoke. "Reach out with your power. Your mind is a good place to start, though you should feel it in your soul."

"Matty using his mind? That may prove more difficult than you'd think, Amber," Vin chided. Amber didn't reply, but a grin gripped at the corner of her mouth.

She continued, "Feel the Earth around you. This is your element. Focus on it." With a graceful motion of her wrists, water broke from the heads of the sprinklers. She brought it above her head to create a large bubble. Then stretch it until it resembled a flat disc of transparency. She brought all five of her fingers to a point facing down, tensing her arms. The disk shattered into millions of tiny drops, then, relaxing her hands flattening them out so that the droplets rained down on the courtyard.

"Did you feel the new element enter yours?" she asked Matt.

He cocked his head and hesitated. "Yeah, I think I do. It's like what you were teaching me in the park that day, Vin."

"Good," Amber said. "Now imagine trying to push on that element with your powers. Not to fight it, but merge with it. Soften your touch on the Earth and imagine it growing, working with my element."

Matt's brow was furrowed and he looked like he was concentrating hard. Vin looked from him to Amber whose face was smooth and peaceful, arced slightly toward the sky. He placed a hand gently on Matt's shoulder.

"Relax," Vin said to him. "It's a part of you, don't think so much, just feel."

Matt's eyebrows smooth out as he exhales, his features growing considerably calmer. Vin looked back to Amber and could tell it worked. Her expression changed, as if something finally clicked and she was registering a change.

Together the two bowed and their hands came down to their sides. Then simultaneously they slowly raised them again, extending themselves back into the world. Then down again. Vin grew fascinated.

"Match your breaths," he suggested to them.

They began to exhale together as they came down and breathed in deeply as they raised their hands again. Vin could feel a pressure building, but it wasn't uncomfortable. It almost felt like a beacon, like the natural energy around was being drawn in. After almost two minutes of nothing but the sound of Amber and Matt's breathing, Vin crouched to one of the planters. A small prick of green broke through the soil.

A laugh escaped from Vin. He looked up to Amber who was already smiling. "It's working!" he exclaimed.

"What? Really?" Matt asked surprised, his eyes snapping open.

"Don't break the rhythm, Mateo!" Amber quickly said. He wasn't happy about it, but Matt quickly shut his eyes again and continued to work with Amber.

Vin made his way around the courtyard with an uncontained smile. His eyes sparkled as he examined the plants. Colors came alive in the courtyard. White bells sprouted alongside every shade of tulip they could find. Flowers that looked like little suns burst to life. Vin thought he remembered the packet being labeled Gaillardia. The bushes around the courtyard began to take on a healthy green again. New ones began to spread out, these had little bright red berries. Vin looked to the trees as they started to let out creaking noises as they too began to flourish, their leaves grew and small white flowers sprouted across them like a fresh snowfall.

Orderlies began to come out into the courtyard, staring around in awe.

"Quick," Vin told them, "start taking some of the flowers inside. I think they can grow more if there's room." The workers, after getting over their initial awe, began cutting out some of the full-grown flowers and bringing them inside, distributing them to rooms and halls.

It took about thirty minutes but the whole center was awash with colors and fragrances and, as Amber suggested, life. Everyone looked notably cheerier. The residents had a little pep in their step, and the orderlies seemed to go about their duties with more gusto.

"That was crazy," Matt said.

"Incredible," Vin agreed.

"Well, what we can do is incredible," Amber replied.

A young orderly walked by and Matt made eye contact with him. H winked at Matt as he walked by with a flirtatious smile. Matt looked a little prouder. "I didn't even know we could do that."

"I don't think it's heard of much, but there's always expeditions out into the Amazon and other densely forested areas to help restore the life there. I heard of a massive event in Iceland a few years back where they planted and grew a huge assortment of plant life there. I think we just hear more about natural disaster relief and what we can do for that."

"Yeah, no kidding," Vin mumbled, but more to himself. He took off toward his grandfather's room, Amber and Matt following.

"I can't believe we can Weave together like that. It feels like a whole part of our life no one's told us about," Matt continued.

"We're still new to this. It's only been, what? Seventy years since we started doing this? Who knows what we're all capable of?"

"Yeah," Vin agreed. "And it looks like we're capable of a lot more together."

"Ciao, mio figlio!" Vin's grandpa called as they walked through his door, his arms open expectantly.

"Ciao, papa," Vin responded, returning the hug. His grandfather lay in his bed, a warm quilt up to his hips and his wheelchair by his bedside.

"I see you haven't gotten rid of this one yet." Vin's grandfather motioned to Matt, cracking a devious smile.

"He's tried many times, but I'm too wily," he responded, shaking the old gentleman's hand. "Good to see you again, Mr. Deluca."

Vin put his hand on Amber's shoulder as he introduced her. "And this is our friend Amber." Amber also shook his hand, telling him it was a pleasure to meet him.

Amber and Matt took a seat on his sofa while Vin fell into an armchair next to the bed. His grandfather then pointed to a vase in the room that wasn't there previously. It over spilled with bright colors of various flowers.

"Do you know what this is all about? The scrubbers have been running around like chickens with their head chopped off." Amber looked to Matt and mouthed Scrubbers? Matt tugged on his shirt and pointed to the direction of the front desk, indicating he meant the orderlies that wore scrubs.

"That was mostly us," Vin answered. "Amber had a great idea to make use of our Weaving." He gave his grandfather a smile, but he did not return it. Instead a shadow crossed over his face, the old lines seemed to deepen.

"Ah, yes. I'm sure it would be nice to get out there and make a connection again." The three exchanged looks, wondering which would continue the conversation. Vin took the lead.

"Well, actually, that's partly why we wanted to come here. We were hoping to talk to you-" he hesitated for a moment, "about the Fading. We're researching it for a Senior Project."

His grandfather thought about it but inevitably let out a sigh. "Might as well, I suppose. Not like avoiding its name is going to make it any better." Vin and Matt leaned closer, and Amber pulled out a pad and paper to take notes.

He started by laughing. "Now that is an interesting topic. Most people my age don't use their Weaving much, so I wouldn't assume there is too much research into it."

"Why wouldn't people be Weaving just because they're older?" Matt asked.

"Well, I suppose it's like any other things humans can do," Mr. Deluca responded. "How many people have legs but choose not to run, or eyes who don't read? It may seem like something new and fresh at first, but inevitably we do as humans do and take for granted our gifts." He sighed after finishing.

"Now I've had my fair share of gifts that I've taken for granted, but not Weaving. No, I've never forgotten about my Weaving…not until I didn't seem to have a choice. Now I'm not quite the expert on the Fading, but there have been plenty that come in and like to speculate. They say it's when we get older, we feel heavy." He stopped, patted his stomach, and added, "And I don't think they meant the beer belly." He made an attempt at humor. The trio tried to play along but they knew he was just trying to cover for what was coming. His eyes began to glisten, and his lips shook. Vin reached out and grabbed his hand, steadying him.

"Every summer I spent feeling so alive," he said, changing his original approach to his story. "I would lay in the sun and draw in the heat. At night the skies would dance with the flames and I would dance with them."

"I don't know what happened over the years," he continued. "They say life takes a toll on you. You feel heavy and you lose…things. But what

I've lost doesn't feel like just things. It's not like my inability to move these old legs anymore. Or being able to see more than five feet without glasses. It feels like I've lost a part of myself." His hand tightened on Vin's but refused to meet his eyes. "I can't get warm anymore, Vincenzo."

His grandfather came from a time when men didn't cry, and even in this he refused, and Vin was at a loss for words. He hadn't noticed Amber get up until she unfolded his grandfather's chair and her kind voice broke the silence.

"Well, then let's go get some sun."

The courtyard had more residents now that it was beautifully decorated. Two men were playing chess on one of the available tables, a third, a woman with bright white hair and a brighter knitted pink blanket on her lap, sat on a comfy chair reading a book. Amber steered Mr. DeLuca's chair to a spot in the sun and freshly grown wisteria dangled above his head, allowing a soft and beautiful aroma.

"This is awfully kind, young lady, but I think I'd rather talk inside. Being in the sun just reminds me of what I can't do anymore," he said as confidently as he could.

"You're not here to talk any more, Mr. Deluca. Let's just enjoy the nature for a moment," she said. Mr. Deluca, being too much of a gentleman, chose not to argue with her. Then she turned to Vin and spoke to him so that his grandfather couldn't overhear.

"Can you dance?" she asked. Vin looked caught off guard and looked to Matt, but he provided no further encouragement as he just sat back with his arms crossed, indicating he lost any control of the situation long ago.

"Uhm, what're we talking here? Hip hop? Salsa? Two-step?" he asked. Amber just giggled.

"Never mind, I think you'll get it after I start. Follow my lead? Ok? We're going to bring the element to him." Without waiting for Vin's response or giving further explanation, she went to the center of the courtyard where there was the most room.

Amber discarded her shoes then lifted her arms, like before, water breaking from the area. Following a beat that only she could hear she began to dance. At first they were soft movements of her feet. Rhythmically moving in small circles, the water travelling with her. She picked up the tempo, feet pounding the pavement. She moved her arms low, turning them hand over hand then raised them again. Then she began to move toward the center of the courtyard then back again. The water flowed with her, ebbing and flowing with her movements.

Vin watched, moved by her motions and the beauty of the dance. It looked tribal and the dancer at peace. *Follow my lead.*

He didn't think he could copy her dance, but that might not be what she meant. Vin went to the middle of the courtyard to join Amber. He closed his eyes and reached out with his senses, the energy she Weaved moved in waves and motions that he could follow. He reached up with a hand, and with a quick motion of his wrist, he grabbed a draft. He didn't try to think about it but moved with Amber's manipulation, the air wrapped its currents around Ambers water.

For once he was using his abilities for something other than fighting or rescuing. He circled and swirled like he was used to. Dropping low and sweeping his legs, the wind picking up fallen petals and leaves. No noise was left in the courtyard except the flow of the water and whipping of the wind. Colors flowed in and around the streaming water. The courtyard looked like the canvas of an abstract painter, flicking every paint he had at his work of art.

Vin and Amber's connection drew on the elemental energy,

strengthened it as it was permeating the area. Like with Matt and Amber before, their Weaving became a beacon for elemental energy. Vin could feel Amber's dance begin to crescendo. Without any communication but their elemental bond, they drew the dance to a close releasing the elements and ending their performance. Vin finally opened his eyes, his breath heavy but face happy. He looked to Amber and she was smiling too, but she was looking elsewhere. He followed her gaze to his grandfather. He sat in the sun with an arm raised, basking in its glow and he stared at it in awe. Flames flickered on his fingertips and tears streamed his face.

Chapter 13

I HATE YOU TWO," Matt sat, once again back in Vin's Durango, with a surly look on his face. "If I had KNOWN we were going to break out into an impromptu dance off I would have brought my carboard box."

Vin flashed a smile from the front seat.

"Oh, so you can break dance?" Amber asked.

"The only thing he'd break if he danced is his hip," Vin retorted.

"Ha ha, Vin," Matt replied sarcastically. "Maybe you spent a little too much time with the old folks if you're already reciting their jokes."

"OH, LEFT THERE!" Amber quickly cutting them off to point down a street they almost passed. The three were making their way back to Amber's house. Her mother had to use her jeep for work, and Vin said he'd have no problem taking her back. Matt rolled down the window and stuck his head out feeling the wind as they went down the back roads. He stuck his arm out as the trees came so close to the road they began slapping at his hand along the way.

"This is pretty cool. I've never been to this part of Rockwell," he added as shadow flooded their car from the canopy of trees overhead.

They arrived and Matt immediately hopped out.

"Whoa whoa whoa, where're you going?" Amber asked, hopping out next.

"Obviously inside your house. You can't just expect us to NOT come in. What kind of hospitality is this? You know if I-" Amber cut him off by throwing her bag at his face, which he caught.

"Alright, geez. Don't go having an aneurysm on me. But you can be the gentleman that carries my bags in." They sneered at each other as they walked up her path and she took out her key, letting them in.

Vin entered after them, giving himself a moment to take everything in. It was decorated unlike any home he had been in. Beautifully colored tapestries hung on the walls, wood sculptures of animals dotted spots around the room.

"This is just excessive," Matt said.

Vin looked to Amber who he saw making a motion to a photo on the wall. She made eye contact and blushed. Vin quickly looked away feeling as if he'd caught her in a private moment.

"What's excessive, Mateo?" she asked, not hiding the annoyance in her voice.

"You have a mountain lion AND a wolf on the same shelf? And is that a buffalo next to a hippo over there?" he chided.

"It's a bear you dolt, and by all means feel free to make yourself at home by insulting mine."

"I'm only kidding, it's really cool. And don't worry, I tell my mom all the time our furniture is ugly," he added as he went up to a painting of two

Native Americans on horseback. The horses drinking from the water and a mountain towering into the clouds in the background.

"Seriously though, these are all really cool where did you get them?" Matt admitted.

"These hands, young man," Amber's grandmother said coming into the room. Amber had to double check the clock on the wall as she was sure Wheel of Fortune should be on.

"Grandma, I'm surprised you're up. Isn't Wheel of Fortune on?"

"Bah," she answered. "The Second Amendment, fifty thousand dollars." Vin and Matt looked at each out confused.

"The answer, and how much they won," Amber added, uncomfortable with her grandmother's strangeness.

"Well they're amazing, Ms. Aldrich," Vin offered. He now understood where some of Amber's artistic interest and talent came from.

"Please, call me Enola, Aldrich is Ambrosia's fathers name." She sat in one of the comfy armchairs splayed with a thick wool blanket in a brown and white pattern. "And thank you. You find you have a lot of time when you get to be my age."

The three squeezed into the sofa on the other side of her not knowing what else to do now that Amber's grandmother made it apparent this is where they were going to be.

"Can I ask what inspired you?" Vin asked.

"Well my people of course," she said, closing her eyes and nodding like it was obvious. "We're Cherokee. And this world seems bent on forgetting us. Figured I might as well do something to remind them. That's the best what's left of us can do. I, Halona, and Ambrosia have a duty to those who came before."

Vin noticed at the mention of Amber's name she seemed taken aback. But her grandmother drew his attention again.

"So, what were you kids up to today?" she asked.

"We were just visiting Vincent's grandfather. We had a project we were doing." Amber answered quickly.

"Yeah, speaking of which," Matt added. "What part of our project do we put in you and Vin dancing? I guess it would be some good padding to stretch out the time limit." His words looked lost to Amber as Vin saw her eyes go wide in panic.

"Dancing?" her grandmother asked. "You were dancing, Ambrosia?"

Matt finally caught up with the mood in the room and realized he may have said something wrong.

"It was just a meditative experiment, Grandmother. It wasn't anything official." She looked worried, Vin and Matt confused.

"Well, which dance was it?" her grandmother asked. She seemed cool and her voice even, but the way Amber was reacting Vin expected her to explode any moment.

After some hesitation Ambrosia finally answered, "The Sun Dance." Vin could have sworn she was bracing for an impact, but her grandmother stayed the same.

"And you danced it with him?" She asked pointing at Matt.

"NO!" She quickly said. Matt snapped his head at her, looking offended. She returned with an apologetic glance but continued.

"It was with Vin," she gestured to the other side of Matt. "But I wouldn't say danced *with,* at least not really. He doesn't know the dance. BUT-" she quickly added, "He was great. I mean really understands the elements. Like I do," she finished, admittedly looking defeated.

Her grandmother sat silent for a moment before finally saying, "You trust him?"

Amber looked up, caught off guard but looking hopeful. "Yes."

Her grandmother stood, "Well, then we might as well teach him." She left coming back with what looked to Vin a pipe and some kind of whistle, heading for the door.

"Wait, what?" Amber asked. Standing up looking flustered, "Are you sure?"

Her grandmother stopped at the open door and turned, looking between Vin and Amber. "If he's willing to learn, and you think he's worthy of it. Why not spread our people's traditions?

Especially if it betters him."

"Was that unusual?" Vin asked, switching his phone being tucked under his right ear, adjusting it to his left. He began losing patience with his t-shirts as they overflowed from the drawer as he was trying to shove them in. *Why do I have so many? I swear I wear the same 3 shirts every week.* He thought.

"Oh, definitely so," Amber's voice replied from the other end. Vin had called her as soon as he got home to go over the eventful evening they had, stopping only so his mother could shove a basket of his clean clothes into his arm before he made it to the stairs.

"Grandmother is such a traditionalist," She continued. "Teaching someone our ways isn't normal. Especially for my Grandmother she doesn't even like my-" she abruptly stopped, and the line went silent. Vin took it as a hint she was about to say something she didn't want to.

"But why would she not want to teach people about your culture? Wouldn't you want other people to understand your history?" Vin asked. He thought to most of his family gatherings where his uncles wouldn't shut up about which one of their restaurants had our Great Uncle's famous marinara. Or how they used to spend every morning making cannoli's back in Cefalù and then pasta at night to sell to the local market. He frowned at the thought, realizing it was mostly food related. Italians love family and food.

Amber hummed in thought picking the right words, "You may not understand. Indigenous people have been mostly appropriated in media and so many of our rituals and histories are sacred. Most things don't leave the reservation let alone willingly taught to an outsider. They aren't even filmed."

"You seemed caught off guard when your grandmother mentioned you, when talking about passing down your heritage? Can I ask-" he paused as he sank down into his bed feeling uncomfortable to ask. "-is there something going on between you and your grandmother?"

There was another pause and Vin assumed she was reacting to the answer the same way he did to the question. She finally responding saying,

"There pretty much has been since I've been born. My father wasn't Native American. It's where my brown wavy hair comes from. Genetically speaking," She added. "She was always kind of upset I didn't take the traditional look of my heritage. I guess to her I always seemed like the start of the dilution of my bloodline."

The words struck Vin hard. It was clearly something she has felt and dealt with by now in her life, but to Vin it sounded so harsh. He laid back on his bed turning off the lamp, letting the darkness of the night consume it until all that was left was the familiar soft glow of the streetlamps.

He reached his arm up and began tugging the air into his room from the open window. Absently circling the draft around, fluttering loose papers and posters tacked onto his walls. He recalled his night, the dance, the music, and the drums. Amber's grandmother's pride in the song, the movement of their bodies. He felt a part of something bigger than himself, and bigger than just the three of them.

"Well, I thought it was beautiful what you and your Grandmother showed me tonight. It's crazy to think your ancestors had such a connection to nature and the elements before we awakened this ability."

He thought he could hear her smile on the other side of the phone. "Yeah, it sometimes makes me sad to think they never got to really feel it. I kind of think that just because they couldn't move earth, wind, fire and water doesn't mean they weren't apart of it. It's why I trust you so much. I know you understand that already. Even if you don't have our blood, you have our heart and spirit."

Vin turned red with embarrassment. He even attempted to hide it, turning over. Which just felt silly to him considering she clearly couldn't see him.

"Thanks," was all Vin managed to say sheepishly.

"Well I'm heading off to bed, today was a long day," she said yawning. "But a good one."

"Yeah, it was," Vin replied. "Goodnight Ambrosia."

"Goodnight Vincenzo."

Chapter 14

THE SUMMER HEAT had yet abated, even going into late September. The windows were down in Vin's Durango as the wind whipped by on highway 45 toward Dallas.

"I still don't understand how you beat that Mercedes," Matt half yelled over the sound from the backseat. He laid in a massacre of beef jerky wrappers and empty soda cans.

Amber smirked knowingly from the front seat. Vin mischievously grinned back at Matt. "I'm just that good bud, what can I say?" Matt didn't accept that, barging his way onto the armrest between the two.

"No seriously. Did you install NOS when I wasn't looking?" he asked, determined.

"Really Matty? Are you that oblivious?" Vin asked, then he took one hand off the wheel and spread his hand forward. Reaching out with his energy to Weave, the wind broke around a bubble he created in front of them. The vehicle growing increasingly quiet as the wind no longer pounded against the vehicle, but it was still speeding along, faster than before. An old jalopy of a car next them started wiggling slightly as the turbulence began dragging on the old car.

"You're kidding! You CHEATED?" He didn't even fake being appalled. "That's so cool! I didn't even think of that. The best I could do would be break up the road or launch a few concrete chunks to their undersides."

Vin and Amber exchanged glances. "Yeah let's leave the racing stunts to Vin, eh?" said Amber.

The four-hour drive turned into two and a half thanks to Vin. He parked them a couple of streets over and they walked the rest of the way. A big group had already gathered. A lot of people holding signs for equal rights and fair equality. Shirts were being passed out so that most of the crowd was a solid, unified color of deep blue.

"What a simple but nice fountain." Amber gestured to the large flat surface of the fountain outside the entrance to City Hall. It had two red, orb like structures on its surface for some artistic flair. Amber nudged Vin and pointed, he followed her prompt and saw a group of kids huddled together in matching shirts like they were on a field trip. She seemed to enjoy the idea of young kids so interested in Weaving events.

"Not my idea of fun." Vin said, "But hopefully they're going somewhere nice after this. I think there is a place to go kayaking around here."

"That sounds cool, we should check it out sometime." Amber responded.

The crowd formed close to the doors where a stage and podium had been set up, wrapping around the fountain the farther back the crowd had gathered. The three were relatively close to the front, the fountain a few feet behind them.

Vin checked his phone, receiving a text from Blake. It showed a picture of him and his team right by the stage, faces painted, holding signs and wearing the blue shirts they were handing out. Vin smiled at their infectious cheer. Vin's attention was drawn back to the stage as a representative took it and began speaking into the microphone.

"Thank you all for coming!" he started. The crowd cheering at his greeting. He wore a nice tailored suit, middle aged and relatively fit. Vin guessed ex-elemental marine turned politician. He began, in Vin's opinion, quite aggressively listing off most of the negatives Weavers were facing today. Some of which Vin didn't even know about. But it sure was whipping up and angering the crowd. He reminded them of the discrimination they face when getting work. The fact that the government was working to create separate laws for Weavers. Discussed the potential of labeling Weavers specifically and separately. Then moved on to discuss the war that's been going on for years now.

"This war in the Middle-East has gone on for far too long! There is much to discuss about this. Should we, the U.S.A. be in it? Whose fight is this really? Are we even fighting for the right reasons? But this goes beyond that. This is about the fact that *we,* Weavers, are subjected to unfair attention in this war!" he emphasized.

"But there is still hope!" he boomed across the crowd. "We can use our voices! United, we can bring about change. Show them we are just like them. Show them we are still human! That we deserve the same rights!" His speech began to build, pumping his fist with each statement.

"We are Weavers! And we have our Rights!" he yelled.

"We are Weavers! We have Rights!" the crowd echoed.

Vin barely heard Amber yell something to him, tugging at his arm, seconds before a large pane of glass plummeted on to the stage, the impact decimating the platform and exploding shrapnel into the crowd.

Vin grabbed Matt, pulling him to the floor as tiny slivers of deceivingly beautiful rainbows flew overhead. Screams of terror broke out, and Vin looked to his other side sighing with relief as he saw Amber get down before the blast. He stood, helping Matt to his feet. If Vin hadn't seen the stage before, he would say it must be a new art piece; the stage had fallen through, large shards of glass protruding in every direction like a crystal display.

He looked up to see one of the floors above missing its panel, someone standing there. Vin heard screams on either side of him as the group was blasted by water from behind, launching them toward the building. He whipped around expecting them to be hit next but saw a wall of water and Amber's hands spread out, one foot pressed forward as her back kept her balanced, halting the flood that almost wiped them out.

We're being attacked! Vin thought with horror. He spun back around to look up at the building. This time he noticed more people behind other windows. *They're going to send more of the glass crashing down!*

"Amber guard as many as you can and fight back against any Water Weavers! Matt shield as many as you can from the falling glass!" He commanded as he crouched down summoning his energy around him.

"Wait, WHAT?!" Matt called back, but Vin didn't hear, now out of earshot and rocketing to the sky.

Amber watched Vin soar into the air. Briefly stunned, she hesitated for a moment. Turning around to face the fountain she counted the attackers; three Weavers obviously wielding water. One was facing her, the one that Amber initially stopped. Then one to the far left and another closer to her right. The attacker on her right was viciously attacking a group of kids. Recognizing the children from earlier, her anger urged her to attack and protect them. Amber jumped toward the fountain; a wave meeting her to carry forward. The one that was first facing her tried to intervene, Weaving a blast of water. Amber pushed the wave off, using it to propel her into the air. She carried the water with her and began to spin, rotating her body and energizing the water with her power to strengthen the oncoming attack.

Amber let her attacker's blast hit the rotating wall, absorbing it. She continued her spiral releasing two separate blasts. One returned to the first opponent, too surprised by the counterattack, managing a meager defence before it slammed over her, knocking her to the ground.

The male Water Weaver attacking the children wasn't aware of Amber's incoming blast, receiving a hit full force that launched him forward out of the fountain headfirst into the concrete.

She came to a sliding stop at the edge of the fountain in front of the kids.

"Are you all ok?" Seeing there were no pressing injuries, she continued. "You need to get out of here. Run to your bus or parents." Amber rushed out. The kids appearing startled and shaken. Sensing it just as one of the children pointed and yelled, "Look out!"

Amber reached out, Weaving her element to move before even her body did. An orb cast from the third Water Weaver, having noticed what happened, moved to attack Amber. Her wall had absorbed the initial impact, allowing time for Amber to whip around and catch the rest, slapping it away.

"Run. Now!" She called to the kids. Then moved forward to combat her new opponent. Standing on the other side of the fountain, they traded long arcing shots while slowly closing the distance. Amber allowed herself a quick look to the first Water Weaver encountered to ensure she wasn't going to be outnumbered. It appeared that instead of returning to the fight, they chose to turn their attention to attacking the defending crowd. The weaver quickly received her come-uppance as a large chunk of rock flew from the crowd and slammed into her.

Amber brought her full attention back to the opponent before her as they began strafing around the fountain, attempting to bait her opponent until they were on opposite sides of the larger of the two red statues. She let the other woman gather an attack and fire it at Amber. Redirecting the attack by pushing her own energy into the stream of water, she spun and dragged it across the surface gathering more water and propelling it at the woman on the other side.

Having taken the bait, the woman believed the orb standing between them would protect her, but she underestimated Amber's blast. The power fractured the base of the structure and sent it rolling free into the woman. Barely managing a yelp of surprise, it plowed her over. Amber took steady steps toward the woman laying spread out in the water, waiting for her to jump up and strike like in a bad horror movie.

Coming from her flank, she sensed a new energy half a second before the wave of heat, just out of her peripheral. Managing to create a crude wall of water before fire exploded into it, the wall Amber created was weak but cushioned the blast slightly as the force sent her sliding clear out of the fountain. Her side flared with pain and she looked up to see a wicked girl with dark pink hair gather the woman Amber knocked out, carrying her into the fleeing crowd. Amber groaned and fell back to the ground under the cover of one of the makeshift earth shelters, exhausted.

Matt gaped as Vin flew into the air. Turning to Amber, expecting a similar reaction to his own, he was shocked to see her surfing off into the fountain.

"What the f-" Interrupted by a crack issued from above, he snapped his head back up to the building and saw another window shatter. Matt stomped his foot into the ground, sending energy coursing into the earth. Pulling on it he motioned as if hauling something heavy. Weaving the concrete below to stretch up and over a group of rally attendees. A second later he heard the shattering of glass and saw pieces tumble down the sides of the makeshift roof. Another second later two other Weavers showed up, grabbing people they could carry to get them to safety.

Matt was barely able to process the scene before him. He looked on in horror at the bodies covering the ground, many moaning and crying in pain with shards of glass puncturing their bodies. Water covered most of the assembly area, Matt standing in a sticky mix of it.

One of the attackers standing in the fountain recovered from Amber's initial assault. She raised a wave of water and saw Matt's group. It was hard to tell from the reflection of the water, but Matt noticed numerous glass slivers preparing to ride the wave. The attacker threw both hands forward as the wave came rushing toward them. One of the other Weavers and himself both took a hard step forward. With closed fists they motioned from the ground up, Weaving a wall of rock and concrete as the wave broke against it flowing around them. Bringing his back foot forward in a swift decisive kick, Matt hurled a chunk of the loose wall at the Water Weaver, crashing into her chest. She dropped back into the fountain motionless.

The fellow Earth Weaver looked between him and the fallen Water Weaver. "Damn, nice job," he complimented.

Matt was out of breath but managed a smile from the unexpected compliment. "Thanks," he replied between labored breaths.

"Keep watching my back while I try to get more of these people out," the other Weaver said, getting a woman to her feet, one of her arms wrapped around the man's neck. She managed a weak, "Thank you" to Matt before they hobbled off.

Matt turned to look over the assembly scene, a bit more confident now.

He noticed a man walking toward them from the side; he was carrying one of the victims. Matt started to wave him over, but something struck him as odd. The man wore all black clothes and seemed untouched. Most concerning of all, the man he was helping didn't look like he was moving.

The man without remorse simply tossed aside, what Matt now comprehended to be, a dead body revealing a sharpened piece of rock. With a thrust of his fist, he launched it at Matt. Matt's eyes widened in surprise, but fell back on his training with a quick step back to give him just enough distance to plant his foot hard and swing forward like a boxer, his energy Weaving into the spinning spike and breaking it apart. With a quick follow up he brought his other hand forward pulling the fragments of the rock, sending the pieces darting toward the other Earth Weaver.

Unlike the condensed piece that was shot at Matt, these smaller pieces couldn't be completely stopped. Missing his defense as some cut into flesh. Rage consumed the now bloodied face of his hulking opponent. Matt danced back, somehow managing to forget the chaos around him and began to enjoy the idea of a one on one fight with an opponent not holding back.

A flash of a woman with pink hair caught his eye. He immediately lost his form and took a step toward the fountain. "That can't be...," he whispered in disbelief. Matt, too distracted, sensed the vibrations too late. He snapped his head up just as the opponent he had ignored destabilized the shelter Matt was under, causing it to tumble down on top of him.

Vin soared toward the building, one of the glass panes cracked and plummeted out. He threw out a hand Weaving the wind forward catching the falling glass in his current. Rotating his body, bringing the current back around, he slingshot the glass back at the person he had initially seen in the center window. Vin was close enough now to see the look on his face, his eyes widening as he saw the shards hurtling toward him. The man didn't have time to react with his Weaving as he dropped to the ground, the glass shattering around him.

Vin grabbed the lip of the roof just to the left of the man, who had recovered and looked up at him. The man had pin pricks of blood over his face and arms from the shrapnel, one large chunk lodged into his cheek. He pulled it out wincing, but not breaking eye contact with Vin. Blood trailed down his face now, over his rugged features and thick brown mustache. He shook himself, bits of glass falling off his dark clothes and out of his hair styled as a shaved mohawk. He took a wide stance slamming one of his feet down.

The ledge Vin held quivered. The man reached out toward Vin open palmed like one would to catch a ball, then he squeezed his hand shut, pulling back. The ledge of the roof gave way as Vin fell back into the open air. Vin now understood, they were Earth Weavers. He saw another pane of glass tumbling to the ground, but just before hitting the ground concrete broke out, shooting over the running crowd protecting them as it shattered across the defensive surface.

Vin controlled his fall rolling in midair and kicking out as he rotated to send himself back toward the building, two floors below Mohawk. Vin barely balanced on the small lip of the wall; his right palm held out to create a constant circulating vortex of air keeping him up.

He looked up, determining he was right below the man, then he looked back down at the chaos on the streets. The ground was broken up with makeshift shelter from the Earth Weavers below. It looked like there was some Weavers darting in and out, recovering victims closest to the stage. Vin didn't linger on the stage, even from this distance he could see a pool of blood that filled the concave of the stage.

Vin looked back toward the fountain, water having already flooded out, coating the whole area wet and, unfortunately, red with blood. He could easily make out Amber. She was still fighting. Creating a powerful blast that hit one of the red orb structures so hard it knocked it loose and flew into one of the people attacking her.

Vin gritted his teeth, he could hardly process what this was and why. But he knew he could do something about it. Looking back up toward the top floor, he gathered his energy and gave a small hop off his ledge before rocketing back up.

Vin shot up right into the face of Mohawk. His arms braced his ascent on the lip before the window and brought his body into a crouched position, building the energy he used to get up there and redirecting it back out as he swung forward kicking Mohawk with both legs. The man's face barely managed a look of surprise before Vin's kick landed, sending the man careening across the office floor crashing through cubicles and desks.

Vin landed crouched, the two other weavers on the floor started thundering toward him. He stretched back on one leg kicking his other forward while punching one fist backward in a t-pose Weaving two blasts simultaneously toward his oncoming enemies. One was aimed directly for the attacker on his right while the other purposely missed, hitting a cubicle low just as the opponent was about to pass it. The hit caused the top half to explode up and out, showering the man with debris.

The three exchanged blows back and forth, Vin mostly dodging as they ripped whatever concrete they could to toss at him. That however just caused the two Earth Weavers to dodge each other's attacks or repel them. They inched closer to Vin but every time his attacker on the left passed a new cubicle Vin would target it, exploding stray staplers and computer parts at him.

After three exploded desks and four pens lodged into his person, the attacker bellowed in rage and slammed both hands down, a fault line cracking along the floor under Vin.

"Finally," Vin whispered, smiling. Then he launched himself out the window before the floor fell away. There was nothing the attacker on the right could do but manage a "You idiot!" before she collapsed to the floor below.

Vin boomeranged right back into the window the man was in front of, his kick was Weaved with propelling air, launching the man clear across the floor. Vin straightened out, papers fluttering around like a flock of seagulls in the wind. Vin breathed steadily, regaining his composure. It looked like it was finally over. He turned back to the area below.

It was a mess. The whole area flooded. Sculptures lay destroyed and scattered across the ground, which already sparkled like diamonds off the sun, reflecting the glass. One of the three flag pillars was broken at its base, now laying on the ground, the American flag soaked through, red and ragged.

He could hear the sirens wailing as they came closer.

Had this only taken minutes? All of this? He thought.

Then he felt something. A building of elemental energy behind him. He spun to see that Mohawk had recovered. His face contorted and full of rage, he Weaved all his energy into his two hulking fists and slammed down, much like his accomplice had but far more devastating. Vin crouched gathering energy and bounded backward into a somersault. Straightening his body as he began to fall, catching a last glimpse, as the whole floor collapsed. He Weaved wind around him as he slowed his descent until he was back on solid ground.

He landed close to the stage, glass crunching beneath his feet as he made his way from the building toward the emergency vehicles approaching. Something caught his eye. He looked toward a group of fallen victims near the stage. A banner rested bloody and shredded over a boy. Blake's glasses askew on his face as his eyes stared toward the sky, lifeless.

Chapter 15

V
IN FOUND THE ambulance that Amber had texted him
about. She stood there next to Matt, who's arm was in a sling.
He jogged over to them and hugged Amber. She looked fine
aside from a few bruises.

"You guys ok?" he asked.

"Yeah, I'm fine." Amber nodded. "The terrorists weren't too hard to
deal with." She saw Vin's look on his face at the word. "Yeah, that's what
everyone's calling them. The news outlets that are already here, and the
police."

Vin took a quick glance back at the destruction, deciding terrorist was
the perfect word to describe them.

"It was just hard to deal with their blatant lack of aim. They attacked
everything and everyone. I honestly couldn't tell how many there were, who
knows how many slipped out like they were part of the crowd," Amber

finished.

Vin looked to the news crews in the distance, already filming and reporting the incident. Amber followed his gaze and saw what he was looking at.

She grew morose and said, "It's not looking good. I overheard a good amount of them. They're all just talking about the in-fighting between Weavers, and the danger we are."

"What? Even though this was a peace rally about Weaver's rights?" Vin responded, incredulous.

Amber just shook her head sadly and shrugged. "Bad news moves faster than calm winds." Vin frowned contemplating how this could have happened, and why. He thought about the man on the top floor, Mohawk. He wondered if he was the leader, if he was caught, if he even made it out of the building.

Vin finally realized that Matt was being unusually quiet. He looked to his friend who was staring down at the ground.

"Hey, you alright, bud?" Vin asked, going to place a hand on Matt's shoulder, which Matt quickly shook off.

His head snapped up, Vin now realizing how scared he looked. "Am I alright? Of course not!" His voice was devoid of his usual sarcastic humor. "We shouldn't have even been here!" he continued, his voice rising. "Are you crazy? We should have been running, not fighting terrorists!"

Vin blinked, surprised. He stammered to get words out. He didn't even consider how his peers would have felt, how they weren't ready for what he'd been trained for. "Matty, I-I'm sorry-"

"We're not like you, Vin!" Matt shouted finally, cutting off Vin's apology. But Matt's rage quickly receded when he saw Vin's face. His normally peaceful facade began to chip away. His eyes began to well up with what looked like tears.

"Of course, you aren't," Vin started calmly. "How could you be," he continued with an edge in his voice. Amber put her hand to her mouth, she began to reach out a hand to comfort Vin but withdrew it, not sure what to do.

Vin continued, his voice also rising, "YOU got to spend the last three years trying out for sports! Taking electives! Making new friends!" Tears started in earnest now; his words came out choked. "I had to train and take leadership classes. Learn about how important I would be. About the wars I would fight in! About the terrors of the Earth, videos of hurricanes, volcanos, earthquakes. The devastation they'd caused! I was being told how it was my duty to help them, to save them!" he yelled at last, hot tears ran down his face.

He calmed slightly as he continued. "As if that wasn't bad enough, I was finally drafted. I had to go help at a hurricane that hit." Matt remembered when Vin had left. Vin was nervous, and when he returned, he seemed fine, but spent about a month reserved.

"The hurricane had already hit; the water had decimated the coast. I got to stand there, holding back the force of nature as-" he blinked hard, clearing his face and choking on the words, "- as bodies of people *I* couldn't save floated by."

"Oh Vin-" Amber tried to approach him but he put up his hands stopping her. He closed his eyes in an attempt to compose himself. When he finally opened them, he was fully calm again, but he looked cold and his voice was icy.

"No Matt, you're not like me. How could you be. You actually had a normal high school life." With that Vin turned and walked away toward his car, wiping his face with his sleeve.

Matt approached Vin about ten minutes later. He shuffled awkwardly toward him, trying to ignore an itch he had on his arm in the sling. Vin leaned against his car, arms crossed looking up toward the sky, but his eyes were closed. When Matt got close enough, Vin asked,

"Where's Amber?"

Matt did a double take, surprised Vin had known. He swore he hadn't looked at him the entire time he was walking toward the car.

"She's uh…created a distraction so I could get away without making a statement." He paused a moment before continuing, "Subsequently giving us some time." Vin looked over at him with one eye open and changed the subject.

"How's the arm?"

Matt sighed, leaning next to him against the car.

"It's not so bad. Probably won't be playing any intermural sports for a couple of months." He chuckled halfheartedly, but Vin didn't reciprocate.

Matt let out another sigh before turning to Vin. "Look, I'm sorry. I reacted without thinking about the last three years. I'm sorry for basically abandoning you. Also for being an ass, if I'm being honest. Better it happened to you than me."

Vin turned look at Matt. He raised an eyebrow in a question, "Is that supposed to make me feel better?"

"I just mean-" Matt's eyes traveled as if they'd find the words he was looking for. "You're stronger than me. You remember how I was after Maggie disappeared. I couldn't handle that like you did and you didn't even just handle it, you exceeded it! You're top of your class! You're so strong, Vin. If anyone could go through that and end up better for it, it was you."

Matt couldn't look at Vin anymore, his face red with embarrassment at his emotional words. Vin placed a gentle hand on Matt's bad arm and pulled him into a hug with his other one. Matt reached out with his good arm and hugged him back.

"I'm sorry I didn't think about what fighting would mean to you, Matt," Vin said as he pulled back. "But I'm so proud of you for standing your ground and helping all of those people. You make Earth Weavers everywhere proud. I guess I was so confident with you watching my back I didn't think about what it'd be putting you guys through."

Matt rolled his eyes laughing, "Ha! Me maybe, but not Amber. That girl was badass. I think she took out like two or three of those guys."

Vin unlocked the car and opened the door. "Well, I guess we better text her the all clear and get the hell out of here."

Interlude

1 Year Ago – Seattle

T ANYA DROPPED A greasy brown bag onto the pale and stained island counter. She shrugged out of her heavy jacket that dripped with the rain collected from outside. She slapped it down on one of the stools, water spraying the ground. She shook out her long and dark hair. She pulled at the ends, bringing it into her vision, missing the vibrant dye she used to use.

She gave the apartment a once over. It was still shabby, still devoid of furniture, color, of anything comfortable. Tanya could laugh herself to sleep at what she was now, a squatter. Her eyes fell on the doorway to another room, through it she could see a form wrapped in a blanket on a mattress on the floor.

Tanya padded across the apartment into the bedroom. There was little in that room as well. Though the blanket on the mattress was of the finest quality. Tanya picked it out herself when she stole it. She went to the bed and sat on its edge, putting her hands on her head. They had a fun go at first. They had tv's and game systems, laptops, and other boujie electronics. There was only so much you can do without electricity and only so long you could stay in places that tracked internet usage.

She looked back and down at the figure still curled on the bed. She reached a hand out and pulled the blanket down low enough to expose Magdalena's soft features. She was beautiful, Tanya thought. Always was, still is. A queen living the life of a peasant. Tanya stroked Magdalen's wild hair out of her face and let a finger trace her cheek.

Magdalena mumbled a reply, groaning and shifting under the blanket.

"Morning," she managed, barely audible the sleep still in her throat.

Tanya frowned. It was 3 p.m. She slept all day. Sure, they were out late last night but she could already tell what this was.

"Good morning," Tanya said anyway. "I brought food, figured you'd need it after last night." She let out a desperate chuckle. "That was fun right? I think that dude is still wondering what cooked his phone."

Magdalena didn't participate in the recount of their previous night's debauchery. "If you go out again can you stop by a pharmacy, maybe get some- "

Tanya launched herself off the bed. Magdalena hardly reacted. "No Maggie. You don't need that crap."

"It would help. You don't want me like this," she said dryly, turning back into her covers.

Tanya sat back down, then hesitantly laid down next to Magdalena, wrapping her arms around the girl.

"You're perfect the way you are. I wouldn't want you any other way, I just want you as yourself." There was a long silence, but Magdalena seemed to settle into Tanya's embrace.

"If you want to lay here all day, hell all week, then let's do it. We're *free* to do what we want, Maggie," Tanya continued. Magdalena nodded in appreciation.

"But…" Tanya began, "we really need money."

Magdalena sighed, "Fine."

Tanya gave her a squeeze and got back up. "I'll wake you when it's dark." Then she went back toward the kitchen shutting the door softly, sparing one last look at the girl with the wild hair on the lumpy mattress.

She went to the counter and fished out one of the burgers. She unwrapped it and took slow uninterested bites. She stared around again at the squalor they were staying in. She closed her eyes and fell into grand memories. She thought of the lobster, the grand chocolate desserts, the exquisite bathrooms with smells of every beautiful scent in the world. She remembered their strength when they stood at the top of the world. The smile and confidence on Magdalena.

Her hand squeezed around the greasy burger, the condiments rolled out, bleeding down her hand. She gave a scream of frustration and threw it across the room, the contents splattering against the newspapered window.

She slid herself to the floor holding back useless tears and silently wept.

The two girls looked both ways before approaching the ATM across the street. They stayed clear of its camera, standing off to its side.

With a nod from Tanya, Magdalena reached out a hand. It quivered before it came to life with electricity that flashed out and zapped the ATM. There was a spark and hiss, the camera and screen cracked and exploded. Bills started to plummet from its mouth, and Tanya bent down to scoop them up. She took about five hundred dollars' worth until they turned and left the rest to waste on the floor.

Money could be tracked, and they learned they couldn't very well carry thousands of dollars on their person. They jogged away quickly and turned down an alley. She looked over at Magdalena and gave her an encouraging smile, Magdalena pretended not to notice. She was lost in her head; she couldn't stop thinking about their last two years. How every minute felt like a cage that was slowly closing in on them, inescapable. Desperation came to her, late at night in the dark hours of her mind. There was no home for her, no hiding from the disappointment, the hate. Her fist gripped tightly, so hard her nails started to cut into her flesh.

Magdalena was so caught up in her thoughts she hadn't realized a man stood in their path at the end of the alleyway, not until Tanya had a hand on her arm.

"Move it, perve," Tanya called, stepping in front of Magdalena.

The man moved closer. He was tall, with a long coat and hood over his head. He didn't look threatening, but Tanya and Magdalena learned they never did, initially.

He held out his hands in surrender.

"I'm not here to harm you." He spoke serenely, not quite polite but not threatening.

"Well, I can't say the same," Tanya replied, flame leapt into her grasp.

"Please," he started. "There's no need for your fire here, Tanya." Magdalena gasped at her friend's name on the stranger's tongue. Tanya gritted her teeth and tried to take a step forward. Her foot wouldn't lift, she stared down and in shock saw the ground had encased it.

What the hell? When did he do that? She hadn't seen him do it, no movement from him at all. She didn't even hear it.

"I know what your fire can do, Tanya," he continued. "That casino in Vegas. That nightclub in L.A."

Magdalena's eyes widened in disbelief. *He's been following us.* She reached out a hand, electricity answering her call, but before she could throw her hand forward, the closest ladder on a nearby fire escape reached out in a grinding snap, coiling around Magdalena's arm like a snake.

Both girls stared back in shock, then returned their glare to the stranger. Another man came around the corner to stand next to the Earth Weaver, his hand outstretched.

"Another Anomaly," Magdalena whispered. Then with her other hand she summoned more lightning. The Anomaly squeezed his hand and the metal around Magdalena tightened. She cried out, letting the lightning wink out as she clawed at the metal with her free hand.

"Maggie!" Tanya cried.

"Enough," The hooded stranger spoke, an air of authority unmatched. He turned to his companion and put a hand on him, slowly lowering his arm.

"Release them, Alexei," he said. The Anomaly immediately followed the command, releasing his hold on the metal. Magdalena dropped to the ground, massaging her hand. The earth released around Tanya as well and she ran to Magdalena stooping down to check on her.

The stranger walked forward. "I'm not here to harm you. Nor am I any kind of police force here to arrest you."

He lowered his hood and they stared up at his foreign features. His head was shaved, his face calm with trained serenity. "I'm here to help you. Like I've helped others like you."

Magdalena's eyes flicked to the Anomaly behind him. He stood strong, confident with his arms crossed and dignity rested on his shoulders like a knights pauldrons. He wore it so well. But more than any of that, she noticed something he didn't have, something Magdalena longed to no longer have herself. Something in his eyes he was missing, that same something she saw every time she looked in the mirror. There was no fear in his eyes.

"What're you? Some kind of collector?" Tanya asked with poison, but it didn't stop her from taking in the two men. The way they walked, unslouched and with clothes that spoke of a well lived life.

The bald man hesitated for only a moment, and as if he was reading their minds he spoke. "You live in filth. You hide in shadows and fear humans jealous of your power." He paced back and forth in front of them.

"You let *them* dictate how you live. But you have forgotten something important." He stopped to look down at them, in their eyes they saw the look of a man with unstoppable determination. A man with a goal.

"You are not alone." The Metal Weaver behind the bald man said in a heavy Russian accent. The bald man nodded in agreement.

"We are Kings and Queens among men, and you have forgotten your place. Let us help you."

Queens. The word reverberated in Tanya's mind. She looked to Magdalena, who was staring down, as she always did. Down to the earth when she belonged in the sky.

Tanya stood, the same determination from the stranger flooded into her. She took her place next the bald man, opposite the Metal Weaver.

"We don't belong down here, Maggie," Tanya urged with pleading in her voice.

Magdalena looked to them, three strong Weavers. So sure of themselves, so confident. How she wished with all her might she could be like them.

"What must I do?" she asked weakly, eyes to the pavement, her long hair draped around her, hiding her from the world. A gentle hand she knew to be Tanya's brushed her hair aside and smoothed it onto her back. Magdalena looked over to Tanya crouched next to her, and then up to the stranger standing above them, his arm stretched out to her.

"Take my hand," he said.

Chapter 16

MATT TRIED TO SLEEP in the back seat most of the ride back to Rockwell, waking only when a bump shook the car and caused a ripple of pain through his arm. So naturally he didn't sleep at all, just winced and groaned in pain every thirty seconds.

He gave a fist bump to Vin as he was dropped off at his house, and surprisingly Amber got out to give him a hug. Though they didn't necessarily fight side by side, he felt like they now had an unspoken bond through mutual kick-assery. He stood in his driveway waving at them as they drove away and continued to stand there a couple of minutes after that. He looked up at the night sky and sighed. Finally, he decided to face what awaited him inside.

"Mijo!" Matt's mother shrieked before he even had time to close the door behind him. She smothered him in a hug that immediately made him yelp as she gripped his hurt arm. She cooed at him, gently rubbing his bad arm. Before immediately smacking his good one and flew into rapid-fire Spanish about how worried she was and how dangerous it was.

His mother was first generation Mexican American and didn't speak English well. His father was too, but he learned English due to his work. He stood behind his mother in the doorway to the kitchen, a yellow apron on with flowers and swirly text that said Mamacita. He had his burly arms crossed over his chest, looking surly, but grunted his affection which loosely translated to, "Glad you're home, safe" and "I love you." Matt was ninety-five percent fluent in Mexican grunts at this point.

"Dinner will be ready soon," his mother told him in Spanish, before reaching to his face one last time, stroking his cheek. Then turned, joining his father in the kitchen to finish- Matt made a quick sniff in the air - tamales.

"Gracias!" he called after them. Then went toward his room but stopped by their fireplace. His mother went furniture exchanging again. They always had new couches and tables. He didn't know where she always went, but one day he would leave for school with large brown leather sofas and return to modern flat designer lounges. Today was plush couches covered in brown suede. Above the fireplace on the mantle was a new mirror. More for artistic than conventional use. It looked like someone took a square sheet of mirror and cut into smaller squares like a pizza and rearranged them, interlaying them in a black metal frame. Matt looked into his broken reflection, a small cut on his cheek had a butterfly Band-Aid and his right eye had a bruise to go along with his fractured right arm.

His gaze lingered to the right and down, to the only object in his house that hadn't changed in the last four years. A simple wooden end table with a drawer, on top sat a single photo and a small statue of a dark marble monarch butterfly. He went to the photo and picked it up. It was perfectly clean, always is, the only indication of his mother's love. A girl with long wild dark hair stood on a rocky shore, the ocean behind her and the wind in her hair. She didn't smile, but she looked at peace. A picture from their family trip to El Salvador, the last time their family was together and whole.

He set it down and tugged at the drawer, locked, as usual. Matt was fairly certain his parents weren't aware that Matt knew what was in the drawer. He reached in his shirt and pulled out his long necklace with a stone carving at the end. He took a peek toward the kitchen. Hearing his parents talking and the food sizzling on the stove, he moved the necklace to the drawer, Weaving its shape and slipped the makeshift key in and unlocked it.

Inside was a plastic bag containing an object so burnt it was almost unrecognizable, but at one time it resembled a phone. The only indication of his father's love and sacrifice. He heard some shuffling in from the kitchen and quickly put the broken phone in the drawer and shut it. His mother's figured formed in his periphery.

"Mijo?" she asked hesitantly.

Matt mulled over his thoughts before finally asking, "If you knew where she was? If you could go find her?" He looked to his mother, pleading with his eyes. His mother shot a quick glance to the memorial before an attempt at a weak smile.

"Come, dinner's ready."

Tears quickly brimmed in Matt's eyes. He managed to choke out, "I'm not hungry, thanks." Before bolting for his room. Inside he slammed his bag down and fell to the floor in front of his bed. He took a moment of hard breathing and managed to force back his tears before looking up and around his room. Sports posters lined his walls, jerseys from all his past teams hung next to trophies from seasons he had won. Clothes littered the floor, and he looked to his desk. His laptop was still open from his hasty exit earlier that morning. He got up wiping his nose, and went to his desk. He knocked the chair into his desk which awoke his computer. The lock screen shined to life. A selfie with his sister and himself, trees dotted the background. They both looked anxious but excited as they stared at a monarch butterfly perched on Magdalena's finger.

He fought back the urge to do something illogical. Turning from his computer and going to his dresser, attempting to remove his shirt carefully failed and he got frustrated, ripping it off, dealing with the pain and throwing it. The shirt flew across the dresser and took something with it, landing with a thud.

He bent down to retrieve the item it knocked over. Two hollow eyes stared back at him. A mask painted like fire with flames licking the edges. He frowned at the memory of the mask. Himself and Tanya never really saw eye to eye, the mask was the one time they worked together. Designing and making it for Magdalena's birthday.

He lay back on his bed, resting the mask on his bare chest. He stared up into the racing lines of his fan. Matt placed the mask over his face, staring through it with the barest of his periphery obstructed. Magdalena had always been his hero. He gave another look to his past achievements that hung on the walls and cluttered the free surfaces of his room.

His family pushed him and Magdalena to play soccer growing up. She was great, he recalled practicing penalty kicks with her in their back yard. She never missed. Matt still cringed when he remembered how awful he was. He couldn't dribble to save his life. He was teased and humiliated by his teammates and other players. It was Magdalena who had, instead of pushing him to try harder or practice more like his coach and father, started trying other sports with him. He couldn't kick a ball for anything, but his football toss was great. His hand-eye coordination made receiving in football and catching in baseball easy. He was only 8 by the time he stopped playing soccer, but he, in general, just thought he was bad. Magdalena showed him his strengths. Confident-Matt was born after that.

When Matt started to fail English and needed remedial studies, it was Magdalena who pointed out how good he was at Math. He started taking computer classes. His childhood seemed like it would have been nothing but disappointments if not for Magdalena seeing the best in him.

Matt pulled the mask away from his face and went to place it back on his dresser. He traced the bristled orange and yellow feathers that made its flames.

She may have been his hero, but she wasn't only his savior. Tanya probably wouldn't be alive if not for Magdalena. She never told the story, but he heard Tanya tell it too many times whenever they got too much alcohol and cannabis in their system surrounded by their friends.

The day they met, Magdalena could tell something was wrong. Matt assumed it was their father's influence, slowly leaking his cop paranoia into them over the years. Tanya and Magdalena weren't even really friends, but she showed up one day at Tanya's apartment. She had to see for herself. Tanya's brother beat her. When Magdalena confronted Tanya, she told her to leave it, she would handle it. She wouldn't go to the cops. So, one day Magdalena went there. She provoked him, and he beat Magdalena too. He was too much of a dumbass and assumed too little of a 13-year-old girl.

Matt had never seen someone so happy to have their ass kicked as when Magdalena walked in the front door that day. He dropped his abuela's china plate right there in the living room when he saw her. Bleeding and black eyed, worse than he was just minutes ago. His mother didn't even care about the broken china, firing off rapid Spanish to fret over Magdalena. His Dad just calmly got up, got dressed, and went to Tanya's.

Tanya was still too scared to testify. Matt smiled at the memory of his sister. She was fearless back then. Magdalena told Tanya she didn't have to, that Magdalena would. Due to it being a onetime incident and the fact that

Magdalena provoked it, the court almost gave Tanya's brother an easy sentence. Magdalena's courage changed something in Tanya and gave her the push she needed.

Together both their testimonies put her brother away, and since then Tanya never left her side. Matt stifled a sob as he looked back to his computer, first Magdalena, then Vin. He was tired of being saved. *Who was going to be her hero*, he thought.

Matt gathered his resolve, shut his laptop, grabbed his hoodie, and as carefully as he could with his hurt arm climbed out his window and into the night.

Fifteen minutes later he left the semi-dense forest behind his house and entered a clearing. The same one from the photo. Memories came to Matt as he recalled all the times they escaped here. Any manic episode she had, any bad break up Matt went through, they would come here and try to catch butterflies. He crossed to the middle and slowly started to rotate staring up at the stars. He started to feel foolish. He was just starting to think, *What am I doing?* when he turned to see someone standing at the edge of the clearing. Matt yelped and almost fell back.

The figure came forward until the moonlight bathed the form revealing long black wild hair. A sleek black jacket and tight jeans. Her combat boots crunched on the grass as she made her way toward Matt.

The photo came to life in front of him as his sister came closer.

"Maggie!?" He whispered, a smile spreading across his face, but his happiness turned to hesitation as his imagination turned toward reality. It was Magdalena but her hair was no longer lively and full, now dirty and stringy. Her face gaunt and pale. Her leather jacket hung loose on her thin body. On her wrist she wore a plain metal bracelet. The most striking change of all, her eyes looked hard, and haunted.

"Matty," she said. "Baby brother." Her arms wrapped around him in a hug.

He choked out a chuckle as his tears returned. "Today's a day for hugs and tears apparently," he said sniffling. Her hug didn't seem to reach her face as she pulled back and her features remained hard.

She glanced down at his arm. "I came to warn you. You need to be more careful."

Matt stuttered on his response, "W-warn me? What do you mean? Where have you been? Wait-" The immediate happiness of his sister began to sink away as his confusion set in. "How did you know I was here?"

"I mean it, Matty. Take care of yourself, stay out of danger."

"Did you follow me here?" he asked, his voice rising in a frantic nature, but Magdalena simply turned and started leaving the way she came.

"Oh my god," Matt said. "I was right, that was Tanya in Dallas." Horror crept into his voice, as he recalled the girl with bright pink hair streaking across the fountain.

"God…Maggie, you followed me from Dallas? You were there? Are you with them?!" His questions exploded out. But she didn't answer. She just kept walking. Matt ran after her.

"ANSWER ME!" he screamed, his good arm reached out and grabbed her left wrist around her metal cuff. A shock flew through his arm. He yelled as it flattened him on the ground. Magdalena whipped around, her eyes alive with electricity.

"I said STAY OUT OF IT!" With that she was gone.

Matt lay hugging his numb arm into his body, tears pouring from his eyes as he wept. Alone in the clearing.

Chapter 17

THE DRY HEAT and sunny evenings made way for harsh cold rains and chilly mornings as the year moved into November.

Vin locked his phone with a sigh, slumping against the door to his Durango. Amber was absently playing with the water that rested on the pavement of the parking lot. She started to make the past rain fall back into the sky before letting gravity take it back down.

"He bailed again?" she asked casually.

"Yup," Vin confirmed, clicking the remote on his car and climbing in. Amber followed suit getting in the passenger.

"That's like what? The third weekend in the row?" she asked.

"Pretty sure it's been every weekend since Dallas." They let the memory sit silently.

"Well…we don't have to do anything; you can just drop me off at home," Amber said.

"No, we can still hang out. I think the only other thing I have planned is movie night with my family, if that's something you're interested in-"

"Yes!" Amber said excitedly before Vin even finished. They both laughed, Amber trying to avoid turning red from her over-enthusiasm. She had been enjoying the weekends they spent at Vin's grandfather's home, helping him connect to his Fire Weaving. Recently though it had become too cold, overcast and rainy to continue. She worried their time together would taper off because of this.

"Ok then. They said it wasn't mandatory to go, but I'm sure they'll be happy we're there." He pulled out of the parking lot of the school, Vin's thoughts on Matt and his recently developed mysterious ways.

"I wish he could join us on our Weaving meditations," Amber said, as if reading Vin's mind. They had spent at least two days a week just going to the park and basking in the energy emenating off the elements.

"Yeah," Vin said in simple agreement. If he was honest with himself, though, he didn't mind too much. Matt never really focused on the metaphysical side of Weaving. He was a good athlete which made him a competent fighter with his element, but Vin would never say he was a good Weaver. He felt it was a fair assessment. After all, Matt got to spend time competing in sports and hanging with his friends.

Matt never understood Vin's need for some peace amid his stressful schedule. Vin supposed he had his own moments of being too busy for Matt and dodging his requests. Though he didn't remember if he rejected the invitations or altogether never received them.

Amber turned up the volume on the radio as a repetitive but catchy pop song came on. She began singing and bouncing to it. Running her hand through her long curls and over enunciating the heavy rap lyrics, being playfully sassy. He looked to her and smiled and he let his fretting fall away as he joined her in a terrible karaoke duet of the song.

Amber and Vin arrived at his house, walking in they found his father on the floor in front of their entertainment stand slowly picking through their DVD collection. He looked over his shoulder and let out a big smile when he saw them.

"Hey kids!"

"Hey Dad."

"Hello, Mr. DeLuca."

"We decided not to go out, so we're here for movie night," Vin told him.

"Bambini!" Vin's mother exclaimed hearing their voices and coming in from the kitchen. She placed a bowl of popcorn on the coffee table in front of the couches.

After wiping her hands on a towel that hung out of her pocket she went to hug Vin. Amber was pleasantly surprised that his mother didn't hesitate to give her a hug right after him.

"Glad you guys could make it! Go get yourselves something to drink and some bowls to split the popcorn," she advised.

Turning away, Noemi yelled toward the stairs, "Juliette! Popcorns ready and we're about to start the film!"

Vin and Amber heard his father scoff as they headed for the kitchen. "Are we? Because I'm still looking for a movie."

His wife went to him and planted a kiss on his cheek and attempted to say quietly, "Well, I figured we go ahead and tell them now before the movie starts." Loud enough for Amber and Vin to still hear her.

They exchanged glances and silent questions formed on their face. Vin gave a shrug before pointing toward a corner of the kitchen. "Bowls are in that cabinet. We have soda, sweet tea, and lemonade. What would you prefer?"

Amber split from Vin and headed to the cabinet. "Sweet tea, please."

Vin started to rummage through the fridge as Amber pulled out two bowls.

"Are these ok?"

Vin stuck his head out of the fridge, a string of cheese hung out of his mouth and a jug of tea in one of his hands. Amber couldn't suppress a smile at how silly she looked. He mirrored her grin and pulled himself out, closing the door and putting a jug of tea and a soda on the table. He chewed it quickly, but between bites he replied,

"Two is fine, but the other can be for Juliette. We're going to be on the love seat so we can just share a bowl."

He was so distracted by pouring two glasses that he didn't see her blush and smile at the thought of them sharing. She had flashes to cheesy romantic comedies where they bump hands going for the popcorn at the same time.

Juliette broke her brief daydream as she came down the stairs.

"That one for me?" she asked, pointing to the soda on the table.

"You know it," he said, grabbing it and throwing it to her giving it a spin as it flipped toward her.

"Shaken, not stirred," he grinned.

She grabbed it easily out of the air but held it at arm's length like it would explode. Juliette sighed then looked to Amber.

"You're a Water Weaver, right?"

Amber nodded.

Juliette hummed in thought. "I don't trust you yet. I'll need some time to bring you to the dark side." Her eyes fell back on her brother. "You win this time," she said, leaving for the living room without retaliating.

Vin laughed and gave Amber a smile. "Wow, you're quite the deterrent."

Amber shrugged but returned the smile. "I've got your back, what can I say?"

Vin brought in their glasses, setting them on the table, with Amber following behind. She handed Juliette a bowl. Unlike Juliette, he sat on the love seat while Juliette filled her bowl and lounged in the armchair across from him.

Amber sat down next to Vin and they both looked expectantly at Vin's father and mother, who stood awkwardly like they weren't trying to make it obvious that they were waiting to say something.

Juliette immediately hopped on her phone while snacking on pieces from her bowl, oblivious to the situation.

"Juliette," Noemi said softly but with a hint of annoyance. Too softly it seemed as Juliette continued to scroll on her phone. Vin's father cleared his throat and finally she got her attention.

She looked up, taking in the general attitude of the room and the judgmental glare from Vin.

"Oh, I'm sorry, no one told me we were having a family meeting," she said exasperated, shoving the phone in her hoodie pocket and gave her parents her full attention while still eating her popcorn like they were the main attraction.

Noemi sighed and closed her eyes like she was wishing for strength before wrapping her arm around her husband.

"Your father has something he wants to tell you all. Giovonni," she said to him with a nod.

Vin's father looked nervous, his shoulders rising like he was trying to retreat into his shirt. Then he finally dropped them and replaced his nervousness with a beaming grin.

"I got the supervisor position!"

"Oh my god!" Juliette immediately screamed.

"So no more nights?" Vin asked.

Giovonni smiled proudly and nodded. "No more nights or late shifts. I make my hours."

Juliette squealed, launching her bowl off her lap and diving for her father. They embraced tightly; she buried her face in her father's chest.

Vin immediately, to Ambers surprise, reached over and embraced her.

"That's so awesome, Dad. I didn't know you were up for a promotion," he said, turning back to him. Noemi wiped her eyes as they had begun to water, then went to clean up Juliette's mess, not even upset.

Juliette and her father pulled away but kept an arm around her shoulder. "Well, I didn't want to get anyone's hopes up, especially mine."

"So this is like…a celebratory movie night?" Amber asked.

"Basically, yeah," he laughed out.

Juliette returned to her seat as her mother came back from the kitchen with a clean bowl.

"I can believe Dad kept this a secret. I didn't expect it from you, mom," she said, accepting the bowl from her.

"Oh, trust me, it wasn't easy."

Juliette turned back to her father. "So anyway, what did you pull out for us?"

Giovonni turned back to the entertainment center and pulled out three DVDs from the shelf. "Ok, so we have Norman and Hooch." Juliette immediately groaned, it was an old favorite of their dad's, a cop movie about a dog side kick they had watched what felt like hundreds of times over the year. Even Noemi grimaced. She didn't hate it as much as her kids, but she only tolerated it because she knew it was her husband's favorite movie.

"Alright, alright. It was worth a try," he relented. Amber let out a giggle that made Vin smile.

"Cheer It On." He showed the second DVD, which Juliette reacted to by letting out similar gleeful cheer that rivaled her reaction to her father's promotion. A cult-classic that Vin and his sister grew up on about a group of underdog cheerleaders rising to the top against all odds. It was famously quoted by everyone in their generation.

"Thought you might like that," Giovanni mumbled.

And finally, he held up the third DVD, titled "2020" a movie about the end of the world in the midst of world-wide catastrophic natural disasters.

"Really Gio?" Noemi said, disapproving of his choice. "Don't you think we hear enough about that?" She couldn't help but glance to Vin.

"I'm fine, mother. An end of the world video doesn't bother me."

"See?" his father agreed. "He's fine!"

"I feel like I still haven't really heard much about the Reliefs you participated in," Amber said, genuinely curious, thinking back to their conversation that day in Dallas.

"Not much to say," Vin replied defensively.

"Oh please, he's being modest," Juliette chimed in.

"They were awful, he had an awful time," she continued.

"Now Juliette, he didn't have a-" Giovanni started, but Juliette cut him off.

"I live down the hall from him. Trust me, he had an awful time," she said curtly. Then continued to mumble, "Pretty disgusting they'd make high schoolers go at all."

Vin didn't even reply. His first instinct was to argue with his sister, but he was genuinely taken aback by her sympathy.

Vin's father nodded, "Right good point. Alright, Cheer It On it is." He put the DVD in.

Vin felt a nudge on his arm. He looked over to see Amber prodding him with the bowl of popcorn. He lit up at her smile and took some, leaning back to enjoy the movie.

An hour and a half later and Vin, Amber, and Juliette having quoted most of the movie, they in unison sung to the popular pop song from the credits. Even Giovanni was belting out the chorus. Noemi had taken the empty glasses and bowls to the sink. As she came back, she was moving and grooving to the song, her husband got up to shake with them.

"Oh god!" Juliette groaned. "Well, now my nights ruined." She complained, launching herself from her spot and stalking up the stairs.

"Why are you two so weird!" she yelled as she went.

Vin shielded his eyes in embarrassment, and Amber laughed at his expense.

Vin's mother gasped, "I forgot to water the garden! I was so flustered all day about your promotion, sweetie."

"Oh, I can do that for you," Amber immediately offered.

Noemi looked at her like she was about to immediately adopt her. "Really? You don't have to do that."

"No really, its ok. I'm a Water Weaver like you, hardly a trouble," she said standing.

"Oh that's right. Lovely having someone else here who can!" she said, embracing Amber in an unexpected hug.

Vin stood as well and walked out to their back yard with Amber. As the door shut, the credit music faded to a soft hum and they were left with the calm open night. Vin went over to the water faucet and turned it on. Amber pulled at the water and began feeding it to his mother's plants across the yard.

He walked over to stand by her as she worked. After a comfortable couple of seconds of silence, Vin began humming the credit song and moving his hips back and forth.

Amber laughed at his silliness. He began bumping into her with his hips, causing her to relent, and they began swaying in time.

She moved her hands over the yard like a symphony composer. The water raised and dropped at her call, soaking into the soil and the plants. The moon and stars cast over them a serene scene.

"I like your family," Amber finally said.

"You sure? They're kinda crazy."

Amber laughed and nodded in agreement. "That's fine."

Vin watched her as she moved her element. He examined her strong features and gentle demeanor. Her peaceful use of her abilities drew him in like water to roots.

She turned to look at him and he quickly turned away, afraid he'd been caught. He was but she pretended not to let Vin know. She may not have gotten her hand-caressing popcorn moment, but tonight seemed pretty perfect to her.

Chapter 18

NOVEMBER BLEW BY and December arrived, with its constant overcast skies and the promise of a warm and roaring bonfire.

"Ok so Saturday, I say meet at my house," Vin said to Amber and Matt. The three sat in a quiet corner in the school library

"As usual," Amber supplied, flashing Vin a smile. Matt kept his eyes on his computer scanning the screen.

"Yep, as usual," Vin responded to Amber. Then looked to Matt. "Yo, Matty. What're you doing?"

"Huh?" he asked, barely taking his eyes off the screen until he realized they were both looking at him. "Oh, nothing," he said quickly, shutting his laptop.

"Uh-huh," Amber mused, "Is this about one of your secret events you're always running off to?"

"What? Secret events? What the hell are you talking about?" Matt asked, confused.

"I'm telling you," Vin said to Amber, "Definitely underground fight club."

"No way," she replied. "His arm is still in the sling. He would get his ass kicked. I'm still going with cock fighting or chihuahua races." She laughed.

"Nah, he could be faking. Easy. I bet he's hustling those guys."

"Wow," Matt finally said, appalled. "First off," he said looking to Amber, "That's racist, and second," looking to Vin, "I can kick anyone's ass, including yours, with one or both hands tied behind my back."

Matt pretended that he was being sincere and for the most part Vin had let him believe he'd gotten away with it, but he was worried about how much Matt had been AWOL since the terrorist attack. Amber picked up Matt's bag so he could put his laptop in it and make their way toward the doors together.

"So," Vin continued from earlier. "You're meeting at my house Saturday? So we can go to the bonfire together?"

Matt nodded his head, "Sure, sure."

They made their way down the quiet hall. School had been over for almost an hour now and only extra curriculars kept students around, and most had those cleared out as well due to the Bonfire event the following day. Amber quickly stuck out an arm to halt the boys. They looked to her confused before she pointed down the hall drawing their attention.

Against the main window to the entrance of the school they had set up a memorial for those lost back in September. In front of it a lone student stood. She stared at the memorial for a long moment. Before wiping her face, which the trio couldn't but assume were tears, and walked out the door. After she left, the group walked up to the memorial, three photos stood with three smiling faces.

"I know in general this is tragic," Amber said. "But I feel bad for Ashleigh."

"She didn't know what she really had until he was gone," Matt added somberly.

"True, but I don't think the bonfire would even be happening if it wasn't for her. She really took over student council and fought for the continuation of the Weaver events," Vin said, walking up to one of the posters hanging on the wall next to the memorial.

The annual bonfire tradition. All seniors were welcome, but it was commonly known as a Weaver event. The students make the biggest bonfire they can create, have a little mid-year celebration where the Fire Weavers light it.

"Yeah, at least something good came of that day then." Matt said absently mostly to himself. He stared down at the three lost students, bouquets of mostly dried flowers littered the floor in front of them.

Amber made a motion toward the cafeteria, reaching out to find water. She bent and touched one of the bouquets, rehydrating the petals. Looking up to Matt she gave a kind smile. "Come on, Matt."

The three walked out minutes later, leaving behind a beautiful arrangement of colorful and lively flowers.

Matt sat in his room the next day. Dishes piled high on his desk to accompany his collection of empty plastic bottles. He hadn't left his computer all day. His eyes were bloodshot and deep bags beneath them as a result of rarely leaving his monitor and little sleep. He reached for one of his bottles and went to take a drink only to find it empty. He grumbled a swear and threw it into a heap of dirty laundry.

He turned back to his computer. An image of an intersection was on the screen, he clicked an arrow button and it went to another image, a different intersection. Matt had been using the police database for months now, his Dad would probably disown him if he knew he still had access to it. Matt paused at the thought, he *would* probably disown him if he knew he ever had access, he conceded. Scrolling through twelve more pictures, his phone vibrated as an alarm began going off. He picked it up, the phone reading six o'clock. The bonfire started at seven and he was supposed to be at Vin's by six thirty.

He sighed deeply, his head falling into his good hand, rubbing it through his hair. He lazily kept his good arm under his chin while he awkwardly used his arm in the sling to tap the right directional button to go to the next picture. This one was an image from a gas station. Matt scanned the image quickly and what he saw made his eyes widen. A streak of bright magenta. He couldn't tell for sure if it was her, but he saw the vehicle she was in.

He used the license plate to search specifically for that vehicle. He didn't dare hope, but anticipation built within him as he tracked the van. More pictures confirmed it was Tanya and a group of what Matt assumed to be terrorists. No Magdalena, but he could tell it looked like they had followed her south, even to Rockwell. Excitement took over as he jumped up and out of his chair, he paced back and forth trying to calm himself then just as quickly sat back at his desk.

He found the last photo of their vehicle, an intersection close to the lake. Pulling up google maps, he scoured the area around the light. Matt's breath caught in his throat as he looked at an unfinished apartment complex It was never completed due to permits not checking out. It was alone by the lake and far from the road. *A pretty good place to hide*, Matt thought.

He stood again gripped by determination and reached under his bed to pull out a duffel bag and proceeded to walk from his room and out the door.

"Off to the Bonfire?" his dad asked as Matt passed the living room. Matt almost smacked himself in the forehead, he had completely forgot, his discovery throwing him off.

"Uh, yeah, on my way to Vin's now." His father gave a nod of approval.

"Have fun," he said, before Matt left out the door.

He pulled out his phone, it was six twenty-five. He texted Vin.

Gonna be late, I'll meet you guys there.

With his good arm he detached the sling. He reached up with his now free arm, Weaving stones around him to follow. With a hard flex of his hand the stones shattered to dust. Releasing his hold, he grabbed his bike and started off toward the lake.

The air was crisp and cool as Vin and Amber exited his vehicle.

"Should we bring the water bottles?" Amber asked, looking through his back window to the case they picked up from the store on the way.

"Nah, I just stopped for some just in case. If they happen to run out, I'll come back for them."

They were both wrapped up in school hoodies and gave each other shy smiles as they walked together across the large empty field devoid of everything except most of the senior class, chaperones and a three-story high pile of wood and pallets ready to be burned. Earth Weavers had braced it so it wouldn't topple down.

They looked at each other again, brushing shoulders, naturally gravitating into one another for warmth.

"I've kind of always wanted to go to this." Amber eventually said.

"Why's that?" Vin asked.

"It just feels very…tribal. Makes me think of our rituals."

Vin chuckled. "Yeah I suppose school floats and mums isn't exactly the most natural of rituals. Should be nice."

They went to one of the truck beds and got sodas out of a cooler, getting into a conversation with some other Weavers and their prospects at the end of year. Vin was mostly quiet; he didn't like the idea of being stuck in a Weaver profession. Amber listened happily but didn't share her own plans. It got him thinking about what she wanted to do after school. Vin hoped that Matt was still a go on their own plan. After the incident in Dallas they seemed to clear up their argument and Vin had hoped he didn't come off as too jealous or insecure about their friendship.

He had believed Matt would just do his own thing while Vin was busy, and they'd come back together in the end. However, it was possible Matt wasn't as invested as Vin was any longer. He had, after all, spent a lot of time shirking their plans or remaining suspiciously busy.

Speaking of which, Vin thought, pulling out his phone and checking. Five minutes past seven. It looked like Matt was going to miss the start. At this point Vin was just happy he managed to get Matt to complete some applications to a couple of the schools. He considered that great progress.

A nudge jerked him out of his thought, it was Amber.

"I think everyone's getting ready." She said motioning toward the mounting pillar as groups started to gather. They walked toward it, spaced out from the rest.

"You ok?" She asked him, concern written on his face.

He faked a smile, "Yeah, of course. Just hoped Matt wouldn't miss it."

She smiled back, a look he couldn't read. "You're so thoughtful sometimes."

"Ha," He laughed. "If that's true I wouldn't have forced him, or you, to start attacking terrorists."

"Hey." She said, firmly, grabbing his arm. "That was one of the bravest things I've seen someone do. Yes, we lost people. Friends and classmates, but we also saved many more. More friends came back to school than not, wives returned to their husbands, fathers-" she looked down, pausing on the last word, "fathers went home to their daughters." She finished, regaining her confidence. Passion burned into him through her eyes. He thought back to the photo on the wall at her house.

He extended out an arm pulling her in for a hug, she already wasn't very far. "Thank you, Ambrosia."

They had mostly missed the speech student council was giving. They were catching the end as Ashleigh was finishing.

"I know this may be cheesy, but sometimes during moments like we had this year, we could use some good old cliché bliss. When we light this fire, think of it as a beacon to each other. Weaver and non-Weaver alike."

She was right, most were thinking, it was cheesy, but it didn't stop the words from churning something deep inside the gathered students.

"Now," she continued, "Seniors. Let's send up a beacon!" She yelled.

The crowd cheered, Vin and Amber joining their voices with the rising tide of the fellow students. The Fire Weavers gathered around the sides of the structure, a foot planted forward, a small pit of fire behind them. They brought their fists back and in one coordinated movement flung them forward. Balls of fire launched in arcs up and over them crashing into the pillar, the flames burst out and the dark empty lot came alive.

Chapter 19

MATT QUICKLY FLUNG himself and his bike off the road as headlights popped up on the dark horizon. He lay prone in the tall grass watching as an SUV crossed the bridge he just came down and drove into the parking lot of the abandoned building. He crawled closer, also groping for his binoculars that gracefully flew from around his neck during his dive.

His hand smacked them, and he tugged them toward him placing them over his eyes. He saw a group of four get out and walk toward the apartment building. Once the headlights went out, the area plunged back into darkness and he could no longer make anyone out. Matt got up in a crouched position as he stalked his way toward the building. The first floor's windows and doors were boarded up. He tried to peek through but couldn't see anything, Matt assumed they must have covered them all to snuff out any light.

He rounded the perimeter of the building, it looked like three vehicles were hidden behind it furthest from the road. One was the SUV that just pulled in, a large black jeep, and the same van he used to track them.

The only way Matt could see inside was through the same door the men used earlier. He pulled stones from the surrounding area to him and put them in the pockets that lined his combat pants. Taking one last look around he cracked open the door and peered inside. The hallway was mostly dark, two camping lanterns sat on stools illuminating the halls enough to guide your way. Faint voices could be heard but he deemed it to be safe enough to step inside and carefully closed the door behind him. He passed a couple of doors and tried each one except the one the voices came from. Most were empty, save some makeshift beds. Another he opened received a shrill response as a voice hissed,

"Donald! I swear if you come in here one more time while I'm trying to sleep, Ill drown you in that lake!"

Matt, in his shock, grunted a sorry and shut the door before she got up. Then he winced wondering how stupid it sounded for one of them to apologize. He exhausted all the rooms on the first floor and ascended to the second. He was just passing one of the first rooms when the door opened. Luckily, it opened away from Matt. In his panic he climbed up the wall to the ceiling, Weaving his fingers to easily press through the concrete, suspending himself above the two that came out. The poorly lit hallway helped camouflage him as they passed harmlessly beneath him.

"Dedric and his team got back just now. They scouted all the areas," one man said to the other.

"I still think the Space Center should be the main hit," the other replied.

"Nah, what's the message in that? We need to hit an idea

somewhere closer to Earth."

Their voices muffled as they entered another room and the door shut behind them. Matt dropped to the ground and carefully opened the door they came from, seeing it was clear he went inside.

"The Space Center?" Matt whispered to himself. "Are they actually here to attack Houston?" The thought immediately died in his throat once he got a proper look at the room. The walls were covered in stickie notes and papers. A large map that covered most of the southwest of the United States was pinned up in the center. There was so much technical equipment Matt didn't even know what it could be used for. Tall towers held more boxes of the tech, wires spilling out connecting to modems on the tables. He quickly ran over to the computers, there was so much to sift through, he knew he wouldn't have enough time.

He went to the standing corkboard that held the map. He placed his finger on the west coast, a large X was drawn through Seattle. He traced a finger down the map until it landed on another large X drawn through Dallas, with small circles put around spots in the Houston area. Matt's throat went dry. *They are going to attack Houston.* Matt confirmed.

"What the Hell?!" A voice broke him from his horror, only for Matt to realize he was in even bigger trouble now. It was one of the men that had left in the hallway, already coming back.

"What're you-" the large burly man began to say only for Matt to react viciously and throw a rock so hard it cracked over the man's face, blood squirting out. Matt was ninety percent sure he broke through bone. He leapt over the man and made a run down the hallway but unfortunately the other man he had seen didn't stay in his room either. He stood in the middle of the hall, his surprise didn't last as he readied himself and punched forward, Weaving a blast of air toward Matt.

Matt Weaved, pulling all the stones on him out of his pockets. He created a cone in front of him, the stones puncturing the blast, it dissiapated around him. He then began punching forward, propelling the stones down the hallway; causing the Air Weaver to leap back into one of the rooms.

He could hear the man he left behind get up and start yelling for the others. Stopping at the door the Air Weaver jumped into, he turned to it, slamming the door and Weaving the concrete around it to crumple inward, sealing the door. Matt sensed incoming earth and without looking he jumped up, pushing hard off the door he had just shut, flinging himself backward and crashing through the door behind him into one of the rooms. He caught a quick glimpse of concrete flying by in the hallway.

He scrambled up looking around the empty room. He could hear the man he trapped banging on the door and yelling, the loud footsteps of the Earth Weaver charging down the hallway, and the rising voices and commotion of reinforcements downstairs.

"Shit." Matt swore looking around, his eyes finally landing on the window. "Double shit."

He reached out both arms, energy flowed out of them as he Weaved it into and around the window. He pulled both arms back, clenching his hands like he was closing on something extremely durable and difficult. Then he flung his arms forward, releasing his closed hands and the energy he poured into the walls. It exploded outward, rubble and glass flying out onto the ground below. Matt took a running leap out the window.

He landed hard but recovered, Weaving the earth to soften the impact and running as quickly as he could so he could dive back into the tall grass and overgrown trees that skirted the lake. He turned back to see the terrorist standing in the hole of the window. Matt rolled his eyes as he noticed if he would have gone into the next room there would have been a perfectly good balcony he could have gone out.

Noisc from the side of the building drew his attention as men began pouring out.

"Well...triple shit." He pulled out his phone, staring at it as he debated, but quickly made up his mind and called reinforcements of his own.

Chapter 20

EMBERS SPRUNG OFF the towering inferno, the fire light set eyes aglow as they watched in awe. Vin reached out his hand Weaving small gusts of wind that sent the embers spiraling until they winked out. Amber watched, giggling.

"This is beautiful." She said, Vin looking back at her as she faced the bonfire, her face bright.

"Yeah, it is." He agreed.

Vin looked around the circle of students, most people were grouped up with their own teams, the art crew, sports teams, student council. Everyone else, Vin noticed, had coupled up. They held each other close, arms wrapped around one another staring into the fire, smiles on their faces. Vin grew hot as he felt like the distance between him and Amber was much more pronounced now. He was about to turn to her again when she spoke,

"Want to dance?" She asked.

Vin's head snapped to her, "What?"

She giggled again; he'd never seen her this happy. "Maybe nothing my Grandmother would disapprove of. Just some dancing. You, me, and the elements?"

Vin smiled back, he looked toward the fire and breathed in. He felt the large concentration of elemental energy in the area, the lot teemed with it.

Without saying anything, he simply held out a hand and she took it. Together they moved and swirled, Vin lashing out with his energy Weaving the air to create a spectacle of dancing fire and sprouting embers. Amber pulled on the nearby water from one of the many large buckets kept in order to extinguish the flames if need be. She weaved the water around the fire, as it passed in front of the flames it created a whole other experience, like liquid amber flowing like rivers.

They didn't dance to any music, instead following the beat of the elements. Vin and Amber felt other foreign energy enter their own. Other Weavers followed suit and started dancing as well. Flames shot out of the pyre fluttering like glowing creatures. Stones of various sizes floated along, passing like ancient pylons.

Vin and Amber finally stopped their own dance backing up to see the power of the Weavers. He looked down at her and she at him, her eyes alive with the fire. He thought of them like lush soil, full of life.

"Beautiful." He whispered. They had their arms on each and Amber moved closer to him, her eyes darting to his lips.

Vin's phone rang, the buzzing breaking their moment. He had to blink a couple of times like he was disoriented; then gave an awkward smile and he fished his phone out of his pocket. The screen was lit up with Matt's name.

He picked up, "Matt? Where are you?"

The voice on the other side was hushed, whispered, and sounded out of breath. "Vin...I need your help."

Vin's SUV snailed along down the road. He had turned off his headlights before he got to the bridge as Matt told him to, and now Amber had her head stuck out the window guiding him into a shallow forested area on the other side of the lake from the apartment complex. They got out and quietly stalked to the shore.

"There's one." Amber whispered pointing down the lakeside, Vin followed her cue and saw a small rowboat calmly lapping against the shore. They came up to the boat a single chain held it to a concrete pole on land. Amber pulled a ribbon of water from the lake then intensified her energy, Weaving it into a spinning saw. She slowly ran it into one of the links, concentrating the pressure to be so fine as to cut through the chain. It dropped to the ground with a plop as it splashed into the water.

Vin flashed her an encouraging smile, then pulled up his phone.

"Ok, he has his location pinged, so we just have to follow it to him." He showed her his phone and they plotted their trajectory across the lake.

"Easy enough." Amber said. "Now it's time to work on the cover."

Vin nodded, "Let's do it."

They both turned toward the lake, Amber began building up her energy and then poured it into the water. Vin did the same for the air. They had been practicing what they could do together during their time at the park. Together they Weaved the energy, pressing it together creating a whole new form of their element. Visible vapor began to form in the air before them, Vin and Amber amplified their connection building it then pushed their power out. Fog rolled from them flowing across the lake, blanketing the area.

They both grinned at each other and high fived, only to flinch as the slap echoed in the quiet area.

"Cool, whip up a perfect cover and then ruin it. Wow are we smart," Vin chided himself.

They climbed into the boat and Amber began Weaving them across the lake. As they got closer Vin checked his phone to make sure they were on the right course, a text from Matt popped up.

Good thing you can find my location, this fog came out of nowhere. Hella handy though.

Actually, that was us. Vin replied.

…of course it was. Came his response.

Vin smiled, he felt like he could feel Matt rolling his eyes from here.

Their fog plan had really worked. Vin couldn't even tell they made it to shore until the boat road up onto it. They stepped out and Vin Weaved them a path, pushing the fog with his air until they were on top of Matt's ping.

"Thank god you guys made it." Matt's voice whispered out. He came down from the tree he was hiding in, causing Amber to jump back startled.

"Sorry." Matt said.

"What're you doing here Matt? What is this?" Vin asked.

He pulled them down into a crouch, even if it probably didn't matter with the fog. Vin looked Matt over, he didn't look injured, just on edge.

"Ok…it's kind of a lot to explain. But these are the terrorists. From Dallas." Vin and Amber gave the shocked expression Matt had assumed they would.

"Well, why did you call us and not the police?" Amber hissed.

Matt breathed in like he was preparing to confess a crime, "We can't. Because Magdalena is a part of it."

Matt didn't think Vin's eyes could get any wider.

"Magdalena, as in your sister?" Amber asked, she still hadn't heard of them talk about her much.

Matt nodded in reply.

"What? How do you know that?" Vin asked.

Matt explained how he thought he saw Tanya at the Dallas attack. How he spent months trying to track their path back to Rockwell. Lastly, he told them how she came to him the night they came back.

"Matty…why didn't you tell me she came to you? I thought… did you not think us that close?" Vin asked.

It was Matt's turn to looked shocked, "Of course not, Vin. You're my best friend. How could you think that?"

Vin looked away awkwardly. "Just, after everything we talked about in Dallas that day. The way you kind of avoided us…" Vin missed the reaction Matt gave at the word, *us.* But he did look up to see the wounded look on Matt's face.

"No, that wasn't it at all. I just- she wasn't right when she came and saw me. I didn't want to get my hopes up. I just felt like I had to find her on my own." The boys left an awkward silence for a moment. Amber broke it, reaching out and placing a hand on Matt's knees,

"Well not anymore, Matty. We look for her together." They looked into each other's eyes, determination building in Matt's face.

He nodded, then turned back to the apartment building. "Right, well first we need to search there. I honestly don't think she's here, though I couldn't check everywhere. There was this room on the second floor, it looked like all their plans were there. We need their hard drive. If she's not here, their plans should let us know where she might be."

He pulled his bag into the middle of the three of them. Then pulled out two earpieces. "I only have two of these, so…what do we do." They both looked to Vin. He stared back at them both before finally relenting, taking one of the earpieces.

"You know I'm still surprised your father hasn't found your stash yet. Do you have a thumb drive?" Vin asked, putting the earpiece in. Matt dug one out and handed it to him.

"I've creatively hidden it, disguised so he'd be none the wiser." Matt responded proudly.

"That's your excuse for year old gym shorts laying around your room?" Amber teased.

"You two should stick together," Vin continued, recovering from his quick smile at their banter "Ill head to the roof first. Give you an update of the area and anyone I see. Ill sneak in and see if I can get to that room. If we fight, they outnumber us. We'll need to be back to back, I think countering will be the best plan. Wait for them to strike, one of us will block, and another return fire. At Dallas they seemed to barely look out for each other or work as a team. At least the people I fought ended up hurting each other instead of me. I don't think they're well organized so I doubt they will have a plan beyond 'tossing rocks'." Vin smiled at Matt, who just shook his head.

"Be careful," Amber wished him, giving him a squeeze on the arm. Vin nodded and disappeared into the mists.

The fog split as Vin soared up and through it. Weaving a cushion below him, he landed softly on the apartment complex. The building was flat roofed with a border, half a shin high, lining the structure. Vin tracked along its perimeter looking down below, he caught some moving shadows but mostly still too foggy to discern exact numbers.

He gave the rest of the roof a once over, it looked like there was a multitude of squares cut out in the floor. Vin walked to the closest one and peered below, ventilation stretched out below. Vin concluded it must be where they were planning to set the air conditioner units. He raised a finger to his ear and pressed the small button to transmit.

"Matt?" he spoke softly.

"Go ahead." He replied.

"I can't tell much from up here, still too foggy. But I can get in from the roof, I'm going to check out the inside."

There was a pause where he assumed Matt was speaking to Amber before he finally said, "Got it. Go for it."

Vin braced himself against the sides of the hole and began lowering himself down. He began crawling along the shafts until he came to an unfinished section and was able to hop down landing in an empty room on the third floor. He scouted out the remaining rooms until he finally radioed back.

"Third floor's clear. If you bring a rope to the South side, you can toss it up and should be able to climb it."

Once all three were in the complex together they began descending the stairs, they didn't see anyone in the hallway, but could hear people on the first floor. Matt pointed a couple of doors down,

"That one is their staging room." He said.

Vin nodded, "Stay here." He whispered before he snuck his way toward the door. He crouched at it listening for anything but couldn't make it out. He looked back to the staircase trying to think. It was then that something came to him. During their practice with Amber, he didn't only feel the elemental energy they Weaved. There was something more, a connection with Amber.

With that thought in mind Vin reached out with his senses. He could feel the elemental energy he already pulled on. Concentrating harder, he tried to find something more. His eyes snapped open as he felt it, a presence, another dormant entity like it was ready to control elements of its own, and it was coming from the other side of the door. He snuck back to the staircase.

"There's only one person in there, I don't think they're moving. They might be standing guard in case you came back." Vin told them.

"You sure?" Matt asked.

Vin nodded his head, "Yes, do you remember if there was a window? Like was it blocked or boarded?"

Matt took a second to think, "No I think only the first floor was boarded, but they still had a curtain over it."

Vin looked back down the hallway, "Ok, I'm going to head out one of the other rooms and to their window. When I give you the signal, I want you to act like you're sneaking into the room, like wiggle the handle or something. It should be a good enough distraction for me to get in."

Amber looked cautious, "Are you sure Vin?" She seemed to have a million questions. When he nodded, though, they believed him, even without knowing the full plan.

Vin took off back down the hallway, he got to the room next to their staging area and reached out again. His theory strengthened in resolve as he didn't sense anything inside but still felt the presence in the room next to him. He could even feel brief energy signatures from below him. He was sensing the energy from a person, not from the elements.

He went into the room and out the window, using his balance and Weaving he kept himself close to the wall until he reached the window to their staging room. Matt was right, it was completely blacked out. But luckily it looked like the windows didn't have locks installed. *Too early in the development* he surmised.

Vin radioed back to Matt, "I'm ready. Go for it."

"Here goes nothing." Matt whispered back.

Inside the hallway Matt purposely made louder footsteps, and slowly began turning the door handle. Vin reached out with his senses and could feel the presence begin to move, it flared up as they, Vin assumed, started to Weave and draw upon the energies of their element. It made it easier to feel their exact position. They were directly in front of the door, most likely waiting to attack, which put him directly in front of the window. And Vin.

In one quick motion Vin slid open the window and dived into the room, his hands hitting the ground which Vin used to continue to launch himself forward in a front handspring. The terrorist turned, shocked, but before he could yell out Vin's legs wrapped around his head. He twisted the terrorist using his momentum to swing himself up, bringing the man down. Vin's legs still wrapped around the man's throat, crouched and squeezing until his breath went away and the body went limp. Vin raised himself from his crouch and opened the door.

Matt stood on the other side, a shard of concrete at the ready. Matt looked down past the guard and raised an eyebrow, impressed. Matt waved Amber over and they entered the room. Matt Weaved the wall by the lock to jam the door. Amber and Vin made their way to the computer and stuck in the thumb drive.

Matt came after them, taking control of the computer and set to work copying their files. "Well, that went much better than when I did it." He mused.

Amber was at the map; she had a finger on Dallas and traced it south until it hit the multiple circles in Houston. "I can't believe they're planning to hit Houston. What's their goal?"

Vin was taking pictures of the room, coming over to the map. Amber moved out of the way so he could snap a photo.

"I don't know, let's just hurry and find Magdalena so we can alert the police," Vin said.

Amber had her hand over her mouth, hesitant to speak.

Matt came away from the computer, stretching out his back. "Ok, it's copying their info now. Should be a couple of minutes, there's a lot."

"Matt," Amber started hesitantly. "Do you know why Magdalena's with them?"

Matt was silent for a moment, "No." He half lied.

Vin thumbed through the papers on the wall, most of them were political figures, an X was drawn through the speaker from the Dallas attack. "They're terrorists, who look like they're attacking Weaver politicians or events, but…they *are* Weavers." Vin said, turning toward Matt. "Is Magdalena even a Weaver?"

The question was warranted, but it made Matt think of a time he didn't want to. "You know I don't know. I always assumed she might have run away because she was scared her powers wouldn't manifest."

Vin walked up to Matt and placed a hand on his shoulder. He gave a glance to the map, his eyes pausing longer on Seattle. "It looks like their past marks were the same location as some of the Anomaly attacks. I love you Matty, and I care a lot about your sister. You know that. We also thought that maybe…she was bipolar. She left before she could be tested. So there's a chance she left because her powers *did* manifest."

Matt wanted to throw Vin's hand aside. To start yelling at him. But hot tears threatened his eyes and he remembered the jolt she gave him in the forest. So instead he nodded, uncomfortably.

Amber's fingers shot back to her mouth; dread coursed through her. "She's an Anomaly."

A thud came from the door. Someone had tried opening it. "Dedric? What the hell?"

Matt jumped, Vin and Amber spun to face the door.

"DEDRIC!" He slammed against the door. Matt swung around and ran for the computer.

"Shit." He whispered.

"Amber! Go." Vin commanded. She ran for the window, climbing out on the edge.

"Matt, now!"

Matt cursed and took the flash drive out and ran for Vin. Together they jumped out the window, holding on to Vin he slowed their descent. He turned to look back up at the window. Amber still hung out the side. She had one last look at the door as it burst open and the man immediately saw her.

"THEY'RE BACK!" He yelled. Amber released herself from the window, falling until Vin caught her in a draft landing in his arms.

They turned to flee but a large gust of wind cleared the immediate area of fog. The terrorists were waiting below. It was a trap.

Two shots of fire flew at them from their left flank. Vin made quick work of them as he rapidly pulled the air from the hurtling balls of fire extinguishing them before they hit. At the same time, he flipped to the left on one hand Weaving a large circumference of air that blasted the attackers back and put them off balance. He backed Amber and Matt up to the wall of the building.

"Stick to the plan." Vin gritted, looking at the two. Amber remained calm but ready and in Matt he saw none of the fear or hesitation he had back in Dallas. The terrorists stood between him and his sister, and nothing was going to stop him now.

They traded blows with the attackers, outnumbered seven to three. Every earth Weaved at them Vin would redirect or Matt shattered. Matt also kept them from getting closer. Anytime one took a step Matt slammed his foot down and Weaved the ground below, destabilizing the approaching terrorist. Amber was their best offense; any opening, she would attack viciously. She could Weave her ability around their defenses, the snaking water lashing out at them.

One of the Earth Weavers shot a stone right for Amber, she ignored it, trusting her team as she shot a stream of water that wrapped around the man encasing him in a bubble. Her trust was rewarded as inches before it hit her Vin blasted it sideways. It was redirected to hit one of the Weavers attacking Matt square in the face, the rock smashing into pieces and flattening the woman. Matt didn't miss a beat as the opening allowed him to send his own attack at the bubbled enemy which had a similar effect of crashing over him and sending him to the ground.

Four remained; their anger having already gotten the better of them. Vin's original assessment was correct, they seemed to have no love for each other and didn't care to attack in a formation or protect one another. They eventually gave way to unfocused rage and made mistakes that left themselves open. Now the trio just had to take down the remaining four, who finally seemed to realize the tides were turning against them.

A vicious energy came from their right flank. "MATT!" Vin warned trying to create a shield of air as a large blast of fire streaked toward them like a comet out of the sky. Matt barely Weaved a wall of earth before it slammed into them. The energy backfiring and exploding out launching all Weavers present. Matt flew far and away to the right, Amber and Vin to the left.

Matt groaned and shook his head looking around, the four remaining attackers looked to have no defense at all and now lay on the ground, smoke curling from the motionless bodies. He caught a pair of combat boots approaching him. He craned his head up to see a girl with a wicked smile looking down at him.

"Little brother." She mocked.

"Tanya." He sneered, climbing to his feet. He unfortunately thought that, unlike his sister, she looked good. Her hair vibrant with her signature color. She used to fill out her dark jeans and skimpy tops with plump fat, but now her clothes clung to her and her taut muscles. Apparently, terrorism suited her.

"Where's my sister?" He demanded, no playfulness in his tone.

She feigned to be wounded, "Now, now." She cooed. Raising a hand and resting it on her arm wrapped around her waist.

"Beat me, and maybe I'll tell you." She fluttered her fingers, flames bursting to life.

Vin tumbled into the blast that flung them away, rolling onto his feet and used the momentum to continue running. He was Weaving and ducking blasts from the incoming attackers. Amber was right behind him recovering, not quite as smoothly, from her fall. She looked back to find Matt, but he was far down the other side and it looked like most of the terrorists had come their way.

They battled through into the open parking lot. Amber could feel the large source of energy behind her, the lake just over her shoulder. It looked like a new vehicle had arrived at the complex, it must have brought the Weaver who created that large fire blast, she thought. The driver was still in it, a red old-looking SUV, a second terrorist ran for the heavy black SUV.

The red one revved and began peeling out to run them down. Vin bent low Weaving a large amount of compressed air and sent it speeding along the ground toward the incoming vehicle. Right as it started to pass under the SUV, he released it, exploding out and upward, the force launching the vehicle causing it to flip and crashing down. Vin wasn't as prepared for the second vehicle as it came charging toward him.

"Vin!" Amber screamed, reaching with as much power as she could, pulling a huge force of water from the lake. She Weaved it into a powerful wave that crashed into the side of the black SUV, tipping it. As it slid toward him, Vin breathed out Weaving his power into Amber's and the water. The water dropped in temperature freezing the vehicle over until it was covered in crystalized ice, trapping the attackers inside.

Pain flared along Vin's side as something slammed into him. It knocked him off balance and he started to fall. A stream met and caught him in an embrace, falling into a waltz that spun Vin, keeping him up. He recognized the gentle touch of Amber's power. He could see her now and he thought her amazing. Weaving against the terrorists while simultaneously catching Vin. Her control was beyond him. Their dance came to an end as Amber released him and he took off toward her.

The remaining terrorist ran around the upturned vehicles, Weaving their element at the duo. Vin looked to the building and up toward the roof and he pointed, "There! Let's get the high ground." Amber nodded in agreement as they took off together. He looked to Amber, she was breathing hard, sweaty and red faced but her determination didn't falter. She's impressive Vin thought, and he hadn't realized the extent of their ability to synergize and how well they worked together until that night.

She looked to him. "You first," she said. Drawing in a stream of water and gathered it in a spot at the ground below a set of the balconies.

Vin reached it crouching low and felt the water launch him up as he extended his legs. He had already begun Weaving his energy into the air around Amber, pulling her up with him just narrowly missing a piece of concrete the size of a tire. Vin landed on the first-floor balcony, continuing to use his power to send Amber up and past him. As she passed, she Weaved water, connecting both their arms. Vin put a leg up on the railing and pushed himself off.

In their rush it was hard to build the appropriate energy or aim their trajectory. Vin's leap sent him farther out then up. Amber, however, pulled on him hard, using their connected arms. His direction snapped forward as he flew. They grappled together mid-air, his momentum carrying them both toward the roof. They tumbled on their landing, Vin immediately getting his footing first, grabbing her hand and gave a subtle push to keep her up right and on her feet moving. They continued running across the roof back towards Matt.

It was the hardest fight Matt had ever been in. Tanya's fire had such impact it shook his defenses. He realized quickly that he was no match for her. His Earth Weaving was all about standing your ground, meeting the attack and returning. Tanya was too quick, and her power too great. Her attacks also exploding on impact sent scours of stray flames out, singeing Matt.

He kept trying to go for her legs, Weaving the ground to destabilize her but she easily jumped or rolled out of it while creating her next attack which made for a quick recovery for her. Too quick for Matt to respond with. He thought she would have made an excellent Air Weaver as her movements reminded him of Vin.

She got in close and back handed Matt so hard it spun him. He followed the momentum to spin and flip away, increasing the distance as her roundhouse kick missed him by inches.

He held up his fists, Weaving two stones to hover in front of him in a defensive stance.

"So…you Attuned to fire, guess I'm not surprised." Matt said between composing breaths, trying to waste time to gather his wits.

Tanya played along but adopted a casual pace like they were old friends meeting up at the mall. Fire rolled along her fingers as she replied, "Yes, I think it suits me quite well."

Matt glared at her and her passive attitude. "You know, a couple of weeks before the terrorist attack on Dallas, a fire broke out at Hutchins State Jail…"

"Oh?" She mused, still not meeting his eyes as she played with her fire.

"13 inmates died…including your brother." Matt spat.

Tanya clenched her fist closed. The fire smote out draping them back in darkness. He barely made out her shift from pain and anger, to a malicious smile.

"Yeah…I guess I'll be making a habit of killing my brothers," she teased.

"I'M NOT YOUR BROTHER!" Matt bellowed at her.

Tanya's hands erupted, a blast prepared in her hand, and Matt quickly poured his energy into his two slabs of earth in front of him, slamming them together. Too late did he realize it was a feint, she used that fire blast to propel herself forward. Then she dived in quickly, sliding under his wall and launching herself up. Extending her leg into a high kick that snapped his head back and sent him flying. He landed hard; his neck flared with pain. Matt groaned and rolled side to side but managed to look back toward Tanya. She walked toward him slowly, teasingly bouncing flames in her hand again.

Cold touched Matt's back and the confident look on Tanya's face faltered. Fog rolled past Matt; and it was his turn to smile. Tanya didn't know what hit her as Vin dropped down to the ground between her and Matt. The impact came with a blast of Vin's energy as he Weaved the air to spread in a circle around him that cushioned his landing. Then he drew it in and up as he launched himself and Tanya into the air, he quickly latched onto her and kicked, pushing off her so fiercely her form was lost as her body and screams were sent flying into the woods opposite the lake. Vin flew from her, flipping in the air and landing next to Matt.

"That…was so cool," Matt managed.

"Don't kiss me yet, come on," Vin said grabbing him and pulling him to his feet.

"Ow!" Matt let out, reaching for his neck. "Damn, she hurt."

Vin and Matt managed to get to the lakeside where Amber already stood in the boat. She helped Matt in, and Vin gave the boat a hard push with his powers. Vin then grabbed Matt's duffel and launched himself after the boat, landing gently and with as much poise as only Vin could manage.

They all looked back at the complex which was now dotted in fire. Sirens echoed in the distance.

"Well, I guess she wasn't there." Vin said, breathing hard in and out, trying to catch his breath. "I'm sure we would have seen her if she was."

Matt just nodded, finally laying back, already feeling the pain take the place of his adrenaline. Amber bent low and gave him a comforting squeeze on his arm.

"I'm glad you're ok," she said before standing back up and Weaving them across the lake.

Chapter 21

THE TRIO WERE IN Vin's Durango heading back to town. Looking in the rearview mirror, Vin saw Matt laying down holding his head. Amber followed his gaze and her face grew grim looking at him

"He's pretty beat up." She said quietly to Vin, who replied with a nod.

"My bodies broken, I'm not deaf." Matt called from the back.

"As well it should be, idiot. I can't believe you ran off to investigate them alone." Amber chastised.

"Alright mom, I'm sorry! How could I think I could do anything without the wonder twins?" Matt drolled.

Amber sighed and crossed her arms. Matt continued, "I'm sure you'll tell me next to buckle my seat belt? Am I out past my curfew?"

"Matt," Vin cut in sharply. Then softened his features, "Please, tell us next time." Matt looked away out the window, shame creeping in before he nodded.

"I don't understand them," Amber said, in deep debate, thinking about the terrorist group.

"I agree. Back in Dallas they seemed to have no bond to each other." Vin said.

"They just seem so hateful, and angry," Amber replied. "I wonder if they even have a leader?" She speculated.

"I really don't think they could have gotten as far as they have without a leader. If that map is right, they've done a lot of hits and still haven't been caught."

"But why?" Amber asked.

"You already said it," Matt finally spoke up. "Hate. They are hated, so in return they lash out with their own hatred. A vicious cycle." He stated mater-of-factly looking out the window. Reliving all the moments Magdalena came to him, complaining about how people treated her. And now she was an Anomaly, treated as dangerous, crazy and something to fear. *How much could someone take of that treatment before they broke*, Matt began to question. *What kind of fear was she slammed with the moment she realized what she was?*

"So," Amber began, turning to face Vin. "What do we-" she stopped, staring at his arm on the wheel, the hairs prickling and standing straight up. The energy of it hit Vin and Amber before the bolt did.

"Oh shi-" Vin managed before lightning struck the side of his SUV, causing Vin to veer sideways the vehicle couldn't stay upright as it tipped and began to roll. The sound of metal renting and bending tore at his ears. Glass shattered and flew around. This continued until the SUV finally slammed into a ditch. Stars swarmed under his eyelids and Vin managed to pick his face off the steering wheel, placing a hand on his forehead, he pulled it back bloody. His hand accompanied its own pinpricks of blood that stung.

He looked over at Amber who looked fine, all things considered, her airbag deployed but she also matched Vin in spotted shades of crimson. Vin groaned and unbuckled, turning to the back seat for Matt, who was no longer there.

"Oh god," Amber said horrified, her eyes on a shattered side window.

Vin panicked, banging on his bent door to get out before he finally unloaded a blast of Air, breaking it and sending the remaining glass flying, along with the door. He crawled out, Amber right behind him. They got out and looked around at the empty field, it was too dark to see anything immediately. Vin, about to call for Matt, didn't even get a syllable out before Amber yelled for him and threw him down as an arc of lightning soared over them. They turned to look as a figure stalked toward them, electricity running down her arms.

"Magdalena." Vin whispered. *She is an anomaly,* he thought.

"I told my brother to stay out of it. That included you too, Vincent." She sneered.

"Magdalena, please!" Vin began to plead only to have to dodge out of the way as she reached forward, Weaving lightning at them. He used a kick to Weave air that pushed him and Amber apart, the lightning passing between them.

They both stood and readied to fight, Vin didn't know what Amber could do, she had practically no water. Vin launched himself toward her, he had to make sure she stayed focused on him. He dodged one of her bolts, flinging bursts of wind at her which she easily sidestepped. It took only a few exchanges for Vin to have a horrifying grasp of the situation; she was just as fast but far more dangerous. Not only that, but Vin had to constantly be on the defense to evade her dangerous and wild lightning abilities.

She was unhinged and it appeared she didn't have skill, just wild power. Magdalena didn't see Amber until it was too late. Amber had grabbed the bottles of water from the back of Vin's vehicle. She Weaved as much power as she could and crashed it into Magdalena. If she had more water it might have worked. The most it did was unbalance and spin her. Vin made a mad dash for her, but Magdalena reached up, her arms facing them. The lightning she Weaved flew out like a spider's web, she had no need to aim like most Weavers. Vin went into a slide using his augmented air to keep him flying along, but it slowed him and it was all Magdalena needed. Amber wasn't as lucky, she lashed out trying to create a wall of water that the lightning easily split through, striking her and sending her back in a terrible scream, then silence.

Vin jumped to his feet and pushed up forward and toward Magdalena. She simply turned and gripped Vin around the throat, electricity immediately flooded through his body. She wasn't shocking so much as stunning him. He couldn't move, his body wouldn't function. She looked down at him and he was surprised to find pity in her eyes.

"You were always good to my brother-" she paused, and Vin could almost believe that she was holding back tears, but something caught his eyes behind her, a large lump in the field.

"You were always good to me." She continued.

"M-Matt." Vin managed to stammer out.

Magdalena sighed, "Yes he's the only reason why-" she stopped as she noticed Vin slowly moving his arm, fighting her powers. He pointed past her,

"M-M-Matt."

She turned at his words and saw what he was pointing at, then immediately dropped Vin. She ran to her brothers crumpled form. He was unconscious, bleeding and broken. Magdalena's lips started quivering, turning between Vin and her brother.

"Please." Vin pleaded, slowly going to a knee.

Tears began forming in her eyes, she dug into Matt's pocket and pulled out his phone. She looked again between her brother and Vin before standing and going to him. She dropped the phone in front of Vin,

"Save him, then drop this Vincent. Don't make me kill you." she said to him as she passed. Then stopped and said over her shoulder with difficulty, "Don't make me kill my brother." She finally whispered before walking back into the darkness.

Vin's heart pounded furiously, turning between the unconscious forms of Amber and Matt, then finally picked up the phone and called 911.

Chapter 22

V IN DIDN'T KNOW HE could hurt like he did, and he wasn't even the one in the gurney flying through hospital halls on its way to surgery to save his life; that is probably why it hurt even more. He stood in the bright white corridors of Rockwell General Hospital, antiseptic permeated the air and tickled at his nose.

Vin's whole body felt like it had been dragged behind the train tracks by a locomotive. He turned as he felt a familiar presence returning to him. Amber's boots padded along the tile, she had two waters in her hands and an attempt at an encouraging smile on her face. Her hair stood big and untamed, looking dirty and tired. *Thankfully she is at least ok,* Vin thought.

She handed him his water and he took it, whispering "Thanks."

He returned the smile and took a sip from the bottle. They stood together looking down the way they had wheeled Mateo through. They didn't know what to say to each other, or for the last fifteen minutes since they arrived.

The paramedics had cleared Amber in the ambulance, who gained consciousness halfway to the hospital. They said she would just suffer minor nerve damage she would recover from and mostly be sore from the exertion placed on her body. Their cuts were easy enough to clean up and bandage. Vin resisted the urge to scratch at the stitches on his forehead.

"It was for nothing," Vin said sadly, still staring after the way Matt had been taken. He pulled out the thumb drive, it looked unrecognizable, destroyed when Magdalena attacked.

"We have nothing to show for it."

Amber looped her arm around Vin. "It's not the end. We need to believe in Matt, and he in his sister."

"What does that matter, Amber? She almost killed us."

"That's exactly why there's a chance. Almost," she said insistently. Vin turned to look at her.

When had she gotten so close, when did I feel so comfortable with her touch? He thought. It caused his heart to race and for the first time in hours his mind flashed back to the flames of the bonfire that felt like months ago. He smiled. A real, genuine one this time.

"You're right."

"Ambrosia!" A name called out from behind them, she immediately dropped Vin's arm as they snapped around. A woman with long black hair moved frantically through the halls. She finally saw Ambrosia and ran to her, hugging her daughter.

"My girl, what happened?" she asked. Amber tried to pull back, but her mother had her in a death grip.

"Mom I'm fine, it's my friend-"

"I don't care about your friend." She snapped, and a pained expression split along Ambers face.

'I told you what would happen when you-"she finally looked up and met Vin's eyes, "associate with *them*, Ambrosia. We're going. Now." She demanded, turning and practically dragging her down the hallway. She tried to keep up, stepping backward following her mother, Amber's eyes not leaving Vin, but her body was too tired to fight with her mother.

It seemed all the crueler that they couldn't be together now. He almost yelled out that he would call her, he assumed she felt the same. The thought of their fried phones went through their minds, weighing heavy in their pockets and could do nothing but simply watch as they were pulled apart.

Vin slumped into one of the chairs in the waiting hall, head in his hands. It was minutes later before someone called his own name.

"Vin! Mom, Dad! He's over here." He looked up to see his sister coming down the hall, he heard something unexpected in her voice. Standing, Juliette embraced him in a hug and he recognized that what he heard, and now felt, was her worry. He paused for a moment before finally reciprocating the hug, wrapping his arms around Juliette. His sister, whom he could hug. His sister, whom was *here*.

Tears began running down his face as uncontrollable sobs breached his façade once again that year. He expected his sister to pull away but for the second time that night she surprised him, holding him close and stroking the back of his head whispering.

"It's going to be alright."

Matt's mother had come with his parents. His father, unfortunately, was stuck at work and couldn't get off.

They sat together in the waiting hall, Matt's mother praying. Vin tried to describe what happened, lying the best he could, but a stray lightning strike was a hard sell. Luckily the hard evidence was there. His vehicle had been struck by lightning and it was believable it would have caused Vin to crash.

Matt's mother looked furious when they had come to give him a breathalyzer, but to their credit there weren't many other reasons for them to be out on the night of the bonfire. It was tradition to take the party elsewhere away from the chaperones. When they told them he was clean, Matt's mother calmed down significantly and even went over to hug Vin.

The doctor came out almost an hour and a half after they had arrived and gave them the good news. Matt was fine. Some broken bones, head trauma and cuts, but he would survive. They would need to wait a bit longer before they could see him.

They looked at each and embraced, sighing in relief.

Unfortunately for Matt, however, his family wasn't the only one in the hospital to visit him.

Heavy black boots paced around the hospital room; she traced a finger around the bed as she went. She came up and took a seat on the bed next to Matt. His face calm and unconscious, it was purpled by bruises and red with cuts. She ran a finger along his cheek, tsking.

"Poor baby brother," Tanya whispered.

Alarms blared in the hallway. Vin jumped up, his head had been resting on his mother's shoulder. Nurses had begun grabbing equipment, Vin heard one of them call.

"Room 240 is flatlining! Grab the paddles."

Vin didn't hesitate as he took off down the hall, the nurses were rushing for Matt's room. He quickly overtook one of the nurses pushing a crash cart,

"SIR! You need to get back!" she yelled. Vin didn't slow, he didn't stop. He ran until he slid and skidded into Matt's room. The nurses and his doctor had gathered around his bed.

"Why aren't you doing anything!" Vin yelled, pushing forward until he saw what they were gaping at. An empty bed.

Interlude

L IGHTNING SNAPPED AT the surrounding targets. Chips of concrete flaked off as the uncontrolled bolts scattered in every direction. Burnt rubber from the smoking dummies permeated the small room.

"I really don't think you should stand so close." Magdalena said between pants as she attempted to recover from the exertion.

"Your aim. Not so bad." Alexei said in his broken English.

Magdalena let out an unexpected chuckle, "You're saying you trust me?"

Her smile had an unexpected effect on Alexei as his mouth moved to mimic hers.

"It's been a month of training; I still have all my fingers." He jested, playfully holding up his hands and wriggling them.

"Come take a break." He said walking toward the door and heading out.

The two Anomalies paced the long deep halls of their bunker, a bottle of water in hand. Fellow members of their organization passed by and they nodded in greeting. Alexei and Magdalena stopped at a window that overlooked a gymnasium sized training room. There were a few Weavers down below, Tanya among them. She was sparring with a Weaver. They watched as her opponent made a bad move, getting in too close and Tanya parried the attack sending her off balance. With a swift kick to her opponents back side they went flying forward, sprawled on the floor. Tanya grinned pridefully at her victory.

"That one," Alexei said pointing to Tanya, "Seems to be fitting in."

"Angyo will want to be careful, she'll steal the leadership spot in no time."

Alexei grunted at her words. "This thing. Not easy."

Magdalena shrugged. "I just don't understand. Why isn't he here" she said waving a hand at the few Weavers training below, "leading us? Training us or something?"

Alexei hummed a moment in thought, "Like you, like her," nodding at Tanya, "He wants us to want to get better. It's what we want. He's not here to hold our hand."

Magdalena still wasn't convinced it was the best idea. She looked up to study Alexei, his broad chiseled features, narrow eyes and lips that seemed drooped in an eternal frown.

"You respect him that much?"

Alexei just nodded. His simple, plain way of relating his feelings put Magdalena at ease. He, for the most part, was the "what you see is what you get" type.

"I don't think that's the concensus around here." She continued, watching the Weavers trade partners and start sparring again.

"I think for once, I'm not the most feared one in the room." She thought back to his looming presence in the alley that day a month ago.

"I don't get scared." Alexei said solemnly. "Not anymore...but *He* does."

Magdalena quirked her head to look up at him, she assumed he didn't mean Angyo.

"He?" she asked.

Alexei didn't answer, he turned and headed back the way they had come.

"Come little lightning bug, I trust you, but not that much. Maybe one day. Let's return to training."

6 Months Ago | Seattle

"You're kidding me, right?" the Air Weaver yelled slamming her hands down on the table in front of her.

Tanya smirked across the room.

"Selene." Angyo stated calmly.

"You can't let her lead this. She's cra-" Selene stopped her comment abruptly, her eyes flashing to Alexei and Magdalena who stood together in the corner.

Selene gritted her teeth. "She's...unstable," she finished.

Tanya let out a high-pitched giggle, "You wound me Selene."

Selene stepped toward her, reaching out her hand, Air building in her palm. Tanya didn't miss a beat and prepared a flame in her own hand.

"Not yet, but I will!" Selene spew.

A pulse of energy flew across the war room. Both Selene and Tanya's elements seemed to quake and wilt.

"Enough!" Angyo commanded. His cloak fluttered and he took a hand to rub along his bald head waiting for the group to settle.

The two women continued to glare but backed down.

"I don't need to explain why Tanya is leading the attack against Houston. Brutus is heading up Dallas, and Tanya is in second command."

"I just think that if we want to get more people on our side, a Peace Rally may-" Selene was cut off as Angyo set his cold, calculating eyes on her. In submission, she backed away from the center of the room against one of the walls with the others.

"The more pressing concern is the upcoming task here, in Seattle." He looked to Alexei. "You're up."

Alexei nodded and took his spot in the center.

"The mayor and city council are trying to put harsher restrictions on Weavers. Peace talks here will do nothing, we'd be but dogs rolling onto our backs to show our bellies." He avoided Selene's eye contact as he continued.

"We give Weavers a reason to fight back, push them until they have no choice but to rise and defend themselves." He strutted around the table, glancing at the map of Seattle, where strategic points were circled and arrows indicated their group's movements.

"You know your places by now, and you know mine. Just watch for falling buildings." The Weavers in the room could never tell when he was making a joke so they just nodded as Alexei returned to his spot next to Magdalena. Her knowing smirk indicated she recognized it as a joke, giving him a soft elbow and whispering something to him.

Brutus, a man as large as Alexei with a mohawk and mustache drooping off his upper lip, replaced the center spot and began detailing his plans for Dallas. Tanya was supposed to have followed him, but she was busy watching the corner. She saw Magdalena's exchange, the small shift in Alexei's face as he found whatever she said to be amusing. She noticed the tiniest shift in their posture as they leaned ever so slightly toward each other, and she did not like what she saw.

Magdalena and Alexei walked the halls after the meeting had adjourned. She listened to his deep breaths and took comfort in his presence. She had been the happiest in years over the past 6 months, even the idea of their upcoming tasks didn't dissuade her, though it helped she refused to dwell on it for the moment. Alexei looked to Magdalena, aware of her hesitation and spoke.

"Lightning bug," he started. Magdalena stopped to turn to him. "I do wish you could be there. It would…help me."

"I know, I'm sorry. I just don't think I'm ready." She turned away from him and started picking at the sleeve of her sweater.

"Nonsense. You're plenty ready. I made sure of that during our training."

She sighed and frowned at him, "You know that's not what I meant."

Alexei nodded. "Yes…I suppose I do." They continued walking, rounding a corner Magdalena placed a hand on his arm to stop him. He hesitated at the motion.

"Are *you* ready, Alexei?" It was his turn to turn from her. He let the moment sink in for a couple of seconds.

"Do you trust me?" She asked him, and it was a small question, but meant so much more in her implication. Alexei sighed again and released a weight he had been carrying for a while as he replied.

"When I was young, in Russia, my uncle had a business. He was a tailor, sold all types of men's clothing. These men had peculiar tastes, and when the suits didn't fit their tastes, he took them downstairs to survey his…other collection." Alexei paused, closing his eyes and breathing deeply, a practiced meditation he had adopted.

"My father protected me for as long as he could. The day he died I was delivered into the hands of my closest relative. My Uncle." He turned to stare back at Magdalena, who looked upon him with a knowing concern. She took his arm, and he let her.

"I've heard stories of what happened. But I don't remember them myself, *He* won't let me." Magdalena hadn't heard him mention *Him* again in the six months they had trained together.

"Who is *He*?" she asked.

"*He's* who comes out when I'm threatened. When I'm scared. Angyo met him. Mal'chik is the name he gave to Angyo."

Magdalena shook her head, trying to avoid obvious sentiments and *I'm sorry's*. "Is that who is going to lead the charge on the attack on Seattle?"

"No." He said swiftly, almost angrily. "Mal'chik makes no decisions in my life. Not as long as I can help it."

"Do you…do you go to someone for this? There has to be somebody who- "

He tore his arm from her and walked away from Magdalena, "I don't need someone in my head." He looked back to her, the anger in his eyes vanished. "Ever since you joined us, Mal'chik hasn't made an appearance. With you around…" he lowered his head. Looking ashamed, "I feel safe," he whispered.

A lump caught in Magdalena's throat; she raised a hand to his face. She looked into his fearless eyes; she couldn't imagine the pain he endured to create this in him. She understood why he was here, what he was fighting for.

"A worthy cause to fight for, not being afraid," she said to him. She raised his chin, so his head was held high again.

"Then I'm here for you, Alexei. I'll keep you safe." She promised him, curling her arms around him and pressing into his chest. He stood confused for a moment, taking a second to process Magdalena wrapped around him.

He then lowered his arms against her back, and with a rare smile he curled around her.

With their eyes closed in their embrace they didn't see the flicker of pink hair that whipped around, retreating from their stolen moment.

Chapter 23

MATT GROANED AS he began to wake, the harsh winter night nipped his exposed face. His eyes fluttered open as the vision stirred and his surroundings blurred. He was rested against a short half wall, the sky open above him. Matt finally took in what was around him; he was on a roof, and a few feet away a figure paced back and forth.

Tanya turned to look at him, she wore her taut black jeans and boots, with a fishnet top and purple tank underneath it. She didn't look cold at all, she looked confident, powerful as she loomed over him. He tried to move, to stand, but pain shot throughout his body and he cried out.

Tanya rushed to him, cooing him. "Don't move, Matty, you're injured." He sneered at her, trying to cover up his wincing, but Tanya looked unconvinced. He also couldn't stop his teeth as they started to chatter.

"Oh, are you cold?" Flame lit in her palm. She brought it close to him.

Matt felt that he should have tried backing away, not that he could, but the warmth enticed him. He tried to draw closer, but Tanya maliciously smote it out. She cackled with laughter, clutching at her stomach. Matt wished he could get up and really give her a reason to be clutching her ribs, but his own hurt too badly to move.

"What do you want? Witch," Matt finally asked.

She snapped up and looked at him, all humor lost. "That was rude," she said with poison.

"I want her free," she continued.

"Who? Magdalena? YOU'RE THE ONE THAT HAS HER IMPRISONED!" Matt yelled, only to cry out a second later as she launched herself at him so fast he didn't have time to flinch and grabbed him by the throat, squeezing.

"No. It's you. It's always been you. She hesitates, she's stuck, she can't move forward because of YOU! You make her..." she looks him up and down with pure disgust in her voice, "Weak."

The door to the roof slammed open and she released him, spinning on the spot to look over at the noise. Magdalena strode across the roof.

"Tanya. What're you-" she froze in place as she saw Matt on the ground.

"What the hell, Tanya?"

"I brought him here, for you. So we can finish this." She told Magdalena, a smile creeping into her voice, like she was doing her a favor.

"Mags. Please!" Matt called out, immediately pain seared across his cheek as Tanya whipped around back-handing him.

Magdalena yelped, as though it caused her pain too. She took a step forward like she was going to run to him. To protect him, but she paused, now torn.

"Tanya...what is this?" she asked, her voice quivering.

Tanya approached Magdalena, arms out, "This is your freedom. This is you breaking your chains so you can finally let loose. You're so-" Tanya swelled with emotion, pouring it into her words. "Powerful!"

Magdalena turned her head away, shamed, "I'm not." She whispered. Tanya reached for her hands, surprising Magdalena by the tenderness and care. She held them as she continued to speak,

"You're wrong about yourself! I can see it. I've always seen it. You're beautiful Maggie. You can do so much more. THEY DESERVE FOR YOU TO DO MORE!" She cried at the end. Magdalena raised her head to meet Tanya's eyes. She looked scared.

"They think you're a freak, Maggie. You're not! I know you're not!" She danced back closer to Matt. She moved her hand out, palm up in Matt's direction. Then turned back to Magdalena,

"They don't know you, but I do. I followed you. Looked after you." Tanya continued. Magdalena looked back and forth between Matt and Tanya. Matt still looked to be in pain, pleading with his eyes.

"Please Tanya, don't do this. Don't make me do this again," Magdalena said, her arm reaching down to grip the metal bracer on her left wrist with tears in her eyes.

Tanya's eyes flicked to it, and her visage grew cold. "He was a monster, Magdalena." She stated flatly without emotion.

Magdalena's head snapped up, a look of pain in her eyes.

"Don't say that, Tanya."

"It's true, Maggie-"

"NO! They weren't monsters. They *hide* from monsters. *He* was just trying to protect him."

Flame burst along Tanya's fingertips, turning away from their conversation that she heard too many times before. "I have to do this Maggie, for you. Because I love you, and I want you to be stronger." She said with finality, then looked to Matt, increasing the power in her engulfed hand.

"NO!" Magdalena's scream broke out across the open air. Lightning split the night sky. The next moment Tanya's body fell from the roof. It crumpled, broken, against the pavement below.

Chapter 24

AMBER SLAMMED THE door to her Jeep as she got out of the passenger side. She stomped across their driveway kicking up dirt as she went. She hated feeling like a child, her mother treating her like a child, and subsequently throwing a tantrum like a child.

She refused to speak the whole way home, opting instead for the infuriating silence of the night and her longing to be back at the hospital with Vincent, waiting on Matt.

She kept looking at her phone hoping it would magically start working again. There was no telling how she would hear from Vin at this point. Her mother at one point tried talking with her and Amber felt a "for your own good" speech coming along. Amber smashed her phone on the hospital parking lot in response; her mother didn't try again for the rest of the ride.

She had hoped to somehow escape, but now that she was drawing nearer the door, the realization struck her how she was walking into a cage. She swung open the door storming inside; she didn't know where to go. No place was safe to escape. She headed for her room, flipped on her light and stopped dead in the doorway. Her paintings were spread out around her bed, some lay in crinkled balls on the floor. She could recognize some immediately. The forest, the river, and on top, torn clean in half was a painting of Vin. Soaring high in the sky, wind whipping about him, in a beautiful moment of peace. Its beauty a cruel center piece to her collection's destruction.

"Amber! Enough!" Her mother shouted as soon as she came in after her. She towered and raged, and at one point might have been imposing. Now Amber was older, as tall as her mom, thicker with muscle and her hair wild unlike her mother's clean, straight look. She rounded on her mother, causing her mother to hesitate, but continued.

"I've told you what would happen with them! You're going to get yourself killed. Just like him! You want to be stupid? And reckless?" Her voice and words reverberating in Amber's bones. Her face grew hot. She could feel her energy bleeding out, she couldn't control it. Amber's mother didn't notice the bubbling water, a mug left on the table and its contents started to rise. The dripping faucet in the kitchen started climbing to the ceiling.

"I won't let you be a fool like him!" her mother shrieked.

"ENOUGH!" Amber screamed back. The mug shattered causing her mother to yelp and jump back. Amber stalked toward her mother,

"He was a hero. Just like any gun used by a non-Weaver, it was a weapon in the wrong hands! He walked into that fire and his body didn't come back, but his life lives in me and those people he saved! I will not let you dishonor his name or actions. Not anymore." She turned at seeing the pain in her mother's eyes and stalked back into her room, turning to make a last gesture toward the shattered mug and the water that burst from it.

"Don't forget, mom. I'm a monster too, just like the ones that set that fire." she said with finality leaving her mother in silence.

She closed the door to her room, seething, but slowly growing calm. Amber couldn't believe she did that, but she couldn't understand how her mother could destroy her art. She stared down at their remains before throwing them onto the ground and falling onto her bed. Her heart still beating quickly in her chest, she breathed out deeply, then leaned over to her laptop sitting by her bedside and put on some music. A deep steady chant and drums began playing through the speakers. She laid back down eyes on the ceiling, her hand reached for the dream catcher that hung over her bed, the feathers tickling her fingers.

She closed her eyes and trees grew in her mind. She painted the familiar forest, held hands with Vin, and he was smiling at her. They began running through the forest together, no words, just the steady beat of the drums and soft chanting. They weren't alone either, soon Matt ran alongside them as well. His infectious grin plastered on his face. She realized she hadn't seen that in a while and missed it deeply. On the other side of him ran a girl with similar features and long untamed black hair; his sister Magdalena.

A tear streaked down her cheek, and Amber continued to live in this vision until her heartbeat slowed, her breaths became even, and her mind slipped into unconsciousness.

"What the hell? Matt?!" Vin had opened his bedroom door to see Matt laying on his bed, awake but looking weak. Vin ran up to him, putting an arm on him he realized how cold Matt was. He then noticed his window open, the frigid air outside making its way in. With a quick wave of his arms he expunged the air back out the window, walking up to it and slamming it closed.

"Th-thanks," Matt chattered between his teeth. Vin went back to him and helped him under the covers. Then sat next to him.

"What happened at the hospital?" Vin asked.

"K-kidnaped."

Vin raised an eyebrow. "I'm sorry, what?"

"I'll tell you, but you can't tell your p-parents." He took a breath in, huddling closer to Vin and deeper under the covers.

"Tanya came and took me from the hospital."

Vin's eyes widened in panic.

"She's gone now." Matt said quickly, seeing the look on his face. "She was using me, I guess, to get to my sister. She said I'm holding her back."

He stopped there and Vin waited, assuming what came next would be the worst part.

"She was going to kill me, Tanya. My sister stopped her though. She…killed Tanya. Then brought me here."

"Oh my god, Matt." He looked down at him. He couldn't focus on just one emotion. Should he be worried? Should he feel pity?

Vin's parents came up into his room,

"Vin, Matt! What's going on? Your mother's worried sick." She dropped her purse and ran to the bed, sitting on the opposite side of Vin. Vin's father was right behind her but stood at the door, his hand ready on his phone. She put a gentle hand to his face, "What happened?"

Matt looked to Vin, concluding it would be up to him to get them through this, again.

"He's fine," Vin started, trying to buy himself some time to think.

"He, uh," he looked back to see Matt's pitiful expression, "Kind of freaked out in the hospital. After Dallas…well, I guess we didn't all recover as much as we thought."

His parents shared a look, then their gaze fell back on Matt's pathetic form. Vin assumed they were debating how realistic it was that Matt went anywhere in his condition.

"Well, let's go ahead and take him back." His father said.

"No. Please." Matt finally said, "I woke up in there and didn't know what happened. I panicked and ran out. Can I go back in the morning? I'm just so tired, and I feel fine, really, I just don't like hospitals."

Noemi patted him softly then went back to her husband, speaking quietly before his mother turned back and said, "Fine, you can stay here. Your mother looked exhausted, and I'm sure needs some sleep. We'll tell her you're alright and escaped that terrible hospital that worked so hard to keep you alive. In the morning we'll tell the hospital we found you and your dad can pick you up after he gets off. Fair?"

Vin nodded his head. "Fair."

"Totally fair," added Matt.

"Well, get to sleep, both of you. You look terrible." She stooped to pick up her purse then went to Vin. Giving him a kiss on the cheek, she then turned and left. Vin got up to close the door behind them.

He went back to the bed. Matt looked up at him and Vin was struck with how sad and lost he looked.

"I don't want to be alone tonight. I can't."

Vin smiled and climbed into bed with Matt, he put an arm around him as Matt wrapped his broken body around Vin, laying his head on his chest. His body still felt cold to Vin. There was no telling how long he'd been outside or what he'd ben through.

"Thanks…Vinny."

Vin looked down at his best friend, his eyes already closed and his breathing going steady. Vin started absently petting his hair. It felt soft; they must have bathed him in the hospital. How Matt could even stand whatever stink Vin had he didn't know, but he was too tired now and didn't care to disturb Matt to get up. In less than a minute Matt had already drifted to sleep.

Vin struggled to reach over and turn off his bed lamp and then finally laid-back thinking of their night. He hoped Amber was ok. Deciding he'd message her in the morning on his computer, he soon joined Matt as he too drifted to sleep.

Chapter 25

MATT STOOD IN A clearing in Hestle Park, hands up in a defensive position, trying to catch his breath. He was dripping in sweat regardless of the chilly early February weather.

A strong gust of wind buffeted his right flank and he narrowly managed to get a wall up before the attack slammed into his defense. Water whipped at him from his left, he tried to defend against it but was too slow. The water snapped at his legs, taking them out from under him and dropping him to the ground.

He groaned and rolled around on the ground.

"Damn Amber." Vin said running up to Matt. Amber approached slower, with less concern.

"What? He should have been quicker." She said, not with hostility, but with little sympathy.

"Yeah, but he' still recovering from-" Vin began but Matt cut him off.

"No, it's fine Vin. I need to be ready for stuff like this, especially when we run into that group again."

When Vin stuck to that word. There was still optimism in Matt, even after everything. He came to Amber and Vin as soon as he was able to start physical training again, insisting he needed to be ready for the terrorists. He was still going to go after Magdalena, even though they had nothing to track her or the terrorists down.

They spent weeks after the incident brainstorming what they were going to do. All their pictures and evidence had been wiped in Magdalena's attack on them. They decided to send an anonymous tip to the Houston police, but without knowledge of a timetable they doubted they would take it very seriously. It's not like the city could be on guard indefinitely on the chance this one tip was right.

Regardless, they decided their best option was to prepare Matt for whatever came, even if they had no leads.

It was only their first week of training and Vin realized if Tanya and Magdalena didn't kill Matt, Amber probably would.

"Maybe we should take a break?" Vin encouraged.

Amber ignored the question and helped Matt up. "You good?" she asked.

He nodded, not meeting Vin's eyes. "Yeah, let's go again."

They took their spots in the clearing, Amber on his left, Vin on his right.

"Ok, let's try your ability to strengthen your defenses. Use your energy to focus the earth to solidify and reinforce it."

Matt nodded, and their sparring began. He stomped hard with his foot. Two large stones rose up on either side of him. Amber immediately grabbed water from a large bucket they brought. It crashed into Matt's wall, causing it to quiver. Vin started next, hesitantly, Weaving his own blasts. Matt's defenses held, but Amber shot Vin a glare knowing he was holding back. She redoubled her efforts, drawing in a great source of water, empowering it and sending it at Matt. It was so strong the blast made him lose concentration on Vin's side, he was forced to release it to focus entirely on Amber.

She came at him harder, strike after strike, assaulting his defenses.

"Hey!" he yelled, holding up both hands as his wall began to groan and crack from the pressure.

She didn't stop, "Reinforce! Strengthen!" She called to him sending more attacks his way. He began losing footing, the force of them pushing him back. His muscles were strained; he closed his eyes holding on in desperation.

"I. Can't." He said with gritted teeth.

"Amber!" Vin called to her, but she ignored him.

She continued to push him back, "Why not?" She asked.

The question startled Matt.

"Wh-what do you mean?"

"It's an easy question, Matt!" she said in between slamming his defense as it splintered and chipped away.

"Why. Not?" she said with a final powerful burst that sent him to his knees, shattering the wall. He held the pieces in the air, a pathetic remnant of his defense.

"I...don't understand," he said quietly.

Vin could relate. He didn't understand what was happening, and to his horror he saw Amber reach up, another attack gathered. Vin began to summon his own to defend Matt.

Matt looked up, his eyes, glossy with tears, widened when he saw Amber wasn't stopping.

He bellowed out at once, "BECAUSE I'M BROKEN!" finally relenting to the question. He let the rest of his stones rain down around him.

Amber sent her water back to its bucket. Vin was about to go to him, but Amber shot him a look that froze him in place. She, instead walked toward him.

"Because I'm weak," he continued, barely above a whisper. The sun was shadowed as Amber stood over him, he looked back up to see her holding out a hand.

"Let's take a break, shall we?" she said.

They left Vin back in the clearing as Amber led Matt to the familiar spot on the river, where they first met months ago. She wanted to remove her shoes, to dip her toes in but the water was still frigid. She settled for just sitting beside it, Matt next to her. He began immediately playing with the little stones around them.

She let the silence play out a bit longer before she took a deep breath in of the nature around her. She finally spoke,

"Do you understand what we're trying to teach you Matt?"

He didn't say anything at first, but a slow smirk creeped onto his lips.

"I don't know if it's what you meant to teach me, but I'm starting to learn you're kind of a bi-" Amber splashed him with water before he finished.

"Kidding. Kidding! Geez, so abusive."

"A relationship, Matt. We're trying to teach you to have a relationship."

Matt was taken aback. There were a hundred different sarcastic jokes he could respond with but didn't. He hardly felt like himself recently, and just when he thought he couldn't feel any worse Amber continued,

"You really are damaged, Mateo."

He scoffed. "Well, thanks."

"But you're in luck."

"How's that?"

"Because your element is Earth. Tell me something. You've spent the last four years using the Earth right? You've worked with it, learned how to enhance it."

Matt nodded not sure where this was going.

"Tell me what you think about Earth? In general, how would you characterize it?"

Matt's mind immediately went to a comment about how crazy she was, wanting to define inanimate objects, but he was so very tired.

"It's solid. It's sturdy and unyielding, comforting and safe. It's…."

"Strong." She finished for him.

He nodded.

"So let it be more than just a weapon for you, Matty. Let the earth be your strength. You've spent four years building it up, let it build *you* up. You're never alone, and I don't mean me and Vin. You're *never* alone, it's always with you."

Matt met her eyes, hanging on every word. Like a life-preserver plunking into his waters, keeping him from drowning. Tears flowed again from his eyes. She took her hands and placed them on his cheeks, she smiled warmly and he closed his eyes, placing his hands on hers. He let the moment sit there, he let her words build him up as he took what she said to heart. He would be strong again, he knew it.

He lowered his hands, and when she removed hers the tears went with them drying his face. They turned from each other to look back on the stream and the trees beyond.

After giving it some more time Matt finally caught on that Amber must have learned this at some point herself. Realizing he didn't know much about her he finally asked, "So what's water for you?"

She smiled immediately. If she was being honest, she was quite proud of his question.

"I fight with my mom a lot." She started, "It really started after my father died. I grew so angry after we had an argument one day. I left and ran and ran until I couldn't anymore. Then I came to this river. I've watched water my whole life, my father was a Water Weaver too, but this time it was different. It felt so calm...so soothing. I started to just come here after things got bad with my mom and just Weave. I'd let it flow through and relax me.

I feel like it did more for me than just that. Water is all about going with the flow, to accept the coursing river and allow it to take you where it takes you. It helped me see that I can't always choose where my life goes but I learned to accept that flow and the changes in my life." She swallowed hard, thinking about her father. "No matter how hard those changes are."

Matt smiled at her. "Damn that's...beautiful, and kinda freakin' deep!"

Amber laughed, letting the seriousness lighten a bit.

Matt put his hand on her arm. "Seriously, thank you. How'd you get so good at all of this anyway?"

Amber grew thoughtful in the moment, then stilled her thoughts as she reached out with her powers. Her senses flowed along the creek, feeling the water churning and rolling where it met resistance. The rocks and silt along its bedding, packed with minerals. She could feel a family of tadpoles just a couple of yards from them. A rabbit, lapping at its waters just a few feet from that.

"My people. They love the land because they see all of it, for miles around. People get too accustomed to just see what's right in front of them."

Matt studied her face when she talked about this, a small smile crept on his face.

"Vin understands that. Doesn't he?" Matt asked.

She nodded and they returned to looking back at the forest. "For the most part he does. Though I think he's more that way with people, don't you think?"

Matt agreed, if there was anything he was sure of, it was that Vin paid more attention to people than anyone he had met before. He was the most empathetic person he knew.

"So, I'm weak and unstable," he said, changing the subject. "You're a hot head with no chill. Yet we have Earth and Water. So does the element, like, choose people it's opposite or something?"

Amber shrugged, "Maybe it's *us* who choose the element, maybe deep down we know ourselves and know what we need. Who really knows?"

Matt let that sink in. "Well…I think I'd like to get back to training now."

Amber looked over him, raising an eyebrow, "Oh are you now?"

His eyes twinkled with confidence. "Yeah, I think I'm ready to stop feeling so weak."

Chapter 26

VIN THREW HIS BAG in the back of his Durango, landing next to the packed tent, and other camping supplies. He walked back up the steps to his front door and turned to stare longingly toward his new vehicle. Vin knew it sounded insane to complain about getting a new car, after their insurance paid for the replacement, but he had lots of memories in the old beat up vehicle.

Down the road, he saw Amber turning onto his street. She, like Matt, adopted to start riding a bike. Amber didn't tell them what happened with her mom afterward, but Matt and Vin caught on that they'd become her dirty little secret, so she couldn't take her Jeep to their houses anymore.

He smiled, walking back down to the street.

"Hey there," Vin greeted.

"Beautiful day!" Amber returned.

She hopped off her bike and gave Vin a hug then let him take her bag from her, putting it next to Matt's. He turned and looked at her, the winter nights turned into fresh spring mornings. She wore an army gray tank top and short khaki's with hiking boots. Vin tried to ignore the way he felt when he saw her. They had yet to revisit what happened during the bonfire. Amber was busy tiptoeing around her mom and Vin was busy trying to keep Matt out of trouble. They tried their best to keep searching for Magdalena but hadn't had any luck for the past couple of months.

"Matt inside?" Amber asked.

"Doing his rounds."

"Ah." Amber looked up and down the street searching for him.

"Do you think it's good he's been straining himself so much lately?" Vin asked.

"Probably not. I think trying to stop him wouldn't go over well though," Amber replied.

Vin nodded. "He was just telling me last week how ironic it was that I'd spent the last three years preparing for stuff like this, and now he's the one that needs it."

Amber nodded sympathetically, "I suppose there's only so many times you can break before you're tired of it."

She thought to the past few months where they'd been training Matt, to understand and use the elements like they could.

"He's been doing great, all things considered."

Vin nodded in agreement. "I think he always held himself back before. He didn't want to learn. I just don't think he had any real motivation to."

Vin pointed down the street, the opposite way Amber had come, now seeing Matt jogging up the street. Sweat glistened his shirtless torso; he had impressively gotten even bigger since his accident. Vin found working out one of the few ways to keep him distracted from thinking of Magdalena. He still spent most nights at Vin's not wanting to be alone. Vin didn't know if it was from missing his sister or being kidnapped. It took Vin a lot of convincing to get Matt to agree to their camping trip for Spring Break.

"Hey, Amber," Matt said between catching breaths.

"Head upstairs and take a shower, then we can head out." Vin told him. Matt nodded agreeably and headed into the house.

Vin and Amber looked to each other and let a comfortable silence fall over them before Vin finally motioned his head toward the house and they went in together.

"Ambrosia!" Vin's mother greeted as she came in. She grabbed her by the shoulders and led her to the living room couch.

"You'll have to promise me you'll keep the boys in line. Those two, in the middle of unpopulated civilization?" She just shook her head imagining the possibilities. Amber laughed, "Don't worry, I'll handle them."

Vin smiled at their back and forth, he liked how well they got along and how much his mother liked her. Even his sister approved, though he thought she was more disappointed Amber would spend time with Vin at all. Something about being too good for him.

His joy over them getting along came to an immediate halt when his mother stood and went to one of their cabinets, the specific cabinet that held their family photos.

"Madre, no!" he pleaded.

"Don't be like that Vincenzo, you should have known this was bound to happen." She chided, pulling out a large green one, decorated on top were the letters *Le Foto del Bambino di Vincenzo.*

She sat back down next to Amber who looked at Vin giving him an apologetic shrug. Noemi opened the first page and Amber let out a noise Vin thought should only be reserved for small puppies and kittens.

"Yes, he was quite the cute baby. And look at him now, a handsome young man," Noemi cooed. Heat rose in Vin's cheeks and for once wished his sister would make one of her annoyingly well-timed appearances to counter the compliment. She was not there, however, and he was left alone with an adoring mother and a book full of ammo.

"I got to say, when I had him, I wouldn't let him out of my sight. You know baby kidnappers were all the rage back then. Can you imagine if one of them saw him?" she asked.

Vin sighed, "No one was going to kidnap me."

"Of course they would have. Look at your pretty, big green eyes and puffy cheeks. Your fluffy brown hair, even back then you were hairy."

"Geez mom!" He said audibly embarrassed now, Amber laughing up a storm.

Vin resigned to shake his head and go upstairs leaving the two to flip through his past. He plopped down on his bed, window open, letting the cool spring air circulate through the room.

Matt walked in a couple of minutes later with a towel wrapped around his waist.

"My mother is embarrassing me," Vin immediately told him.

Matt shrugged flashing a grin, "Nothing new then." He dug in his gym bag grabbing a change of clothes. He wore clothes similar to Amber, a cut off t-shirt and khaki shorts.

"You and Amber match." Vin told him, "Though she's showing significantly more thigh."

Matt looked down, flexing and rotating his leg, "You think I should cut them shorter?"

Vin laughed, "And make her jealous? No, better to keep her thinking she has the best legs in the group." He said getting up from the bed and heading to the door, "Though you might want to shave yours. We don't want other campers thinking they stumbled across a yeti out there." He added leaving to head back downstairs.

Matt's mouth dropped at the insult before he yelled after, "You're one to talk! Grizzly bear!"

The road trip to Oklahoma was four and half hours of too-sweet sweet tea, every candy at the gas stations they passed and rocking out to Matt's playlist of alternative rock, belting it out the open windows. Though they didn't admit it but every mile away from home the more the weight of their lives alleviated. Vin suspiciously felt like it was the calm before the storm and they were currently cruising through the eye of it.

"So where is this place?" Amber asked as they drove down the forested roads of Norman, Oklahoma.

"Turner Falls," Vin answered, "My family came here a couple of times when I was younger. There's this big cabin area at the entrance surrounding a lake made by a waterfall. We'll camp in the woods above the falls, along the river that feeds it. It's usually shallow enough in most places that we can walk it."

"Not that it would be much of an issue for us if it wasn't." She smirked knowingly from the back seat.

Matt had his feet propped up on the dashboard in the front who sardonically called back to her, "Maybe for you two."

Amber appeared on the console in between them, "Don't worry, I promise I won't let you down when you fall." She teased.

"When? It's a big IF." He retorted. Amber leaned back crossing her arms playfully. Vin kept his eyes on the road but smiled along with them.

They pulled into the park and paid their fair, then took their SUV up into the hills as far as they could go before parking and getting out. Grabbing each of their backpacks, Vin and Amber took the extra gear they brought while Matt hoisted the tent over his shoulder.

The trio made their way along the path, Amber breathing in the fresh air. Vin pulled out his phone to text his mom they made it but didn't have reception. He made a mental note to hike to a good spot later to text her.

"Breathe it in guys, feel the energy from this place. It's amazing." She said as they walked.

Vin closed his eyes feeling what she meant, even Matt who had grown increasingly proficient in his months of training also soaked in the energy of nature around them.

"It's almost too much." Matt commented, "I've never felt it so intensely."

"That's why I want to explore the world after graduation. There's so many places that belong to the Earth and I want to experience them."

"That'll be cool." Matt said, but something else flashed across his face too quickly for Vin to catch.

"River's up this way." Amber said, feeling the pull of her natural element and guiding them off the path until they came to a small area clear of trees right on the water.

It bubbled and gurgled as the water raced down the stream toward the falls about a mile off.

They set their bags down and Vin gave the area a once-over. It was clear of trees but heavily jagged with rocks and roots. He looked over to Matt, "Want to set the scene?"

Matt smiled, stretching his arms forward cracking his knuckles as he walked to the center of the clearing. He drew in a breath, then propelled his energy down into his feet. He dropped, spinning with a leg out, drawing a line with his power. Then stood and punched downward, like a karate student would when breaking a board, Weaving the ground below him. The rocks and earth rolled away like a shockwave.

Matt stood, his arms crossed in the center of a perfectly smooth circle.

"Campsite ready, Captain."

"Cannonball!" Was the last thing Vin and Amber heard before Matt slammed into the water sending a torrent of waves crashing over them.

They stood in the shallows of the river by their campsite, now dripping wet.

"That was selfish," Amber scolded once Matt resurfaced. "We spent an hour getting this together and you just *had* to be the first one in?"

Matt replied with a snooty eye roll, earning a raised eyebrow from Amber and only too late did he realize his mistake. Amber Weaving a large wave pushed him up and out onto the other side of the river.

They had spent the hour Weaving their spot to perfection. Matt carved out the bottom of the river and widened the space so that they had a nice pool for the water to enter first before it drained back into the rest of the stream.

"Hey! I was the one that that dug out a whole damn pool!" he yelled from across the river, "And I dammed it so we could have a plentiful source of water. I think I deserved the first try."

"Well, I was the one that had to constantly Weave a whole river around you so you could actually work!" She argued back. Vin was the only one that didn't have anything to do with the pool, but they both seemed to keep him out of it.

Vin had soared over the forest getting the lay of the land. From far above the forest looked like the scour pad side of a sponge, the individual trees morphed into the landscape of a prickly shell. He enjoyed seeing the mountains and real hills, unlike Texas with its mostly flat, uninteresting stretches of land. A silver ribbon cut through the carpeted forest until it spilled out into the massive swimming lake at the entrance of the campgrounds.

Vin smiled at their continued debate and readied his excuse that he had set up their tent, but it didn't seem like he would need it.

Amber raised her hand like she was ready to Weave again, but Matt was ready and quicker, stomping his foot down. The earth beneath Amber and Vin jutted up and forward, launching them into the air as he had been shortly before. Amber flailed for a bit before she gracefully belly flopped into the pool. Vin used the air to carry himself to their man-made dam at the source of the river which now resembled their own mini falls. He landed gracefully taking a seat on the edge.

Amber resurfaced and flew into a tirade at Matt who argued back in kind. Vin couldn't help but bust out into laughter. Matt and Amber stared at him and then back at each other, starting to feel foolish for their playful argument getting too serious.

Amber released a smirked and pulled with her energy, Weaving the water to drag Vin and Matt back into and under the pool. Once they surfaced, they all laughed together, alleviating the tension. Like the waters they swam in, the stress now flowed from them down the river.

Vin lay there floating on his back with his eyes closed, soaking in the sun. He snuk a peak toward Amber; he couldn't help it. She looked beautiful amidst nature. She wore a tight, yellow sleeveless shirt with matching briefs, her tan skin glistened with moisture. Her exposed arms were strong, and her long hair lay in wet curls folding on her back. He was reminded of the day he first met her, in a place much like the one he lay in now. Vin thought how sometimes the most beautiful things in the world were the random wildflowers you would come across in nature. He hardly gave himself time to really think about how Amber wasn't like any girl he ran into in the school's hallways, and how his life, which revolved around the elements, seemed to co-exist so naturally with her. In this moment of peace on the water, in woods far away from home and everything he knew, he explored the idea of how she made him feel and who she was to him.

She wasn't paying attention, gently moving the water in a small quiet dance all to herself. Vin started as he realized Matt had caught him staring, he quickly dipped his head before Matt could see him turn red.

Chapter 27

T HE SUN BEGAN TO set, and they retreated to their tent
to start the fire. Coming out of the river Amber wrung out
her hair, pulling the excess water from her and sending it
back out into the stream. She reached out a hand, focusing
on the boys, separating the water that rolled along their skin from the
moisture deeper with in. The river water leapt from their bodies and
retreated to its source.

They smiled appreciatively at her as Matt went to grab logs for the pit
and Vin some kindling.

"You know we really need to add a Fire Weaver to our little group,"
Matt commented as he dropped the last log into the pit he dug out. A
current of air circled them, dry leaves and wood chips rode its wind into the
pit to settle amongst the logs.

Amber grabbed their lighter fluid squirting it over the pit. "Because we go camping so often," she teased. "I'll put an ad out when we get back." She added.

Vin bent down with their lighter, "You know Matt, I'm starting think you really like this whole, 'landscaping' thing. First with our pool, now this fire pit." He commented, noticing the neatly placed stones that lined the pit, the perfect, circular, foot drop into the ground. Then he clicked the lighter and put the small flame underneath the wood. It ignited sending a splash of yellow and orange across the camp.

Matt came back from the tent and plopped down on one of the cushioned stones he had also added, giving them some comfort and elevation over the fire.

"You think so? It's kind of fun."

Amber sat down next to him, pulling out the bag of marshmallows from their supply of snacks. "I think so," she said to Matt, "It's pretty cool. None of the other elements can do anything like this, at least nothing that's permanent"

She skewered a marshmallow for each of them, handing out the stokes. Vin taking his and sitting next to her, close enough that their knees touched, but she didn't pull away.

They let silence fall over them as they quietly roasted their marshmallows. The only sound was the crackling fire and the running water. Vin's eyes flashed like emeralds as he stared into the flames. His attention was drawn to Matt as he let out a loud sigh. They turned to him and saw he didn't look annoyed, but relieved.

"This is…this is really nice guys." He finally said. "I'm sorry how tense I've been for the past couple of months after…everything."

"It was a lot, Matt." Amber comforted, "No one blames you."

"Yeah but still, I'm sure Vin would like to sleep alone again." Matt mused.

Vin could have sworn her back straightened a bit in reaction. She knew Matt was staying at Vin's, perhaps not realizing in his bed. Vin almost felt silly hoping that made her jealous.

"Matty you know I'm always here for you, no matter how long." Vin comforted.

"Me too, as long as we don't kill each other first." They laughed together, before Matt withdrew, on the edge of falling back to his worried look.

"I just wish we could do more. For Magdalena I mean." He said.

Vin nodded, "We will, we know this wasn't her idea. She was just a weapon; we can help her. You can save her." He encouraged.

Amber smiled at Vin, then looked back to Matt. "Vin's right. We're getting close." They normally opted for more practical sensibility, but there was something about the woods, something that seemed to drape them in a comforting lull. Like the tongues of flame from the fire, optimism and hope couldn't help but pop off of them.

Matt let out another sigh, this one more exasperated than relieved. "I know, I know! We've gone over it a hundred times. I shouldn't have brought it up again. Let's talk about something else. Someone else must have some issues, right?"

Silence spread through the camp again, this time due to the awkwardness rather than peace. They all knew Matt was mostly referring to Amber, who had yet to talk about what happened at the hospital and why she was now sneaking around to hang out with them.

"My dad was pretty much the most amazing person I knew. He would have had to for my mother to marry outside the reservation." She started suddenly; she grew more vibrant as she talked about her father. "He's where I got my love of nature. We would go hiking all the time. Camping, just like this. He would have loved it here."

Pausing amidst her memories a sad smile crossed her face, "The last time I went camping was with my dad."

She pulled her marshmallow out of the heat and prodded the surface, now have turned brown, it made a satisfying crunch.

"He was a Water Weaver like me. But that day we didn't camp along the water. A fight broke out between two campers. Fire Weavers. I can't even remember what it was about anymore, something stupid I'm sure. Something that wouldn't have escalated to anything if they weren't Weavers."

The air seemed to drain from the area. Vin was surprised the fire didn't flicker out as the ending became clear to him and Matt. It made so much sense now, what it really meant for Amber to help at the Dallas attack. The way her mother reacted after the accident with Matt.

"My father tried to stop them and when he couldn't he ran into the forest trying to help campers stuck inside. It made sense at the time, I'm sure. He was a Water Weaver, who better to assist against a fire."

She still played with the marshmallow, having long lost the appetite to eat it. Matt, surprisingly, reached out first and wrapped her in a hug, their tiny spears dropping to the ground. She leaned into his chest as she tried to hide back tears.

"I haven't told this story to anyone. I don't know why; I feel ashamed not to tell it. He was a hero, and brave." She sniffled, Vin placing his warm hand on her thigh, which she immediately returned by gripping it in her own.

"But more than shame I feel angry, angry at my mother for making me feel most of my life that I should be ashamed by what happened."

Matt choked on his words, then cleared his throat. "I know about family shame," he finally said. "Even if my parents act like she doesn't exist, they carry on the shame of what Mag's did. It's no way to live."

Amber pulled away from Matt drying her eyes with her left hand, keeping Vin in her other for a couple of moments longer.

"I suppose, with the family I have, I have no room to judge, but I've always wondered. Your parents, are they that upset just because she ran away?"

Matt looked away into the fire, thinking. Vin suspected there was more, but he never asked Matt what he was hiding.

"They…we're prideful. My parents sacrificed a lot to get and stay here. I think they saw what Magdalena did as a betrayal to everything they had to go through."

Amber let out a somber chuckle. "Funny, that's how my grandmother thought about my mom's decision to marry my dad for the longest time. I didn't really notice when it changed. But one day she just stopped berating my mother or looking down on me."

"That's why you were surprised when you told her about the dance?" Vin asked.

Amber nodded, "Yeah, growing up she knew I would have to be the one to carry on any of our family traditions and she didn't act like it. It's something so small but I couldn't have a conversation with my grandmother without her looking disappointed and shooting glances at my hair.

That night we told her about the dance, I realized how that must have looked, history repeating itself. I never expected her to go along with it, and even show you."

She looked up at Vin, her soft brown eyes glistening with the remnants of tears off the firelight.

"She must respect you greatly."

"Maybe she finally respects you, and your father." He countered. Amber's eyes widened just the slightest at that. His words always found a way to pierce her shell, then wrap her heart in a warm embrace.

A flapping noise broke their attention as they looked over to see Matt shaking out one of their thick blankets. They looked at him curiously,

"Figured we might as well get comfortable," he said lying down, "Too bad we can't see the stars through these trees." He said casually but expectantly at Vin.

Vin rolled his eyes getting up to lay in the middle next to Matt, Amber joining him on his other side to the right.

Vin raised a hand slowly drawing in elemental energy and then Weaved a pulse of air that sliced through the canopy above revealing the skies beyond.

"You do good work, Vinny." Matt teased. Vin smiled.

"Can't see stars like these in the city," Amber noted.

They sat for a while in the silence looking at the stars.

"I was a coward back in Dallas," Matt said suddenly. "Not for anything to do with the fighting or even for not telling you guys I saw Tanya."

Vin looked to his left examining Matt's face, but he refused to meet his eyes.

"When you told me about how you've been feeling the past couple of years, about our distance and it just being because we were placed in different life classes. I'm a coward because I did that to you, and I couldn't admit it at the time."

"What do you mean?"

"The day of the Awakening I knew things would change when you became an Air Weaver, but I didn't know how much."

"Matt..." Vin whispered. He could see his body tense.

"You had so much responsibility, and you were doing so well. You had such a bright future ahead with so many possibilities. And I was just there, and it hit me. You were all I had. There's no way I could have gotten through Magdalena leaving me without you. So there I was realizing one day you'd have to go too. I started making new friends, joining clubs, distancing myself from you."

He sat up, putting his head down between his knees. Muffled he continued, "I had no idea what you had gone through. I was so scared of you leaving me, that I left you first."

The impact of his shame wasn't lost on Vin, between Matt and Amber a theme began to develop. Vin sat up and wrapped his arm around him,

"You didn't lose me, and I didn't lose you. We're here together, and I don't see that stopping any time soon." Matt didn't reply, and Vin got the impression he would have to prove it. He continued, "Especially since-" Vin got up and left the two going to his bag in the tent. Matt looked up and over at Amber who just shrugged,

"Don't look at me, he doesn't tell me everything." She smiled encouragingly.

He came back with an envelope in his hands, "Your mother gave it to me, she thought it'd be better if I gave it to you." He said handing it over. The University of Florida and its logo the Gator were on the front. The letter had already been opened, and Matt's jaw dropped.

"No…" He looked up at Vin in disbelief and Vin's large grin was all the confirmation he needed but he still tore it open and scanned through letter. Then jumped up and bear hugged Vin.

"I suppose it goes without saying, but I got in too."

"Sun, sea and – "

"School?" Vin finished for him.

"Oh yeah, if we have time." Matt mischievously grinned.

"See? So, you have nothing to worry about. We got this."

Matt fell back down to the blanket, unfiltered glee flowing across his face as he clutched his acceptance letter. "I knew I shouldn't have doubted how good of friends we were."

"I think it's good what you guys went through," Amber added, "I don't think you two would be as strong, most bonds aren't before they go through a little turbulence. I'm sure there's a metaphor in there about being forged in fire and all that."

"Wow, what a poet." Matt teased.

Vin kicked at Matt before taking his spot back between them, "You're probably right Amber, at least now in hindsight."

They talked deep into the night pausing on occasion to listen to the sounds of nature around them.

Eventually breaking back into the marshmallows when they got hungry again. The fire got low and they added more wood to it.

Matt began to stare intensely into the fire,

"You guys, this is going to be dramatic, but I don't care, it's how I feel. This burning fire symbolizes my renewed vigor at saving my sister. My passion burns as hot as this flame before us!"

Amber laughed giving him a shove, "You're right that is dramatic. But I'm glad you're more confident about it."

"I agree, you are dramatic. Did you steal Ashleigh's first draft of her bonfire speech?" Vin goaded.

"Ha. Ha" Matt said between wrestling him into a headlock. "If you remember correctly, *I* wasn't even there. So, for all I know it was an amazing speech, and I'll take that as a compliment!"

Vin relented, tapping out.

"I jest, but seriously. What we've done, and what we might have to do, is scary. It's important to remember what we're fighting for. She isn't a monster, she's a girl, lost and scared, and she needs us."

"You have no idea, Vin. The way she looked after Tanya…she seemed so broken."

"Not broken, just bent. She's tough, she always had to be, you and your whole family are."

Matt agreed nodding, "Sometimes I just wish I would have appreciated the time I had with her while she was around. You never know how much time you have with people, no point in wasting it. I feel like all of us can attest to that."

He gave both Vin and Amber a look but didn't elaborate. "I should be off to bed now." He said smirking as he got up and went into the tent.

Vin and Amber exchanged looks. "Did he just-?" Amber started.

"Give us permission? I think so." Vin smiled. He laid back on the blanket but kept his right arm open behind Amber. She rested back on his arm apprehensive at first, but finally looped her hand in his.

They laughed nervously together but their breathing became easier the more time they gave.

"Well, here we are again, at night, in front of a roaring fire." Vin mused.

"Yes, it does seem to be a reoccurring event. I like it, it feels...primal, raw like everything is just laid bare, surface exposed. If you get too close you can get hurt." She contemplated.

"But just right it keeps you warm, and you feel safe." He said quietly to her, the whisper sent goosebumps along her arm and she clutched him a little tighter.

"It's beautiful, in the natural sense. It's not something you'd find in a Hollywood movie, or in a magazine. It feels all the more real with you, like that first day I saw you in the park. It was a beautiful moment I happened upon in nature, and you the striking center piece."

Amber flushed and her body tensed. Vin finally rested his head on top of hers, breathing in the scent of her hair, like every wildflower he'd ever come across, dotted along a fresh stream. Amber turned into the nook of his neck, her senses flooded, he smelt fresh like crisp spring air.

"You're beautiful, Ambrosia," he told her.

She smiled against his skin, placing one soft, warm kiss on his neck before they fell asleep to the peaceful thump of each other's hearts.

Chapter 28

"I AM GONNA MISS this place." Matt announced as he shut the trunk to Vin's SUV.

"We can always come back. It's not going anywhere." Amber encouraged, sitting in the front seat with an arm hanging out the open window.

Vin started the car, and once Matt got in, they left the park. Amber and Matt watched the trees with longing as they moved further from the park. Matt looked down at his phone, the black mirror staring back.

"I didn't even think about charging my phone, it's so dead." He said.

"Wouldn't have mattered," Vin replied, "Mine didn't even have signal.

"I turned mine off, didn't want any distractions." Amber added.

"Good idea," Vin said turning off his phone, then reached his hand to the back for Matt's, "Give me yours, I'll charge it on the way and we'll turn them on at the same time when we get closer. Enjoy some last moments before the world inevitably returns."

An hour outside Rockwell they stopped at a gas station. Matt quickly tugged on his phone sending the cord flying.

"Careful Matt!" Vin lectured.

"CAN'T, GOTTA PEE!" he yelled, jumping out of the car and running for the restroom.

Amber and Vin exchanged a humored glance as they got out themselves.

"You know, I think I'll be ready for parenthood when I'm done dealing with him." Amber mused.

"It is like dealing with a child, isn't it?" Vin replied. He opened the gas cap on the side of the SUV and fed it the nozzle. Amber joined him, leaning against the vehicle. She crossed her arms and stared wistfully at the sky. It had grown colder the farther south they traveled, and they exchanged their t-shirts and shorts for hoodies and comfy sweats.

He rested against the SUV next to her, their arms touching. He looked at her profile, tracing the lines of her face and reached up to play with a strand of her hair. Then looked back to his phone as it began to start up.

"You ok?" he asked her.

She sighed, relaxing as she felt him against her. "The trip was wonderful, don't get me wrong, but I still have to deal with my mother. And I have no idea how to deal with her."

"Oh, shit." Vin said, breaking Amber's calm, she looked over to him, but she didn't get to ask the question as Matt came hauling out of the bathroom, franticly holding up his phone.

"She called me!" He sputtered.

"Who?" Amber asked worryingly, looking back and forth between the two.

"Magdalena! She left some cryptic message."

"What did the message say?" She asked.

"It's like she's saying goodbye. I think they're going to attack soon!"

Amber looked to Vin. "Did she call you too?" she asked, studying the worry on his face.

He silently shook his head staring at his screen, contemplative.

"Why would you think that?" Matt asked, "We have to find her. Now."

"We can't," Vin said, finally speaking.

"What the hell do you mean, we can't?" Matt shot incredulously.

Vin held up his phone, a weather app showing the Galveston coast. A large tropical storm reported on the app.

"A hurricane is heading for Houston. I just saw the missed message. I need to be there as quickly as possible. I should have already been on my way this morning. The last bus from Houston leaves in a couple hours. I was drafted."

Vin flew down the highway, would be wind and rain attempted to pelt his windshield, but Vin took intervals of repelling it as he drove.

"Matt, I know how important it is, of course I do! We can find her afterward. I promise."

"There may not be time afterward, Vin!" Matt had grown only increasingly frantic as they headed back to Rockwell.

He looked over to Amber for support but she had yet pull herself from her phone, remaining quiet most of the ride.

"We will, I promise. We'll find her." Vin responded, looking at him through the rearview mirror.

"Pft, your optimism is all well and good." He sarcastically spat, folding his arms and withdrawing to pointedly stare out the window.

Vin sighed, letting the silence spread. He stared out the window trying to focus on just driving.

He looked back to Amber. "I'll drop you off at your house first, you shouldn't be riding your bike in this weather anyway."

"You can take me to my mom's first, but you're not leaving me there," she said, finally clicking the lock on her phone, laying it to rest on her lap. "I'm coming with you."

"To uh-?" He didn't know what she meant.

"To Galveston. I just finished registering. I'm approved to help; Water Weavers are never turned down from a hurricane or tropical storm."

Vin's mouth dropped. He didn't know what to think, his first instinct was that he should be worried or concerned. The more he thought about every moment they'd had together, whether it was a terrorist attack or a high school celebration, he realized he had come to take comfort and reassurance from her presence. He concluded he didn't trust anyone more than Amber for something like this and found it a relief not to go alone. Not again.

He reached for her hand, squeezing her fingers. "Ok, to your mom's first then."

Chapter 29

AMBER HOPPED OUT of the SUV, a hand held above her head that parted the slight rainfall that was coming down, it split over her like an invisible umbrella.

"I'm going to grab some stuff, and I'll be right back," she said to Vin.

"What if your mom tries to stop you?" he asked.

Her face drew tight, determination in her eyes, "She won't be able to."

Amber went into her house, found her grandmother in the tv room watching her shows but no sign of her mom. That was until she went into her room and there, on her bed, was her mother. She held the dream catcher above her bed and the picture of her father.

Amber started, surprised at seeing her mother, but recovered quickly, putting her bag in her desk chair and tossing out her camping clothes preparing to replace them with clothes she'd need in the rain.

"Mom," she said as a greeting. It took a couple of seconds of her mother watching her go back and forth between places in her room before she finally spoke.

"What're you doing? Running away?"

"No." Pausing for a moment before finally finishing. "I'm going to Galveston to help in the Hurricane relief."

A laughed barked out of her mother's mouth as she put the things in her hands down and stood,

"So that's it, you're just going to run off with the Weavers. Be just as foolish as your father. LEAVE ME JUST LIKE HIM!" she ended in a scream.

Amber threw down her bag and rounded on her mother, tears already in her eyes. She hesitated when she realized her mother was also crying. It caused her to hold the initial insults that sprung to mind, thinking of Matt and their talk along the creek in Hestle woods. She practiced what she preached, and reached out, communicating with her element. She felt it calmly fall from the sky, followed its path as it took off in different directions on the roof, unable to control where it drained to, but continuing nonetheless. The soft patter massaged her emotions, soothing them. Amber released her anger, letting it roll down and away.

"He wasn't a fool, he was brave." Amber spoke softly. She could see her mother's eyebrows rise slightly in surprise. She realized her mother prepared a defense, ready to battle Amber's anger. She had to admit now that was what her mother always did. Now she seemed more susceptible, "He wouldn't have wanted to leave you. I know you miss him. I do too, but he wouldn't have been the man we knew and loved if he didn't go back into the forest that day." Amber began to choke on a sob.

"I still dream about it," Amber continued, her eyes flashing to the dream catcher clutched in her mother's hands. "I have nightmares of the fire, but he finds me and takes me to safety. Just like that day with the people he saved. I can't keep letting you say what he did was anything less than an act of love, not just for our family but every person in those woods, and even the woods themselves." Her eyes narrowed, "I won't."

Her mother just stared, her breathing slowing, and the anger began to leave her eyes.

"I don't know what I'll do if I let go of this anger, Ambrosia." She whispered.

Amber reached out and grabbed her mom's hands, "Replace it with something else. He's all around us. Even if he isn't Cherokee, I believe he lives with our ancestors watching over us and our world."

A voice came from behind them causing them to both jump.

"He may not have our blood, but he has our spirit." Amber turned to see her grandmother in the doorway. She shuffled over and lowered herself into Amber's wicker chair, her hands resting on her cane. Her grandmother fingered the eloquent eagle carved into the handle.

"I thought- I thought you didn't care for him, grandmother."

"Oh sure, maybe at first. How could I have. My only daughter muddying our blood, producing the girl known as my granddaughter with that brown hair of his."

She looked up to meet Amber's eyes, who then lowered herself to the bed across from her grandmother.

"That day he went into the woods to try and save not only those people but all the wildlife, not to mention the forest itself." She closed her eyes and just nodded her head, almost humming with pride.

"It allowed me to truly see my beautiful granddaughter and be proud of her and her father's gifts. I started to listen to you and what he taught you. He has as much Cherokee spirit as the rest of us. Heck, sometimes more. He really understood the elements, and our people. That bond that binds us together, and how he saw our land. It was something so silly, some brown hair."

She reached her hand out to her daughter, grasping it. Looking deep into her eyes and she said words Amber never thought she'd hear her grandmother say.

"Be proud of him Halona, he was a great man."

Amber had her packed bag over her shoulder and headed back toward the car. She could see Vin through the rain specked window. He looked to her, and he could already tell hope was brimming in her eyes. She kept replaying the words her grandmother had said about her father. *He really understood the elements, and the people. That bond that binds us together, and how he saw our land.*

She kept her eyes on Vin realizing she had the same thoughts about him.

Vin ran up the steps to his house, rushing inside. He didn't make it to the stairs before his mother came out of the kitchen.

"Vincenzo!" She shouted, going to him and wrapping her arms around him. He returned the embrace, he could tell she was shaking, she looked like she hadn't been sleeping.

"Did you get our messages? You never returned any of my calls. The hurricane- they drafted-"

"I know, I know. Its why I'm here. I'm sorry I didn't call you back, we've been rushing back from Oklahoma. I'll be right back. I gotta get my Draft Bag and then I gotta go." He said rushing up the stairs, his mother's eyes following after.

He burst into his room and threw down his camping bag, going under his bed and grabbing for his Draft Bag. It was an emergency pack issued to

Weavers on Draft in case they needed to leave quickly. It had essentials, supplies, first aid, rations, water. When he pulled it out, he turned to see Juliette standing at his door. She looked him up and down, and Vin could have sworn she shared a hint of her mother's look of worry. She simply strolled in and sat on his bed.

"I have bad news." She said casually.

"Uh…yeah I know about the hurricane." He said, confused.

"No not that, you'll be fine. You've done like two of these already, you're practically an expert. I'm talking about me."

Vin rolled his eyes. He should have assumed it was about her, it usually was. He adjusted the heavy bag on his shoulders, sighing.

"Right, well, I really should be going I'm-"

"I'm failing one of classes." She interrupted.

"What?"

"Its stupid Economics, like I want to know how money works. I mean, I thought college was supposed to be about doing what we wanted."

Vin started, looking around the room wondering if there were hidden cameras and he was a part of a joke he didn't understand.

"Can you believe that?" She continued. "I'm failing friggin community college." Upset, she flung herself back on his bed, ams behind her head.

He was thinking of going into the importance of economics and why finance was vital, but he got the feeling that wasn't her point. He started to piece together that his sister had come to him for comfort. Vin lowered his bag to the ground and sat in his desk chair.

"Well…that's fine. I mean you still have time to turn it around. It's just one class."

She returned his sigh and sat back up, facing him without meeting his eyes.

"Maybe, but then what?" She flashed a look to him, but he just shrugged.

"I don't know, Juliette. What do you want to do?"

"Million-dollar question right there, isn't it?" She didn't continue the thought after that but had something else she visibly struggled saying. Her eyes rested on his desk. Laying open for her to see was his acceptance letter to Florida State.

Finally she spoke, "I'm going to miss you when you go off to college."

Vin snorted a laugh. "Yeah right. You'd have the house all to yourself. You'll be happy I'd be gone." He spun in his chair, heat rising in his cheeks, preparing his defenses for a snooty come back.

"No Vin, I won't." she said seriously.

Vin had to rotate back around and make sure her face matched her voice. Unless she had had been taking acting lessons, Vin was sure that she was indeed being serious.

She got up and walked to his dresser, feeling the need to break his eye contact. She fingered through his trophies until she landed on a picture of himself and Matt, it was at one of his birthday parties and Magdalena was photobombing it in the back with a funny face.

"You know," she started, "I could never admit this because people would think I'm insane, or just plain insensitive, but I've always been jealous of Magdalena."

"I'm sorry, what the hell did you just say?" Vin asked, face dropped in shock.

She didn't turn to face him as she continued. "I don't think anyone saw it for what I did. When I first heard, I just thought, 'Damn. She did it. She got out of here.' I don't think I'd ever have the courage to get out. To be on my own, away from the safety net that is Rockwell, and-" she glanced at him over her shoulder, "family."

"Jules..." Vin started but couldn't think of what words to reassure her with. He'd never have guessed his strong, cool, popular sister was secretly jealous of Magdalena.

"I only tell you this little brother because you're probably going to run off and die in a hurricane," her normal cool sarcastic tone returned, and a slight smile formed on the corner of her mouth. She fully turned to look him in the eyes. "But if you ever had done what she did, I would have been devastated. So try not to leave me like that, okay?" She had clearly gotten the last words she wanted to say out and headed for the door.

After thinking about it for a brief second, Vin shot out his room and called to her down the hallway,

"Hey!" She turned, about to go into her room. "Maybe volunteer sometime at Grandpas home. You never know, a bunch of old people, hearing their stories about what they did with their lives might give you some direction on your own."

"Gross," she immediately said but Juliette hummed in thought before finally saying, "eh, sounds boring." Cracking a sincere smile anyway, "Thanks Vin. I'll see you when you get back."

Back downstairs he saw his mother staring out the kitchen window into the rain, holding a towel in her hand. She kept clutching and releasing it.

"Tell Dad, I love him, and I'll see him when I get back." His voice startled his mother who quickly pretended to be drying the dishes in front of her.

"He was sorry he missed you." She put down the towel and went over to him. Putting her hands on either side of his face, she rubbed them softly with her thumbs, "Be safe, my baby boy." Drawing him into a hug.

"Don't worry, it's not that bad. We caught it pretty early." He pulled away, "You don't need to worry." He tried to reassure her giving her a kiss on the cheek before heading for the door. His hand on the doorknob he heard his mother call his name, he turned back to look. Even his sister came downstairs, sitting on one of lower steps while holding their mother's hand, watching him leave.

"I'm your Mother, I'm never not going to worry."

He mustered as much confidence as he could and smiled. He could never admit that each time he walked out the door after being drafted, he was afraid it would be his last. Readjusting the weight on his back from his bag and he finally walked out.

Chapter 30

THE RAIN WAS coming down a little bit harder at the bus station. Members of the National Elemental Disaster Relief, NEDR for short, stood around the last two buses headed for Galveston.

"I'll get us checked in and get some seats." Amber said, then turned back to Matt. He had remained uncommonly quiet the entire time. She placed a hand on his arm, causing him to look away from the windows to meet her eyes. He looked like he wanted to remain stubbornly silent but finally broke and gave the best smile he could.

"Be safe Amber." He said. All three of them got out, Amber heading across the lot to get them checked in. Vin and Matt stood together under a lip in the roof to shield them from the rain. Vin handed Matt the keys.

"Just wait at my house if you need to, but please don't do anything. We'll look for her as soon as we get back."

"If it's not too late by then." He said under his breath.

"It won't be!" Vin tried to encourage. "Remember, back at camp we said we'd find her, bring her home-"

"Don't you get it!" Matt snapped, glaring. "That was just a fanciful dream. Even if we stop her, you think she's just going to come running home? My parents will just accept her back and we'll all be a big happy family again? That the terrorists will just let her leave? That's only IF some FBI, law enforcement agency isn't already on their trail. Oh, and of course there's the whole Anomaly thing, who are notorious for destruction and basically losing their minds. WAKE UP VIN!"

Vin stood silently, letting Matt get all his frustration out, but the look in Matt's eyes worried him more than anything. They almost seemed hopeless.

"You know why you became an Air Weaver?" he continued, "Because you're always up in clouds. Looking down at a pretty picture, but you don't understand. You don't know what it's like to live with your head and feet on the ground."

The rainfall was all that could be heard as they stood together, no more words to say. Vin looked up and saw Amber urgently waving at him, they were about to leave. Vin wrapped his arms around Matt, holding him tightly, trying to push every hopeful thought and happy memory onto him. He could almost feel his inner energy wrap around his, and just the slightest sensation of something rejecting him.

"Please Matty. Don't do anything until we get back." He whispered before finally hoisting up his bag and heading through the rain onto the bus.

Matt sat in Vin's Durango, the hum of the engine and pelt of the rain being swept away by the wipers as his only companion. He watched the buses through the wet streaked windows and with Vin now gone he felt the most alone he'd been in a while. Which he considered to be poetic considering he spent a majority of the last four years pushing him away. Vin's admission of feeling left out while Matt joined sport teams, and made friends, hit him strangely now. He couldn't rely on any of them even a fragment of how much he relied on Vin. And now Amber.

He was absently flipping his phone in his hands until he finally looked at it. Turning it on he went to his voicemails and for what felt like the hundredth time that day he pressed play. The voice of his sister, tired and worried crackled out of the speaker.

"Matty, it's me, Magdalena…I wanted to call you to tell you how sorry I am, for any pain my leaving may have cost you. I wish I could go through and explain why I did it, it's just everything after the fi-" she broke off for a moment before returning, "It doesn't matter. Just know I've done some bad things. Things you could probably never forgive me for, nor would I deserve it if you did. Whatever happens, know I love you…" there was moment at the end, a long pause where Matt wondered what she was going to say but she ended with a single, mournful, "Bye, little brother."

Matt put the car in gear and began his drive back to Rockwell. He kept repeating the message over and over. As he reached the city limits, he began to really think about something in the message. *Everything after the fi-* He had a pretty good idea what she was going to say. On a whim he turned and started heading to the Rockwell Memorial Auditorium.

Chapter 31

A MBER LAY BACK IN her seat with ear buds in, eyes closed. Vin had his own headphones on and leaned his head against the cool glass, watching the landscape wash away in the pouring rain. He looked up and made a quick scan of the bus, it wasn't particularly filled. He figured most people were already there, the first responders had to have been there most likely a couple of days earlier.

Water Weavers would have been the most important, to stop majority of flooding. Either diverting it or pushing it back. A team of them and Fire Weavers would have set up in heavily flooded areas, preparing the whirlpools. These pools had the Water Weavers creating great currents of rotating water that the Fire Weavers would then burn off. It was usually a last resort as this threw off weather patterns and caused a huge excess of rainfall afterwards. Later was the idea though, to take care of the immediate threat first.

Earth Weavers would have created ocean trenches and back up canals for excess water to flow. The hardest part was going to come soon after Vin and Amber would arrive.

Vin noticed Amber had opened her eyes and was watching him,

He smiled and mouthed *Hey.* She took out her headphones and smiled back.

"Hey. You doing ok?" she asked.

"Yeah. For what we're about to do, yeah. Just mentally preparing. What comes after…not so much."

She placed a comforting hand on his arm. "One step at a time."

He put his hand on top of hers, "I'm really glad you're here. These aren't exactly the most fun times and I'm glad to have company."

She nodded, bit her lip in thought, then changed the subject, "Really cool about Florida, eh?"

Vin managed a chuckle, relieving some built up tension and thankful for the change, "Honestly yeah. It'll be so cool to get out and go somewhere new."

"What're you most looking forward to?"

Vin looked away in embarrassment, "I mean, there's so much to do in college, but If I'm being honest…" He laughed trying to alleviate his apprehension, "Well, its gonna sound a little weird, even a little holier-than-thou, but I'm hoping to find more mature or lost people. After this year meeting you and training Matt, it would be kind of cool to find Weavers who are more like-minded in our view of our abilities."

Amber's smile turned from an encouraging one to sincere delight. "I think that actually sounds pretty cool. You'll find people of all types, and most of us will definitely be lost."

"Us?" Vin asked.

It was Ambers turn to look bashful. "Yeah, I mean, some of us don't know what we really are going to do, or even go."

"Ha, you mean a Water Weaver doesn't just go with the flow?" Amber gave him a glare at this and then a playful shove.

"But seriously," Vin continued, "You don't know where you're going to go?"

"Not really too sure. I don't know what else I'd like to do besides travel aimlessly."

"Well…have you given any thought to Florida?" Vin asked.

"Like…going with you?"

The implication would have embarrassed him just a week ago, but their night in the woods finally confirmed that she felt the same way about him that he did for her. "Well, sure. I mean, for your own reasons. I would definitely like the idea of you being around. I can't be the only one to argue with Matt, it'll get old."

Amber let out an unfiltered laugh and it lit up Vin's face.

"I think it's already gotten old." She replied, "I have, though. Florida has, for obvious reasons, a big pull with Water Weavers. In particular, there's an association that's working with the Everglades that would be interesting."

"Yeah, that sounds really great! You should do it."

"I should? I mean, we should? Go to Florida?"

They looked at each for a moment, letting the connotation sink in before Vin flashed his teeth in a genuine smile, full of hope.

"Yeah, we should." Amber settled in against him and his words of the future. Vin laid into her and with a gentle hand he put her headphones back in, then put in his own. Together they lay, basking in what calm they had as they drove deeper into the storm.

Amber stepped off the bus, and almost immediately her breath caught in her throat. She stumbled herself out of the way of the bus, Vin running over to her.

"Ambrosia? Are you ok?" He had a hand on her back, and she put one up to his chest as he steadied her.

"Yeah, I'm fine, I just…didn't expect this." The energy in the area was so palpable. On the drive she wondered if it would feel different, feared it would feel wrong. All these Weavers, trying to control the elements, she imagined a discomfort. Instead she was in awe, the combination of all the Weavers, working together with nature to guide it. She thought back to when her dad would play recordings of whales, something that seemed so majestic and mystical, but it was here in their world. The best word to describe what she felt was connectivity. A connection between the elements and humans.

"It's actually kind of beautiful," she finally said.

Vin smiled. He didn't need to ask what. "I thought so too, once I got over the initial shock and nerves. It's actually always made me think, how different are Weavers and Non-Weavers. You hear stories about how people get that feeling when something bad could be coming, like a storm or something. It's not so different from our own senses." He guided her along, "Come on, we better go check in and get our stations."

As they walked Amber marveled at the feeling, she assumed it should be raining hardest here but on the contrary, with all the human energy in the air, it caused the rain to fall slowly and more like a mist. It was as if time had slowed and the rain fell gently. Amber raised a finger and scooped a droplet out of the air.

Vin went to the main staging area where the organization was giving out their stations.

"Perfect, another Air Weaver," A woman in a NEDR uniform said, after Vin gave his name, scrolling through along her tablet.

"We're just about to start the Rotation." She looked over at Amber. "You two together?"

Vin nodded, "Yeah, she volunteered. Ambrosia Aldrich, it's her first time." The lady made a humming noise as she searched her tablet again.

"Water Weaver, I'll put you two near each other on the beach. Vincenzo?" She tried to pronounce, missing the CH- sound.

"I see you've been in at least two so far, but I'll give you a refresher anyway since I got to explain it to Miss Aldrich here."

She flipped round her tablet so they could see a radar of the storm. "Air Weavers are currently above the storm approaching the eye. Your jobs along the perimeter of the storm are to Weave the winds in the opposite direction, countering the storm." She spoke as she whirled her stylus in the direction to exemplify. "A secondary group is keeping the storm centralized in the water right now before it breaks land."

"That's amazing." Amber whispered in awe. The worker actually smiled at this, amused.

"Indeed." She agreed, then continued, "Water Weavers are helping with the rotation. At least pushing the water back out to sea." She clicked her tablet closed and held it to her chest as she finished,

"Once the storm is disrupted enough the Air Weavers above the storm drop into the eye and break it apart. This will create multiple smaller storms but nothing so severe as the hurricane. Once that's been done, you two, along with any Volunteers or Drafted members are free to go. Of course, Volunteers are more than welcome to stay and help with flooding and possible aftershocks."

She looked between the two, "Got it?" Vin and Amber both nodded. "Good." She stepped away from the staging area to look to the coast.

"Head down that way and report to someone looking like me, the tablets usually a dead giveaway. They'll point you to your spot."

"Thank you." Vin said as they left her heading for the shore. In the distance they could make out the gathering darker clouds in the distance.

"Is it dangerous you think?" Amber asked.

"Not this one, they caught it really early on. We're especially good here on the shore. Since we need a pretty good hold on most of its circumference, just be glad we aren't out on the water. There are ships that have Weavers out there doing the same thing we are.

They found one of the tablet-wielders and had their spot pointed out. Amber was positioned on the actual sand of the shore while Vin was about half a mile behind higher up on some staging ground that the Earth Weavers had created.

Vin gave Ambers hand a squeeze, "Have fun, good luck."

"Pft, easy for you to say, you're not going to get perpetually pelted with sand."

Vin laughed as they parted and took positions. He jumped up to his stone perch, he barely had to gather the elemental energy as it flowed heavy and rich in the area. There was about a mile and a half gap between him and the nearest Air Weaver. In front of him, along the beach, the Water Weavers were more plentiful and spaced about a mile apart. An announcement erupted across the area; emergency speakers sparked to life.

"Commencement of the Rotation will begin in five minutes." Vin stood, the air whipping around him as he stared out into the tumultuous breaking waves, dark clouds shifting in the sky. It was quite peaceful; a calm lay about the land, disregarding the approaching storm.

Vin raised his arms as the countdown began at thirty seconds. He started leaking his energy into the air, painting it into the wind.

The countdown hit zero and he began Weaving the air left, against the initial spin, which was going right.

He began to feel a buildup of pressure as the rest of the Weavers began pushing against the wind as well. It at first hit resistance, but the more they pushed the more naturally their energy began to bleed together until it wasn't just him pushing, but all the Weavers together. Vin liked the buildup, he felt almost empowered by their coordination.

It got to the point where Vin recognized he didn't have to think about the push. It naturally occurred now. It gave him moments to be able to appreciate it. He could practically feel the rotation of the storm. He closed his eyes and breathed in the insatiable currents, able to sense both the elemental energy and the human.

Something tickled him different, his face distorting at the feeling. He cocked his head as he felt the touch of something familiar. He redoubled his focus to pull on this feeling, locking on an energy that seemed to stand out from the rest. He followed it until he found the source, opening his eyes he saw a familiar figure. Wild brown curls whipping around, riding the wind.

Vin felt dumb for not noticing it sooner. He could sense her energy specifically amongst all the others. All the time they spent combining their own energies made an impression, and her energy had a unique signature.

He began looking around, the other Weavers now having an interesting outlook to him. Like fingerprints, human energy was unique to each person. Vin became fascinated by the idea. He was further intrigued and tried testing something of his own.

Reaching out, he found Amber's energy more easily this time. Attempting to do what he normally did to perform his Weaving abilities, he tried to combine his energy with hers. It wasn't as natural as with the elements. Nevertheless, he increased his focus, prodding at her power. Watching her and waiting until something finally seemed to click. It appeared she sensed it, like when you get the feeling someone is watching you.

He could see her head move, like she was looking out of her periphery.

She turned to the left and then the right, clearly searching. Vin could then see her close her eyes in concentration and Vin's breathe caught in his throat. She reciprocated, melding her energy into his. Her eyes snapped open and immediately whipped around to find Vin's.

They had Weaved, not the elements but each other.

Interlude

5 Months Ago / Seattle

T HE CHEERS ROARED in Alexei's ears as he returned to the bunker. Most of the groups having returned from their battle for Seattle. Recognizing a few faces were missing, they would need to relocate soon. Trucks were already being loaded; plans had been made to begin travelling south.

Fellow group members patted him on the back, tried shoving victory shots in his face that he politely, but sternly pushed away. He felt invigorated, alive and full of power at his accomplishment. Seattle was now in chaos. He kept looking for the one face in the crowd he had yet to see.

Magdalena should have returned by now, Alexei thought. She wasn't part of any of the offense forces, but she had been sent to disrupt communications.

"Alexei!" A voice called to him. He saw Tanya at the end of the hall. She looked frantic and was ushering him toward her. He jogged to her and without waiting Tanya started down the hallway, he followed.

"Tanya? What's going on?"

"It's Magdalena!" she said hurriedly. "She got hurt in the chaos."

Alexei's heart thrummed fast and he picked up the pace running down the hallway, passing her and throwing open the door to the medical room and stepping inside. It was empty. His mind started to catch up from when the adrenaline had taken over. It was odd he thought, if someone was really injured, especially Magdalena, why was everyone just in the main room celebrating.

"Tanya?" he said confused, turning to face her. Pain ripped across his chest. He yelled and tumbled back onto the floor crashing into a gurney. He looked down at his chest, searing claw marks etched onto his body like a brand, his skin still sizzling.

He looked up at Tanya, whose hands and fingertips were alight, like molten gloves.

"Come out and play, *boy.*" Was the last thing he heard as her two hands, like miniature suns, closed around his face.

Magdalena didn't even shut the door as she jumped out of the car and ran for their facility. She gave another quick glance to the text she received from Tanya.

GET HERE NOW! WE NEED YOU!

She had sensed it as soon as she pulled up. The whole area felt like it was quaking, but not like Angyo's Earth Weaving, it felt like Alexei. She threw the door open and sprinted down the stairs. The whole facility was shaking. She burst through the doors at the bottom that opened to a foyer of the bunker and immediately slipped on something wet and fell. Her head smacked against the floor and she groaned, trying to sit back up. She felt at her head where it hit the floor and when she pulled it back, she saw red.

Her eyes widened in horror as she realized it wasn't hers, but that she had run in and slipped on blood. The rest of her senses played catch up as she recognized yells and screaming from further within, bodies had collected in the entrance way.

"No…" She said to herself in disbelief. Launching herself up she carried on further down the halls, going until she found the source of the yelling. Throwing herself through the doors to the gymnasium, her fear manifested in front of her.

Alexei stood in the middle, his arms flailing and moving in no way she'd ever seen him Weave. Members of the organization were trying everything they could to defend themselves as metal from the floor, pieces of equipment and bars that moved as fluid as snakes attacked them. She saw more members injured or dead, pierced by his metal or bludgeoned from something heavy.

Magdalena met Tanya's eyes from across the room, and Tanya saw her in return.

"Maggie!" She yelled. Everyone in the room turned to look at her, even Alexei, though what she saw she didn't recognize.

He looked frantic, his body twitching like he was expecting blows at any moment.

"Alexei…" Magdalena whispered.

Their eyes met and she saw, for the first time, something she hoped to never have encountered in his gaze, fear. He continued to throw his arm in mad chaos knocking the Weavers aside and battering them back to their last defenses.

"MAL'CHIK!" She called to him. Recognition caused him to pause as he turned back to Magdalena. The hesitation was all she needed. She could calm him down, let him know he was safe.

A blast of fire plowed into him from behind, and Mal'chik roared. The whole room came alive as metal sprayed from walls and ceilings, weights flew and bent around the Weavers, collectively screaming and struggling to break free. Magdalena tried to go to Mal'chik but the door frame broken off, the door shattering and throwing her forward. The metal bent around her wrists and kept her there.

She could only stare in horror as the Weavers were slowly being squeezed to death. She found Tanya who matched her gaze.

"Please Maggie! End this!" she pleaded. Magdalena heard a snapping noise come from one of the men on the ground as he screamed, the metal constricting and breaking his body.

She looked back to Mal'chik, she cried out, calling for him, hoping to break through, but she could see fear overpowered his other senses. They stared at each other again, gruesome burnt skin around his terrified eyes. She didn't recognize him anymore as Alexei, those eyes reminded her of the ones she used to stare at in the mirror every morning.

"Please." She choked out, barely above a whisper. She found the faces of Tanya and the rest of the Weavers. They weren't going to make it, they couldn't stop him.

"Maggie!" Tanya called once more. "Do it!"

A scream ripped out of Magdalena, the likes of which she had never felt possible. Power surged along her veins, rippling out around her. Lightning flew from her, attempting to pierce Mal'chik's defenses. She couldn't break through. She didn't have time for discretion. She watched him struggle with the attack. She could see it in his face, he would soon grow desperate to save himself. She had seconds to end this, or everyone would die. With a last push she unloaded everything she had, power tore through his defenses and struck him. Letting out a blood curdling yell, he fell, smote in the middle of his former comrades.

The Weaving stopped immediately; Magdalena fell to her knees with metal still wrapped around her arms.

Tanya's feet landed softly on the floor as she fell from the metal she was trapped in, having melted through its grip. She ran to Magdalena and slid down to embrace her.

"You did it, you saved us." She told her before she began working on cutting off one of her cuffs. She didn't comment on Magdalena's silence, or her dead-eyed look.

"That was amazing." She continued, "I've never seen you so powerful." A loud clang rang out as her cuff fell from her right wrist. Tanya moved to start on the left one, but Magdalena held out a hand to stop her.

"Wait…don't worry about me. Go help the others, I'm not injured." Tanya hesitated but Magdalena then looked up, giving Tanya a glare she had never received before.

"I said I'm fine." Tanya nodded and got up to go release the others.

Magdalena looked up at her arm, a protective hand reaching around the metal wrapping around her wrist. Regret pummeled her insides. She should have gone with him, she thought. She should have kept him safe. Silent tears rolled down her cheeks as she was forced to say goodbye to a friend, then an old one she hadn't faced in months wriggled its way back into her mind.

Chapter 32

MATT ALMOST DROVE off the road when he saw it. He had reached Rockwell's Memorial Auditorium and was about to pull into the parking lot when he saw a figure, hooded, standing at the cross. The memorial for the janitor who died in the fire almost four years ago.

His heart started pounding harder in his chest, he was almost too scared to hope. Pulling over, he drew his hood over his head and jumped out of the car. Approaching the figure, he cautiously called out over the rumbling thunder, "Mags?" no response. He walked closer and noticed no lightning in the sky.

"Magdalena?" He called again. The figure didn't turn but he walked up and looked into her face. His sister kept staring at the cross. A photo of the man with his daughter now speckled with rain.

"Hello, Matt," she finally replied. Her dark eyes not leaving the photo, they looked haunted, and Matt was afraid to admit she looked even more unraveled. He hadn't thought about what losing Tanya might have done to her. *Had she been there with her since the beginning?* He thought.

Matt knew Tanya was crazy and hoped Magdalena didn't regret saving him, but now realized how alone she must feel. His stomach felt tight as all too late he realized that losing Tanya would have been like losing Vin after he helped him through his sister running away.

"What happened that night, Maggie? The night you left."

She bit her lip, trying to keep the words from falling out.

Matt knew; he knew for a long time. Ever since his father brought home the phone, a piece of evidence. The only evidence that went missing from the fire. The evidence that haunted his father every day until he couldn't take the guilt.

"It was an accident, Mags. I'm sure it was," he offered.

She let out a dead laugh and raised her face open to the sky. What were tears and what was rain Matt couldn't discern, assuming she did it on purpose.

"It doesn't matter," she said coldly, shaking her head. "I left a daughter fatherless." Matt tried to reach out to her, he wrapped her in the briefest hug before she pulled away.

"Please don't go. Don't do this, Maggie."

"This world doesn't want me, but someone does. They understand my power, they want others to understand my power."

"I want you! I understand you, Magdalena, please!" Matt begged.

"You can't truly understand, and I honestly don't want you to. I'm an Anomaly. There's something wrong with me." Her words struck Matt harder than any blow he's received so far in his life. "I'm broken, and you can't save me Matt," she then turned to him, looking him dead in the eyes, "and I don't want you to." She said with finality.

Matt did nothing as she turned and walked away, getting in her car and leaving. He somberly went back to his own, sitting there, soaked, and lay his head against the rest behind him. He eventually looked down, at a phone that didn't belong to him. Swiped from his sister's pocket during their brief embrace.

He opened it and there was one outgoing call, to his number, and a single received text. A location and a time.

Hope returned to Matt, determination rekindled so fierce a Fire Weaver could pull flames from it. He started the car and peeled out, heading back to Houston.

Chapter 33

THE DISRUPTION OF the eye took just little over an hour. For those leaving, a crowd began forming back toward the busses. Amber quickly found Vin in the mess, following their link. Reaching him she quickly jumped him in a massive embrace. She was laughing, taking Vin aback.

"What was that for?" he asked.

Amber pulled away, shrugging. "I don't know, that was all just kind of amazing. All of us working together...and what we did." She said the last part hesitantly. Vin agreed, giving her an encouraging smile.

They got to the busses and noticed people in line bunched up around the outside.

"What's going on?" Vin asked the people closest to him. One of the Weavers, tall, in his mid-thirties with dark hair, turned. Vin already didn't like the fear in his eyes.

"The Houston bus isn't leaving. There are reports of an attack. Like there was in Dallas. They're saying it's terrorists."

Vin's heart dropped as he looked to Amber who shared in his shock, eyes wide. Vin immediately whipped out his phone and pushed himself out of the crowd. Amber was hot on his heels.

He dialed Matt's number and put it up to his ear. He frantically rushed farther from the crowds heading down streets and shops.

The phone rang and rang until it went to voicemail. He finally shoved it back in his pocket, swearing.

"Vin," Amber called to him, worry in her voice. "What're we going to do, do you think Matt actually went to Houston?"

Vin shook his head, hands on his hip, he thought his head would explode. "I don't know, but I wouldn't doubt it. We have to get there, now."

Amber looked resolved, growing confident, "Not 'we'. You can get there faster, right?" Vin seemed hesitant but looked to the sky. He really could, he thought, there was enough wind from the storm he could easily fly to Houston.

"I could, but then…leaving you here."

She shook her head, shaking away his worry. "Don't worry about me. I'll be right behind you."

She said then looked around until she saw a motorcycle, jogging up to it she made a secret prayer that whoever she was about to steal from would forgive her.

"Help me with this." She said as she pulled water from the air and fit it into the keyhole. Vin went to her and together they cooled the water until it froze solid. She turned the key to make sure it worked, and the engine roared to life.

"I'll be right behind you, go!" Vin started pulling away their fingers latched together until the last second. He backed away from her, their eyes locked, rain continuing to pelt down.

"Good luck." She whispered to him. He nodded as she turned away about to get on the motorcycle but felt a warm hand on her arm, spin and hug her. She got a quick glimpse of his leafy eyes, droplets hanging onto his long lashes before his lips cascaded into hers. Like waves breaking upon the shores they crashed into each other in a warm embrace.

She had been waiting for this, silently hoping for the moment their lips touched, and it was everything in that moment she could have hoped for. It wasn't until they finally pulled away did the rain resume, crashing down on top of them. Amber didn't even realize she was holding it back, it felt like the rain too had lost its breath. Red in the face and breathing hard they both looked at each other. A final piece of themselves seemed to have fallen into place, and they felt whole.

"OK…I'm going to go now." He said backing away getting ready to bolt into the sky, but Amber reached out one last time, grasping his arm.

"Vincent," she called his name, so many feelings in her ready to burst. "When my father died…he was the bravest man I've ever known. No one compared. I've never met anyone as brave as him, not until you." Her eyes quivered as she spoke.

Vin couldn't find his voice, as the impact of her words fell on him. His first instinct was to shake it off, to reject this honor that Amber bestowed upon him. Instead he nodded, he thought of who he had become over the past three years. The responsibility expected of him, and for the first time he wanted to be this man that Amber saw in him, that Matt thought he could be.

He gave her hand one last squeeze, crouched down, and launched himself into the air. Weaving the winds around him as he rocketed off toward the city.

Chapter 34

AMBER WATCHED him go, her nerves finally settled. She allowed herself to open up to someone, she couldn't be afraid of losing them, not if it got in the way of living to the fullest. She marched back to the bike ready to follow him, but a chill ran down her spine. That sensation of someone watching her, but instead of coming from the warm place Vin's had, this was in the air, in the elements around her. Someone else was Weaving their power into the water around her.

She spun and there in the middle of the road stood a man, tall and bald in strange foreign robes.

He was unmistakably looking straight at her. She couldn't tell why, but she sensed menace in his attention.

If it wasn't for the lack of it, she would have sworn the water around her turned to ice as the next two words out of his mouth froze her in place,

"Ambrosia Aldrich."

His cool tone made her shiver. "How do you know me?"

"I've been keeping an eye on you. Originally Vincent intrigued me." The voice was cool and calm, but it held no warmth or comfort to Amber.

"After the Dallas incident, I became interested in his abilities. I suppose you could call me a recruiter."

"I doubt he'd be interested in joining," Amber shot back.

"Possibly, but like I said, he was what originally intrigued me. I'm here, now, for you." She hated how still he stood; his body may not be moving but power was flooding from him into the water.

"Your power and skill in Dallas, then at the lake," he continued. Amber tried hard not to show her shock at the idea of him following them.

'You're a terrorist." She said evenly.

"Possibly, but I'm not here to promote the fight and uphold the rights of the Weavers. I'm here to end them."

Her expression broke, confused. "What? Why?"

"I figured of all people to explain it to, you'd be the last. Weavers," he said, finally raising a hand and with it a large orb of water formed. He stared at it passively as he spoke,

"Are a blight against nature. They abuse and destroy," Amber wanted to ask why her of all people, but she had a shaking suspicion and she didn't need to ask as he revealed more of her past than she would ever have wanted a stranger to know:

"They destroy, just like that forest. The day your father died trying to save the same people that waste their beautiful gift."

The top of the orb began pouring off, as if sliced by a knife, letting it decend like a waterfall. Layers of it slowly flowed away, his elemental control, under other circumstances would have amazed Amber, but instead it worried her.

"I see the hesitation in your eyes, and I understand you're young." He softened his tone and looked sympathetically at her.

"But you need to think of your future. Of our Earth's future. You know nature, Weavers are like a poisonous thorn, are you going to sit there and let it fester? Isn't it better to burn away the rot, so that new life can grow anew?"

"I-" Amber started, so many thoughts raced through her head. Almost all her life these same words echoed from her mother, these same fears, same dark thoughts.

She thought of the forest she would run through, and her father there in it, his kind smile and big heart, Amber gritted her teeth.

"You use my father's sacrifice against me? You want me to turn against him? I can't, and I won't!"

The final bit of water finally fell from his hand, he closed his eyes pained. Amber looked down; water was draining away from her feet. Then he opened them, any softness gone, "Pity."

A wave exploded from him, huge and tidal falling on Amber. She raised a hand quickly Weaving out a barrier. The water crashed into it, forming a bubble around her. Noise became deafened, like she had cotton in her ears.

She split it down the middle and spun, dragging the water with her in her rotation. She pulled the left half into a powerful stream shooting back at him and then followed up with the second half.

Her opponent copied the move, rotating faster and sending the water around him, pulling even more of it into his stream as he sent it back at her.

Amber was off balance, distracted, conflicted. Her concentration held, however, as she pushed on the first streamed, splitting it past her but the second broke her hold, collapsing into her and sending her skidding down the street.

She groaned and rolled to her side. Her enemy approached her down the street, he now held two orbs in his hands casually letting them cascade down around him.

"I was hoping you'd join me, but I can't let you or that boy get in the way," Amber's eyes widened at the realization. She was his target now, but not his only target. He was the one that must have recruited Magdalena, and was now looking for Vin. She thought of these people that began to mean so much to her, and she thought of her father, as they fought with as much courage as they could.

The moments in nature she spent with Vin and Matt, and so far back as to her time with her dad. She recalled the earliest moments when they sat by streams and felt the power of the water, when she first began to really understand the connection they felt to the elements.

She slammed her hands down into the water, anger flooding her, and rose to her knees. Water had always been her calm, the gentle flow that eased her frustrations in life. It could be so much more, a tempest and an undertow that drowned those in its wake.

"I don't know why Earth chose us." She muttered, face still toward the ground, her hair hanging like a curtain. The bald man cocked his head at her trying to hear her whispers,

"I don't know why it chose to give us this gift, but it did. Nothing you do will stop that."

Her hair pulled back from her face, Amber manipulating the water to twist the hair behind her ears. Her eyes snapped open to glare at her opponent,

"But I will stop you!" She clenched her fist under the water, the orbs next to the man exploded, she barely caught his surprised face before he was slammed by her attack. He began coughing and sputtering as the water clogged his nose and mouth.

Amber launched herself up, using the water to carry her farther and faster. Driving a knee into the man, he bent over coughing up the rest of the fluid in his lungs. She rounded on him, using her momentum to sweep him off his feet, causing him to crash heavily onto the flooded street. Amber drew her arms up, creating a large column of water up and over her head.

The bald man's eyes went wide when he finally opened them and raised a hand as Amber let it crash down on top of him. He deflected the brunt of the impact, using the rest to wash him away from her. He stood, completely soaked and breathing heavily.

Amber, no longer hesitant, her concentration absolute, glared daggers at him. Her stance became solid and ready, rain pouring around them.

He launched wave after wave at her, which she rode letting the attacks pass around her rather than stop it head on. His control, which at first overpowered hers, she now rivaled. Amber had created a revolving wall of water around them, that steadily grew higher and drew them closer.

Every time he tried to reach out to disrupt the walls the pressure knocked his hand away and he was forced to use his concentration to block Amber's attacks.

Panic grew in his eyes as he saw the passion in hers as they drew closer, her confidence flooding her with power. They were perhaps feet apart, and Amber focused her energy, ready to attack.

A force erupted from her opponent. He bellowed and blasted Amber back along with all the water in the area. He jumped away, riding an arc of water he created. She followed his movement, confused. It felt like he used more than just Water Weaving to disrupt her attack.

He looked back at her, and to Amber's horror, he gave her a smug satisfied smile before launching himself away from her. She recovered, shaking her head and running to the motorcycle which had tumbled down the street during their fight. Amber hauled it up, turned the ice key, and the engine revved to life. She pulled out a wave of energy, Weaving the water around her, propelling it so the tires stood on dry land.

She pointed it toward Houston and cranked the throttle, flying down the road. A constant flow of her power Weaved the water in front her, it rolled around her like a speed boat slicing a path on the open ocean.

She didn't need to worry about slippery roads as she gave the bike everything she had. Resolve on her face, her hair whipping around her as she rushed toward Houston. A hurricane was coming after all.

Chapter 35

MATT DIVED INTO an alleyway to dodge incoming debris as concrete and light posts were ripped from the ground. Fissures tore along the earth. It was chaos in the streets of Houston; police and emergency responders were in a frenzy. He turned away from the street he dived from as it seemed a lost cause and ran through the alley. Someone turned the opposite end and the person immediately raised their hands in surrender.

"Whoa whoa, man. Please done hurt me." Matt examined the pleading man but had recently learned to not rely solely on his eyes. The senses granted to him as a Weaver spoke clearer, and Matt could feel the man building energy preparing to Weave.

Instinctually Matt dived low before the man could launch two fireballs from his hands. Matt Weaved the ground beneath him to propel him along, extending his slide. The man barely had time to widen his eyes in surprise before Matt, gathering stone around his fist, slammed his enhanced punch into his face. Matt stared down at the unconscious man then rifled through his pockets.

Swearing under his breath Matt confirmed they didn't have anything. He supposed it was a safety precaution in case any of them were captured.

Matt rose from crouching over the body.

"Guess all that training with Vin was worth it after all," Matt said casually before throwing himself back into the fray. He found it quite amazing the lessons Vin and Amber had instilled in him. He couldn't go back to how he used to fight even if he tried.

He sensed the searing fire before the flames even hit him. Nimbly rode broken waves of fracturing concrete before they split apart below him. He used to just fight like any two physical opponents would; make your move then counter theirs, using your eyes and ears. Like two boxers or fencers. Their weapons were nothing compared to the power the elements bestowed upon them.

Screams caught his attention. He found their source, a corner coffee shop. Two terrorists were outside Weaving streams of water at the windows. They laughed gleefully, even Matt could tell they were just playing with the frightened workers and patrons inside. They gradually increased the pressure so that cracks began webbing across its surface.

In an action he was sure Vin would have approved, Matt bolted for them, looking for the source of water. He located the broken fire hydrant. The two Water Weavers, still distracted by their mayhem, didn't see Matt approach. He stomped one foot down, Weaving his energy into and through the ground toward the hydrant, making a twisting motion with the same foot to fold the earth closed in around the pipe below, cutting off the flow of water.

The two Water Weavers looked back, dumbfounded, then noticed

Matt charging at them, while chunks of concrete flew at them. The closest Weaver went down on one knee as a piece of rock cracked against their leg, letting out a scream. The second snapped back and fell, sprawled on the ground as it smashed against his shoulder, he lay face down in the flooded street.

The woman, whom was upright breathing air instead of water, began Weaving an orb into her hand. Her concentration was weak, though, and as she winced at the pain, the gathering of water was slowed. Matt took his next step hard, right foot forward, Weaving energy into the ground that lifted a large but flat chunk of concrete into the air. Keeping his running momentum, he somersaulted forward, landing on his hands and launched himself forward into the surface he created and rode it forward.

The orb of water that was launched splattered against the approaching stone and she watched helplessly as Matt crashed into her. Making the stone brittle, he landed on top of her, correcting his position. It knocked her out and crumbled around her instead of crushing her.

He continued his launch forward, immediately jumping up and off the downed female Weaver, flying in an arc over the second. He reached down Weaving the rock below, cracking and dropping it about two feet, concrete teeth closing over the man to lock him in place.

His flow of energy dissipated as he flailed and struggling, to no avail, against the bindings. Matt smugly walked away from them. He felt good, alive and strong, after months feeling weak and unable to do anything. He unabashedly relished in his skill and competence. That confidence evaporated immediately when he heard the man speak, not to him, but to an earpiece he hadn't assumed any of them carried.

"He's here on my position, Polk Street! The Earth Weaver from Rockwell base!" the man stuck in the stones yelled, still struggling to break free.

Matt swore and took off down the street. It was then that Matt's plan began to fall apart when it fully dawned on him that he had no plan at all. He didn't know where to run to, he didn't know where their base of operations was. He had just planned to run around the city looking for Magdalena, assuming she'd be easy to find. The location from the text had apparently just been where they were supposed to have met up, not the location of their hit, and so far, no lightning. He did not, however, plan to be actively hunted, he assumed he could make his way around the city and blend into the chaos.

How fast can they really find me? Matt asked himself.

He was immediately given an answer as a familiar white van skidded around the corner, headlights flaring onto him. Matt cut quickly toward the alley of two tall buildings, risking a peek over his shoulder.

Realizing the van would easily run him down, he made a leap forward Weaving energy into his legs and the earth below. Upon landing he launched himself up, the earth jutting out with him increasing his height. He flew up, luckily the buildings were made of stone, and began Weaving the structure, making it brittle enough for Matt to slam his hands and feet into the wall. He hung there in his impromptu climbing holds, he risked a glance downwards. Below the van slammed on its breaks, goons jumping out.

Matt turned back to the task at hand as he deftly began scaling the side of the building. He was out of range within moments, he noted, as fire and water attacks flew wild and hit feet below him.

Unfortunately for him, he sensed an Air Weaver take to the skies. He focused hard on the pulsing air rising toward him, feigning ignorance of the Weavers ascension.

Stupidly, Matt thought, the Weaver wanted to get in melee range of him and Matt let him. As soon as he was behind Matt, he manipulated the stones, launching himself backward. Spinning, Matt lashed out grappling the Air Weaver, feeling all too cat-like in his movements. Matt was able to wrap himself around the now struggling Air Weaver, hanging on his back as the Weaver drooped and flailed trying to keep right.

"Get off me you son of a-" the man began to yell. Matt waited until his back was once again toward the wall then launched himself off. With a swift kick and push with both of his legs he sent the Weaver mid-sentence flying forward as he got back to the wall, gripping the stones as he did before.

The Air Weaver didn't have the control to stop himself from smacking straight into the building across the street, his air dying around him as he slid from it and crashed into a parked car on the street below.

Matt winced, thinking it looked far less painful in cartoons. He was too used to Vin's competence and forgot how hard it really was to ride the winds. He quickly resumed his climb ignoring the shouts from below. A tremor began crawling its way up the wall, an Earth Weaver attempting to shake him off. Matt gave himself two big jumps before he grabbed the lip of the roof and hauled himself up, seconds before the wall crumbled behind him, exposing the bones of the building.

He allowed himself a brief reprieve, trying to catch his breath before climbing back to his feet and jogging toward the other side of the roof. He let out a yelp and slammed to a halt as someone appeared in front of him, flying up from the side of the building, holding a larger man in her arms and releasing him as they both dropped to the roof in front of Matt. The large man was bald with an eye-patch and a dark brown mustache with a bald spot, revealing a scar. The girl was lithe but muscled, hair cut short, with an asymmetrical design, the front falling longer than the back. Her skin and features suggested Asian descent.

Matt started stepping back slowly, the larger man matching pace walking forward. His accomplice in the back playfully Weaving the wind around her hand.

"So, you're the one giving us so much trouble?" She said coolly, with striking confidence. She flicked her wrist sending a tight compact blast toward him. Matt grabbed the closest piece of earth he could, stone chimney-like fixtures littered the roof. He pulled them near to shield his path, the air blast shattering it flinging dust and debris in every direction. Matt shielded his eyes, when he lowered his arm again, he saw the larger man dive through after the attack.

Matt couldn't react fast enough as the man wrapped his hand around Matt's neck and lifted him into the air. Matt's hands flew upwards trying to claw the bigger hands away, he could see now the man in front of him was littered with scars. He was unable to comprehend the strength the man had; he was easily two feet taller than him and, while Matt was bulky himself, was easily dwarfed by this giant.

"Brutus," his companion called, "You know I like to play with my food." The large man, named Brutus, let out a dry chuckle before tossing Matt down, sliding across the roof like a sack of potatoes.

"You're almost as bad as Tanya, Selene." Brutus replied to her.

She scoffed, "Don't compare me to that psycho, I just like to have fun, I'm not crazy." She gracefully stalked toward Matt who was still massaging his throat as he climbed to his feet.

"It's rare we get to test our gifts. It's a pity, like a lion trapped in a zoo." She continued.

Matt looked her up and down; she went from gazelle to mountain lion in seconds. Selene sprung at him shooting gusts of air from her feet as she dove at him with a flying kick. Matt side-stepped her, punching chips at Selene. She pushed them away and continued the prowl, quickly closing the distance on Matt. He fell back to his martial skills. She was already within his defenses and he couldn't Weave fast enough to keep up with her.

His punches too slow as Selene bobbed and weaved, he felt like he was trying to punch the air itself. She let her own punches fly, not as powerful as Matt's but they connected and each one spread the pain throughout his body.

He took two on the arm, one in the rib and, after a playful slap in the face, Matt grunted in frustration. Jumping at her, he threw his arms open wide to cover as much area as possible in hopes of grabbing onto her.

In a flash, she ducked below his right arm, grabbing it and throwing herself up and around, feet landing on his back. Her kick came with a blast of air that sent Matt flailing forward on his face. He stifled a yelp, drawing on his power, he leapt up and turned to hurtle the closest chimney at Selene.

He should have expected her to be in his face, but her speed continually overwhelmed him. Her hand lashed out and struck his throat, he dropped his offense as he reached for his neck. The immediate lack of air burning his lungs. A swift kick from Selene to his legs dropped him to his knees. He struggled to look up at her through teary eyes. He managed to see her leg come back around in a kick that turned his vision black and sent his body crashing to the floor.

He lay there groaning as he tried to hear the words exchanged between the two terrorists.

"Finish him, Selene. We need to get back before she starts," Brutus said.

His vision swam but he stared up at the two, the playfulness in Selene's face evaporated. She seemed to agree turning back to Matt as she ran back toward him. She jumped gathering air behind her, Weaving the blast above her head. Matt attempted to grab what rubble he could, but it was too slow before and he was even more incapable now.

He watched, unable to stop the attack that was coming. She, however, wasn't looking down at him anymore. Her face was turned up and behind him, at the last second she tried to toss her attack in that direction but wasn't fast enough. An air blast, not belonging to her, hit Selene square in the chest. She let out a strangled noise as the wind was pummeled out of her and she plummeted back the way she came.

Feet touched down gently behind Matt, and a familiar hand went to his shoulder. He looked up to see Vin's face, serious but gentle, his hair wild from riding the winds.

"You ok, bud?" He asked.

Matt couldn't contain the smile that broke out over his face, "Well, now I definitely am. Sorry I had to start without you. You were a bit busy."

"All's good. I'm here now." He replied, holding out his hand to help Matt up. Vin stepped up beside him, getting into a ready position.

One hand forward, palm open, and the other holding slightly behind it.

"I see you met my friend; he had a mohawk in Dallas," Vin added.

Brutus looked furious on the other side of the roof, glaring at Vin.

"Eh," Matt offered. "I doubt the haircut did him any favors. Were the beauty marks there before too?" He said in reference to his scars.

"No." Vin grinned, pulling back his right hand Weaving a focused blast of air, "That was when I kicked his ass." He finished the sentence, launching a blast. Selene attempted to blow it off course but couldn't Weave her energy with enough force to; causing her to dodge sideways to the ground.

Mid-dodge she returned with a weak blast of her own, which Vin stopped with his firm, open left hand. Brutus bellowed running toward them hands out to either side as he charged, passing the stone chimney columns as they cracked and broke off, pieces flying with him.

Vin continued pouring energy into the blast he held in his left hand.

"Matt, give me something precise."

Matt nodded, "Like a scalpel," he said, bending low making a sweeping motion that dragged all stray earth toward him. He then began Weaving the stone, compacting it until it was a solid spear of stone. He was still amazed by what he could do with this level of control. Before he just assumed rock was rock, now he could influence the density and precisely mold its shape.

He looked to Vin, who nodded back at him. He took a stance, like one would use to throw a javelin, and with an enhanced push he launched the spear.

Brutus barked a laugh as he drew his rocks together forming a wall that moved with him. Vin fired his shot after the spear.

"DON'T TAKE THAT HEAD ON YOU IDIOT!" Selene bellowed, quickly Weaving her own wave and sending it at the spear.

Like with the frisbee at the park, Vin's air blast caught the spear, shrouding it in energy that rocketed it toward Brutus. Selene's attack was miscalculated, missing the spear due to its enhanced speed.

The impact wasn't anything devastating, no big blast or intense knockback. The spear instead sliced cleanly through Brutus' weak wall like a needle through flesh. Brutus managed a few more steps growing all the slower until he crashed to the ground in a heap of his stones, spear piercing his shoulder, coated in blood.

Selene sat slack on her knees, a look of defeat already in her eyes. They flashed between Matt and Vin; tension stilled the air.

Brutus barely stirred but wasn't dead. Vin met Selene's eyes across the rooftop. Her hand jerked up to her earpiece. A noise gurgled from Brutus' own ear. Vin and Selene's eyes matched in realization as they both thought the same thing. She reached out with her power, snapping Brutus' head back as his earpiece flew toward her on the wind.

Vin Weaved his own air to catch it. Hovering in midair, attempting to be pulled by both Weavers. Matt looked between the two before he dug in deep and launched himself forward.

Panic spread on Selene's face, biting on her lip, she summoned as much energy as she could. With a quick flick of the wrist the wind snapped the earpiece.

Vin let out a gasp as their tug of war ended. Selene danced back to the edge, put a finger to her ear replying to the communication. She then took one look over her shoulder and leaped, catching her body on the wind and disappearing below.

Vin relaxed his stance.

"Huh," Matt said, walking toward the edge she jumped off. "I gotta say, I didn't think she'd back down. I don't think any we've fought so far have backed down."

Vin peered over the edge at the street below, empty, no signs of the Air Weaver.

Vin knew Matt was jesting, but it did raise a disturbing thought. Why were they terrorists? It was easy to just smack a label on them and assume them evil, but how many were like Magdalena? Lost and broken, feeling they only had this kind of option remaining.

Vin looked over to Brutus' body, now completely unmoving. He stored away the guilt for later turning back to Matt.

"Guess she's the only smart one in their group." Vin replied deciding to keep those thoughts to himself for the moment. "Speaking of which." Vin smacked Matt on the arm. Which he reflexively brought a protective hand up.

"On a list of unintelligent and stupid things to do!" Vin scolded.

"I'm sorry ok- I was-" Matt started, but Vin cut him off.

"It doesn't matter." Vin said, his face growing smoother, Matt now noticing how worried he looked. Vin similarly noticed a change in Matt, he didn't want to push his reasoning, their fight hours ago now seemed like nothing. Vin could tell Matt finally felt good, doing something distracted him from his despair.

"I'm here now, so let's hear it. What now? What's the plan?" The rain began again; a light sprinkle. The storm finally catching up with Vin.

"Honestly," Matt began, walking to another edge of the roof. "I'm not sure. I think I was always depending on you to come up with something." Vin joined Matt at the edge as they looked out across the city. Smoke rose from the streets; some fires had even reached the heights of the buildings. Sirens echoed from every direction of the city and they had no idea where to begin looking.

For once, they had really hoped to see some lightning.

Chapter 36

V IN'S FEET TOUCHED down gently on the rooftop, Matt's falling hard half a second after their landing. They had been moving from rooftop to rooftop trying to avoid most of the terrorists and responders. Vin was able to sense Air Weavers before they got too close, allowing them to hide. At this point they were wary of enemies and emergency personnel both, they couldn't afford to be presumed terrorists by the police.

"What's that?" Matt pointed to a rooftop two over. Vin followed his gaze, together they could make out more Weavers.

"I don't think they're the police," Matt cautioned. Vin looked back, biting his lip. He debated going, the terrorists would have the advantage of the high ground, and probably doing a lot of damage. He looked to Matt, but he seemed determined to help as well, seeing the distress on his own face.

They nodded to each other, then Vin took off toward the enemy, sprinting along the roof with Matt right behind him. As they had been, Vin went into a slight slide, gathering air behind him. Matt leaped when he felt the wind below, then Vin launched Matt up and over in a tall arc. Quickly following, Vin flew out afterward but with less height and with more speed. He would quickly outpace Matt, just above him, allowing Matt to grab onto Vin's back as they rode the winds back down to safety.

"There's no purpose to what they're doing here," Vin continued their discussion, still trying to determine where they could look for Magdalena.

"Well, what would ever be the point to aimlessly attacking something?" Matt asked. Vin grew silent in thought as they performed the same maneuver on the next rooftop, their fight would begin after the next jump. He thought back to his military classes, going over different strategies they learned.

"Well a reason to aimlessly attack somewhere, is to disguise what the actual target is." They landed, Matt a little harder that time and he stumbled. Vin kept him on his feet as they continued to charge ahead.

"A distraction then, all this a distraction?" Matt asked.

Vin nodded, "Could be, could just be for the sheer chaos. The Dallas attack had a point, a message." Vin and Matt could now easily see Weavers on the next roof, they launched fire balls and chunks of bricks into the crowd below, who mostly seemed to be police.

"Also, back at their base in Rockwell," Vin continued. "They were discussing specific buildings. It doesn't seem like they've hit anything of meaning yet, at least nothing impactful."

"So we just need to figure out what their real goal is."

"First thing's first," Vin responded, sliding low and launching Matt.

This time Matt dragged chunks of stone and brick from their building, taking it with him over the edge. As soon as they were up in the air the two closest Weavers on the edge facing their jump noticed them, looking up. Matt immediately let the rocks fly from him, pelting them indiscriminately but forcing them to duck for cover.

Instead of landing on Vin's back Matt dropped lower behind him. He grabbed at his legs, decreasing his fall and allowing him to release closer to the roof, flipping and landing. Vin continued to hover past the two Matt began to deal with, taking a brief count. There was one to the right facing north, another facing West and two in the center that looked to be feeding them the elements. Vin and Matt arrived from the East.

Vin inspected the two in the middle, they had opened a hole in the building and were pulling rock and water from broken pipes up and to the surrounding Weavers.

Take out the source *first.* Vin thought. Hovering over the hole he could see that out of the nine-story building, they had dug four stories deep.

"This will work." He said to himself before wrapping his hands across his chest in an X, closing his feet together, pointing his toes, and plunging down into the building. As he spun, he rapidly began Weaving air in and around him, like a falling vortex he dived down. The two above were completely unaware having no time to catch themselves as they were pulled in and fell toward the ground.

At the last second before hitting, Vin broke his fall with a powerful blast of air suspending himself inches from the ground. Quickly drawing back on the wind he shot back up, passing the falling, screaming Weavers and out into the night once again. Vin could see them moving four floors below, but barely.

Matt made quick note of Vin flying off farther along the building. He then glanced left and right, both Weavers now rising from their protective cover. Matt felt the pull of Earth from the right and Water coming from the left. Matt stomped a foot toward the Water Weaver, causing a tremor to grow in magnitude in her direction. She raised a hand to throw her attack but the ground beneath her cracked and then shot up around her legs destabilizing her and causing her to lose concentration on the attack. At the same moment the Earth Weaver behind him flung a chunk of stone that Matt jumped and backflipped over it. It sailed below him and too late did the Water Weaver register the boulder before it crashed into her face.

Upon landing, Matt pushed his momentum and energy into the ground, his back still facing the Earth Weaver. He came up, Weaving the stone to follow him, the floor breaking beneath him in a large piece. Matt angled it toward the Earth Weaver and pushed off. Matt leaped forward from the push and the rock flew backward.

The opposing Earth Weaver attempted to punch into the stone and shatter it. A cracked impact crater appeared in the slab, but Matt had reinforced its density, which left Matt standing in between two unconscious bodies.

The noise of the chaos in the city deafened the Weavers on the rooftop, who ignorantly still fired into the police below. Unaware of Vin, who first launched himself toward the fire Weaver facing north. He almost felt bad when a simple kick sent her flying forward and easily off the edge of the building. He Weaved a current that sent her into the building across from them calculating she most likely would be out cold but not dead.

Vin was distracted as he looked down and didn't register the other Weaver noticed what was going on and attacked Vin while his back was turned.

He whipped around fearing he was too late. The impact of the opponent's attack should have already hit. The presence he felt from behind was no longer that of an enemy but Matt, who stood with an immutable stance, arms extended protecting Vin.

Vin smiled and put a grateful hand on Matt's shoulders. The Earth Weaver immediately began launching the walls and foundation around him. Vin vaulted passing Matt toward the Weaver, diving and spinning around the stones. The Earth Weaver quickly ran out of ammo, so he began targeting the roof below Vin as he ran. Pieces of the roof kept jutting up attempting to displace Vin, or worse. Vin was too agile and could sense the fluctuations in elemental energy. Instead of being hindered by the rocks Vin would use them as steppingstones, like Matt used to launch himself.

Vin leaped the last couple of feet toward the Earth Weaver, who stood dumbstruck as he succumbed to the fact that he had nothing left to throw, lest he risk taking the very ground he stood on. The man could do nothing as Vin came hurtling at him, a swift kick to the chest sent him flying off the edge. Vin reaching forward, created a funnel of air to cushion the man. He still fell hard onto one of the police cars with a sickening crunch, but he would live.

Vin and Matt jogged toward each other and rejoined in the middle; Vin was surprised Matt wasn't out of breath. His skill had grown considerably and hadn't even hesitated to let Matt take on two Weavers on his own.

"Electricity," he immediately spat out when they were in range.

"Huh?" Vin responded.

"If they need to cause havoc, and something more permanent, and they are using Magdalena. It has to do with lightning. Like with most of the anomaly attacks they are usually using something innate to their abilities. The one in Rio used their power to erupt and control a volcano.

"Nova Iguaçu," Vin agreed, remembering the same event. "That makes sense." Vin looked to the edge of the city where the chaos hadn't reached.

They originally wished they could have recovered the photos from Vin's phone but even if they had it probably wouldn't have done much good. There were so many options, and the guards had been arguing as though their plans hadn't been solidified.

"Look for the largest plant or transformer station that's farthest from this area. With any luck," he turned back to look at Matt, who was already drenched in hope and anticipation. "We'll find your sister."

Chapter 37

THEY WERE RACING toward the power grid on bikes, hoping they had it right. Vin didn't have the energy to fly them all the way there. He hadn't wanted to admit how exhausted he felt. Practicing endurance of his abilities had never been something he had done prior to today. The amount of control he exercised allowed him to not waste any of his stamina while Weaving, unlike those that don't have as strong a connection. They are likely to expend too much trying to Weave or their little control causes excess energy to leak out, unused and wasted.

Regardless of Vin's skill, he was growing tired, but he redoubled his efforts as he saw the resolve on Matt's face. They had been able to take public rent-a-bikes almost all the way, thanks to Matt. Vin had left everything but his phone back on the bus. They were coming up on the station; it was eerily quiet, all the more enhanced by the chaos that echoed in the distance.

Arriving at the entrance, two guards stood at the gate. Vin gave Matt a glance and they both thought the same thing,

This didn't look right.

They got off their bikes as one of the guards approached, the one on the right got there first. A man with dark copper hair and mustache, he was thin and wispy. The other guard remained back in the shadows, looking like she was doing something on a tablet.

"Hey now, what're you kids doing here?" he barked. Vin took note of his uniform being all too generic, no logo or visible allegiance. Matt immediately morphed into a whiney adolescent that almost took Vin by surprise.

"We got lost! There's all hell breaking loose in the city! We were just trying to get help, we can't get home!" he whined.

The man just shook his head, "Listen kids, this isn't where you need to be. Go find a police station or something" He answered waving them off.

"Well, can you point us the way?" Vin quickly retorted, his voice cool, an edge of judgement in his tone. The guard looked back, a hint of losing the assumption that they were just simple kids.

"What do I look like? A map? Get lost kids."

Or he doesn't know, since he's not from around here. Vin thought. "Hey, wait-" Vin continued approaching toward the man. He audibly grunted turning to glare at Vin. Matt tackled Vin, spinning around his body and pulling him down. He Weaved a wall of earth to block a blast of air. Vin nodded his thanks. He really was off his game. They poked around the wall, the second guard finished what she was doing and they recognized her.

"Donovan, what the hell are you doing?" Selene called.

They hid back behind the wall, Matt staring toward the ground his hands shaking. Vin reached out gripping them, Matt raised his eyes to meet his. Vin wasn't one hundred percent sure if he saw anxiety or excitement, or perhaps both. Matt whispered one thing. Surer of anything in his life,

"She's here." Matt said.

Vin nodded. "Go save her."

At this Matt kicked back, launching the wall toward the two terrorists. Vin immediately began Weaving a large force of wind drawing the air under Matt and launching him up and over the walls of the facility.

Selene used her powers to Weave a break shield for most of the earth to split around her. The red-haired man, Donovan, flew back slamming against the gate.

Donovan grunted, "Go get the boy Selene!" He yelled. She made attempt to leap into the air, but Vin already met her there, batting her back down to the ground. While falling he Weaved attacks at Donovan who dove and rolled away from the gate to avoid them.

Vin landed lithely, exchanging positions with the terrorists, standing guard between them and Matt.

Good luck, Matt, He thought.

Matt knew nothing about the looming towers of metal and countless wires that were strung about as he ran through the forest of walls and extended pole. He ran past a small building that probably served as a work or break room. He didn't see anyone inside, but it had been disturbed recently and he assumed the stuff inside belonged to the terrorists and not the workers.

He finally found a clearing in the metal trees, the largest of the machines standing in front of him. Large towers rose high above him, clearly the center of the whole operation. Standing there, staring up into the sky was Magdalena.

She was shaking her head, sighing, "I told you to leave it alone, Matt." She said turning. Surprise quickly escaped across her visage as she saw, not an emotional, desperate looking boy, but a rigid and determined man. Matt no longer came to her as the loving, pleading little brother. He stood firm, brows knit together in a scowl.

"I'm not here to talk you down, Mags." He widened his stance, slamming down the left foot, two chunks of stone flew up to hover above his hands.

"I'm here to take you, whether you come willingly or not."

Magdalena shook her head, wiping away her initial shock; replacing it with a scowl to match Matt's. "You think you can bring me in? TAKE ME DOWN?"

Matt didn't flinch. He thought about Vin and Amber, and what she did to them. He knew Vin was good, no great, but even he couldn't bring her down. He realized now however, that he could, the earth around him pulsed as if telling him it was ready to help him. He was her match.

"Yes," he said coolly, confidently.

Disgust flicked across her face as lightning arced around her, she began summoning her energy. No words were left between them. She threw her bolt of lightning, Matt launched his attack preemptively, the lightning crashing into the stone, obliterating it, but the debris hit an invisible wall as Matt Weaved a field to stop it. Matt grew in confidence, *Earth might be the only element that can counter hers*, he thought. Launching for her he threw stone after stone; she, flinging bolt after bolt.

Donovan was a fire Weaver, his flames racing across their little battlefield. Vin clapped his hands Weaving out a force of air to break against. He didn't like his odds, Fire and Air Weavers were usually the ones quick enough to counter and keep up with Vin. His wrist already ached as a blast from Selene had snapped his arm out of one of his prepared attacks, smacking it against the brick wall lining the facility.

He had kept his back to the wall, rotating back and forth along it as they traded blows. The storm continued its way across the city and now began to sprinkle here. Vin was quickly getting whittled down, he only had enough time to dodge or redirect their incoming attacks. Smacking down a blast of fire, igniting a patch of grass close to him, he now stood both arms forward, palms up, breathing heavily.

They stood watching each other in the pause of the fight, Vin's eyes flicked to Donovan, who's then flicked to Selene, who's flicked back to Vin's. He knew he would need to end it soon, somehow. He began recalling his battle strategy classes, but nothing could help him, not with how tired he was now. He glanced over to Donovan and a thought struck him, maybe battle strategy couldn't help, but something more natural would.

He sent a weak blast at Selene, as a feint. Donovan summoned fire to him, but Vin reached out, using what he knew about how the NEDR handled forest fires, he created a suction bubble around Donovan. Vin had to really focus, creating a vacuum that pulled the air out from around Donovan, with no air the flame quickly sputtered and died in his hand.

Donovan looked at it in shock before registering it was also being dragged out of his lunges. Even Selene had looked over in surprise, mouth opening in shock. She eventually recovered turning to stop Vin, but she had once again been surprised to see Vin charging at her. She didn't have time to Weave as Vin entered melee combat with her. She was a good match for Vin, just as quick and just as strong. Every impact shook them, but Vin had the advantage as she kept glancing over her shoulder to see if Vin's Weaving had broken; it hadn't. This was something Vin excelled at; the manipulation let him focus on his Weaving while not needing to directly look at it. He could feel his power and control it while in combat with Selene. She grunted in frustration, Donovan turning blue as he fell to his knees clutching at his throat and chest.

Selene tried to break from the fight to throw a disrupting air blast, but Vin was able to refocus and double the strength of the swirling vacuum to deflect Selene's attack.

She screamed in frustration, "WHO ARE YOU?" screeching as she let all her reserves go and flew at Vin tackling him with her enhanced speed, causing them to roll and tumble away.

They both looked up to see the vacuum finally fade away, Donovan dropping to the ground unmoving. Vin let out a breath of relief. He had taken out one enemy, one more to go. Bringing his attention back to Selene, he saw rage beginning to take over and realized he may not be making it to Matt after all.

Lightning fell from the sky as Magdalena Weaved it. Matt grabbing the power from below, Weaving the earth's energy through him, bringing his arms above his head creating an umbrella of stone over him. The lightning crashed down onto it, the impact causing cracks and pieces flying off, but this time Matt kept it whole. Magdalena started, "What?" she muttered. She was caught off guard as Matt then launched the stone at her. Diving out of the way, she watched as it crashed into the large box behind her.

Matt winced as he realized the poor decision that had been. The transformer began sparking. Magdalena looked at it, then reached out and began Weaving it, causing bolts to fly indiscriminately across the area. Matt's eyes widened in shock as he took his turn to dive out of the way. As he rolled, he Weaved the earth to follow and created a small lip to hide behind as the electricity sparked and crashed against it.

A couple of seconds after he couldn't feel the electricity colliding with his makeshift cover, he peaked over. Magdalena's fist flew toward him, electricity crackling in her fingers. Matt gasped, reflexively he snapped his hand out. It smashed through his small impromptu defense; Weaving the stones to act as a glove around his hand as he caught her fist.

The electricity had no effect and she let out a cry as she snapped back her arm after the crunch her hand made in the impact. She cradled her hurt hand in her good one, she doubled over breathing in sharp gasps.

Matt crawled to his knees, "Maggie, I'm- I'm so sorry." Losing his will to fight. Magdalena dropped to her knees, she sounded like she was crying, tears fell across her cheeks and raindrops joined them. Then her cries turned to laughter as she raised her face to bark her laughs into the air.

"You think this is pain, Mateo?" she stopped laughing to glare at him. "I'm quite familiar with pain, brother. Every laugh, every judgmental glare. Every dark depressing day where I felt so truly in that moment that I'd never be happy again." She shook her head.

"Don't you understand? I *need* to do this. Justice for me and my people," her eyes flashed back to sympathy, "our people. It's the only thing I have left."

"Maggie, I-" his words lost in his throat. Her pain overwhelmed him. Matt didn't want to hurt her, never wanted to. She had to know how much he loved her.

His hand slowly reached toward her, "Mags, you have me. I love y-" pain flared through his body. So quick the shock flew through him that the pain was gone as quickly as it came, and the words died on his lips as he slipped into unconsciousness.

Vin's head snapped back hitting the ground below him as Selene's fist smacked into him again. She was on top of him, her legs on both of his arms pinning him. Blood leaked from his nose, draining into his mouth. He turned sideways to cough it up, trying not to breath in his own blood.

"You're kind of amazing, whoever you are," she smiled down at him.

She was bleeding on her face too, a busted lip, her left arm hung back, Vin bent it at a wrong angle earlier in their fight.

"Please stop punching me, if you think I'm so amazing," Vin coughed out. The rain fell on them, washing the blood away. A sly smiled escaped her lips and admitted,

"I wish I could. You could do amazing things with us. I wish more of the Weavers would understand what we're doing, how we can't let *them* treat us like this."

"By striking fear into *everyone's* hearts?" He tried to summon his energy, to Weave, but he was tired, and the pressure on his arms was disrupting his flow.

"If that's what it takes! We have to fight; we *can't* stop fighting."

Vin wheezed out a laugh. "I gotta say, Selene? Right? I'm so tired." He closed his eyes as he whispered, "So tired of fighting."

Selene looked at him sympathetically. "I wish I could stop, Vincent, but he told me to kill you, and I won't go against him."

Vin's eyes snapped open; she knew his name. "Wait, who?"

Selene didn't get to answer, her face drew in surprise and she looked around as she began to notice the rain stopped falling and water was pooling up around them. Too late did she try jumping back, the water surging up and around her. She was caught in a mini waterspout that began spinning her around. She let out a yell as it whipped her around before the tip finally released her, Selene's body launched into the wall crashing into it and falling silent.

Vin just stared in awe at her unmoving form. He winced, raising himself to a sitting position. He scanned the area, not realizing how little his senses were working until he finally felt her. Amber jogged toward him; Vin falling into her as she wrapped her arms around him.

"You made it." He whispered. She just shook her head, lips pressed against his head.

"Where's Matt, Magdalena?" she asked.

"They're inside," Vin managed. She pulled back and looked at him.

"Vin, we have to go. Now. Someone's hunting you, hunting us."

He looked over to Selene's form, "She mentioned someone was after me." Amber nodded in agreement.

"He attacked just after you left Galveston." Vin's head snapped up to look at her, concern on his face. She shook her head, "I'm fine, he ran, and I left right after him. He was some foreign-looking guy, I don't think he was from around here. He was bald, like a monk or something."

Vin's head raced back, almost four years ago, to the day of his Attunement.

"Bald monk?" *It couldn't be, could it?* Vin thought. "What did he Weave?" Vin asked.

"He was a Water Weaver." Amber answered, with hesitation in her voice at the relevance.

Vin let out a sigh of relief, recalling the Fire Weaver monk that day of his Attunement, then Amber helped him to his feet, urgently. Vin hadn't noticed it at first, but he now felt it, a powerful source of energy.

From the street a figure walked toward them, so smooth he almost looked like he was gliding. Vin almost choked; his memories came to life as the monk that helped him years ago arrived before him.

He looked to see Amber panicked. "Amber it's alright, he's different."

"Who are you?" Vin called out. "Are you here to help us? Is the man that attacked Amber an old member of your order or something?"

He didn't respond, but Amber clawed at his arm, dragging him back. "Vin...that *is* the man that attacked me."

Vin looked back at her, terror on her face, "But you said he was a Water Weaver?"

Amber slowly nodded her head, "He is."

Vin focused back on the man; his two arms were raised. Both hands with an orb of water draining like a waterfall. His gliding wasn't a trick of their sight, his feet didn't touch the ground as he suspended himself with air. The ground cracked beneath him as stones rose, rotating in a tight circle around his abdomen. Then, just above his head, a spark lit a bright flame flickering like the gem of a crown on his brow.

Vin understood Amber's terror now, he understood that this man, was Weaving each element.

Chapter 38

IMPOSSIBLE. VIN wanted to say, but this man was clearly standing in front of him, all four elements at his control. If he couldn't believe his eyes, he trusted his senses as he felt the monk drawing on each of the elements.

"I don't understand," Vin said confused.

Amber's brace shoved him back as she strode forward, no longer looking scared, just determined.

"He means to kill us Vin," she lashed out, Weaving a flood of water that broke against an air shield surrounding the monk. Amber now understood what had happened back in Galveston when he broke free, it wasn't just water he Weaved, but air to escape.

"I see we are apparently behind schedule, the girl has still yet to take out the power to the city," he drolled, "I'm assuming the brother interfered." He gave them a once over, a look of disinterest. "I suppose I'll have to go check on that." He turned to hover off, but Vin finally recovered from his shock, jumping toward the monk, Weaving a blast of air from two forward kicks and then a palm thrust.

The monk looked over his shoulder, a smile on his face as he weaved to the right dodging the two kicks and then catching Vin's third attack, the same move he had used on Selene back on the rooftops.

"Oh good, I was hoping you'd want to fight. It looked like it had been beaten out of you." He sneered before returning the air blast, amplified with more energy. Amber pressed forward, drawing her hand up Weaving the water to follow then quickly raised her second hand up in a chopping motion. The water followed her call as it thinned and sliced upward, splitting the air blast disturbing its formation and allowing it to diminish before it hit Vin.

Vin used the dying winds, reaching out with his own two hands Weaving more blasts. The monk drew fire from above him shooting two flames, forcing Vin to use his attack to defend against them. The monk following up with a forward stomp with his right foot, shooting a fissure of rock. With his left hand he launched an air blast that hurtled for Amber.

Vin leaped forward passing over the fissure, spinning he sent a wave to push the blast off course, but he didn't have time to react as water from underneath him shot up hitting him square in the front launching him up spitting and sputtering. Amber slammed her hand forward, launching the Wave the monk just used, speeding it toward him, quickly pulling the water from Vin's lungs.

He was able to recover midair, spinning and floating back toward Amber. The wave broke around a wall of earth, then the monk pushed forward, breaking through the wall and sending the stones and himself flying toward Amber and Vin. A wave of water from Amber spun around them, slapping the stones away. The wave was then broken as the monk tore through it, now placed between the two of them.

It was so fast Amber couldn't do anything, having been left wide open from the water wall, a palm smacked her hard in the face at the same time Vin reached up to strike, but never connected after receiving a kick in his chest. They both flew from the monk, sliding against the ground. Vin looked to Amber who still seemed unharmed and quick to return to her feet. Vin wished he felt even a quarter of the same. He reached for his chest as something warm and wet fell from him. The monk's foot laced with earth that punctured his skin. Everything in him flared with pain, he was so overwhelmed he didn't know how to continue fighting, so he decided to change tactics.

"Matt stopped her," Vin said, more into the ground. Trying to ignore the wound in his chest, still struggling to get up. "He stopped Magdalena; your plan failed. Whatever brainwashing you tried failed, she won't continue to help you destroy the peace Weavers are trying to create."

He looked over to Amber and he saw concern on her face, and he only now comprehended how wrong his words were.

"I don't really care," the monk said, "I don't care about her. Her abilities were simply a means to destroying her and her world." He made a motion to Amber, "Like I told the young Water Weaver, I'm not here to save Weavers from the oppression of those without power." He looked over to Vin and he saw in the monk's eyes unadulterated disgust and hatred. "I'm here to destroy them and all of you."

How? Vin thought. *How had he not sensed this those many years ago.* A crackle in the air disrupted his thought, his attention brought to the gates.

"Angyo!" Magdalena shouted. Electricity rippled along her skin, tears streaked along her face and a rage so deep poured out from her.

"You. Used me?" she asked, "You told me-"

"Yes, yes I know what I told you. Guess you finally heard the truth."

He smirked and spoke heartbreaking words, "I don't care about you or your pathetic little plight, child."

Magdalena roared a guttural scream so violent Vin fell back, pushing himself away as she shot forward, riding lightning. The monk, Angyo, began countering her. Blocking with Earth and returning with Air, Water and Fire attacks.

Vin hadn't seen Amber, using the ensuing battle as a distraction, get around to him. She crouched holding onto him, her cool demeanor shattered, fear and worry lining her face. Vin could only assume he looked ten times worse.

"Are you ok?" She asked, shaking her head at the ridiculousness of the question. Her hand went to his bleeding chest. She then pointed back from where Magdalena came.

"Look." She told him. Vin did so, but couldn't see what she was looking at, then he noticed it. Someone laying, unmoving, on the ground inside the gate. With help from Amber they got up and ran to him, hoping the stray lightning wouldn't strike them. Vin's eyes quickly followed the battle, it was more intense than anything he had seen before, and he faced hurricanes.

Lightning flew from Magdalena, shattering trees, exploding walls. She was wild, a force of destruction. Angyo was a scalpel; Vin once thought he was too, but not like that. He stepped aside as lightning passed him by just a hair, returning each strike with careful precision, slowly whittling her down. Vin thought how astounding his elemental affinity must be, it wasn't luck, he was sensing the lightning and dodging it. If Vin hadn't also fought Magdalena, he wouldn't have known how impossibly insane that was.

They reached Matt and looked him over, Vin checking his pulse. He looked up to Amber nodding,

"He's fine. I think just shocked unconscious or something."

"Can you do something?" Amber asked.

"I…don't know, actually." He thought about it, *Could he?* He reached back out to sense Amber's energy, he could still feel it, they were connected. He looked back to Matt and tried the same, he could sense Matt's energy. The same way he Weaved into the elements, Vin made the attempt to do the same as he had with Amber back on the beach. He tried to wrap his own energy around Matt, poking and prodding trying to connect with it. He started to sense more from Matt than he initially anticipated. Fear, apprehension, loss. The idea of hope gone.

Matt's energy began stirring, reacting to Vin's. He thought of every happy memory, every positive experience, every wish of the future and willed it through his power. Suddenly the connection slipped together, combining their energy. Matt's eyes shot open in a gasp, they looked around frantically before seeing Amber standing above him, then finally settling on Vin.

"Vin? I-I feel y-" he was disrupted as Amber shrieked.

"VIN!"

A body crashed into the wall of the complex, close to Selene's. Vin looked over to see Magdalena's crumpled form, electricity briefly sparking over her body before stopping completely.

"MAGGIE!" Matt screamed, running to her. Vin looked over to see Angyo, standing smugly without a scratch on him. Vin stood, his hands out in surrender. Amber right behind him, a hand on his shoulder. Her energy and his thrumming powerfully, Matt's and his still connected as well. He huddled over his sister, cradling her but he appeared to understand their new bond, energy flowing together. Vin didn't know if he was mistaken or not, but he felt better. His pain seemed to dim; strength returning.

"I still remember what you told me that day," Vin spoke to Angyo. His confidence stunning even himself, but he felt peace, for the moment; surrounded by his friends.

"Before my Attunement. What you said changed me. It helped me understand the elements. *You* helped me understand the elements. I wouldn't be the Weaver I am today without you. You see? We can be taught, we can change." Vin urged.

Amber stepped forward, with Vin. "He's right. And he's not alone. Vin used what *you* taught him to help Mateo. I've seen it." She bit her lips in thought, trying to understand even herself what she was trying to say. "Humans were given this power, by Earth itself, it chose *US,* to be its guardians."

Angyo closed his eyes in thought. He almost seemed pained, finally speaking.

"I stood on top of mountains, meditating and being taught that inner-enlightenment was the answer. I sat on top of mountains, feeling the destruction humans caused running rampant with this amazing power."

He opened his eyes again, and Vin knew he failed.

"The Earth chose wrong, child."

Angyo stomped forward, his hands raised, fingers spread. The earth behind Vin, Amber and Matt trembled before large spikes of rock shot out and forward. Vin and Amber dropped before they were skewered, Matt and Magdalena already being low enough to avoid being impaled. The wall of Earth spread long claws above them, no escape.

Angyo gathered wind in his hands and then spun before a full force of it slammed against them. Vin barely managed to create a wall that lessened the blast in front of him and Amber, but it couldn't completely stop it. It took everything he had to stop them from flying back to their death. He looked to Amber whose head was bowed against the wind, she was now a foot or so from him. Looking to Matt he saw that he had raised a wall in front of him as he held on to his sister's body trying to keep it from helplessly falling back. He looked strained as he struggled to keep it together, pieces of the wall breaking off and smashing against their doom.

Angyo stood, hands forward perpetually calling the wind, no longer smiling, just stone-faced and determined.

Amber slipped backward, "No!" He yelled reaching for her.

She reached for him in return, but they were too far away. He looked into her eyes as she slowly inched backward. She wanted to keep her own open, if there was going to be one last thing to see, she wanted it to be Vin and lose herself in the forest of his eyes. However, her eyes began to water due to the harshness of the wind.

Vin watched her close her eyes against it, he thought maybe if they could use some water, they could ice her a hand hold. He reached with his power, but it was hard to grasp hers. Angyo's power wasn't just disrupting them elementally, but the force of it blurred the human energy. Vin opened his eyes again as he stared in horror at Amber's inevitable fate. He wouldn't hold her anymore, never sense her energy again. He shut his eyes once more, reaching again with his power and hand, trying against all hope to link with her one last time.

Vin's eyes snapped open in shock realization as a thought struck him. Vin looked back to the monk. He didn't need to attack elemental energy.

Vin couldn't feel Matt and Amber anymore. Just the overwhelming force of Angyo. He reached out, but instead of trying to find the force of his elemental energy he found something else; Angyo's human energy. Vin pushed forward, not Weaving his ability against the air but to the source controlling it. He began pushing against it, forcing it back. Vin felt something, physically, and he almost laughed out loud with joy. The wind was losing its strength.

He looked back at Amber, who had opened her eyes realizing the same thing.

"I can stop him!" Vin shouted. He looked over to Matt who was poking out over his wall. "Attack him! Now! With everything you've got!"

Vin pushed harder against Angyo's power, forcing it back. Amber didn't hesitate. As soon as she was able, she launched herself up and began dragging the water that had been pushed to the spiked wall behind them. In a powerful blast she Weaved a constant stream of pressurized water. Matt placed Magdalena down gently and hopped over his wall. He stalked forward, rage enveloping him, each step pounding deep into the earth, then he ground his position and began Weaving a stream of stone, pulled from around him and the spiked wall.

The two waves crashed into Angyo's wall of wind. His eyes widened in surprise and confusion. He tried harder to push the wind, and Vin could feel him fighting to regain complete control. Angyo began to fathom he couldn't continue the wall anymore, grunting and retreating to a more condensed defense. The abilities of Matt and Amber struck relentlessly against him. Angyo was using everything he had: hardened rock, whipping winds, rotating waters. Vin grunted in frustration as his energy pushed onto his, becoming so difficult now to hold his back. He couldn't do anymore. He couldn't staunch his abilities anymore. They needed something more.

Electricity crackled in the air. From his peripheral he saw a bolt fly past and hit Angyo's defenses. Magdalena stomped toward him, shooting bolt after bolt until she reached the line Matt, Amber and Vin held. She seemed to draw on everything she had and launch a constant torrent of plasma into Angyo and his elements. With this added strength, the group's attack became strong enough to push him back.

Vin could immediately feel Angyo struggle to hold the power back. He began pushing again, flooding everything he had into battering down Angyo's energy, lashing back at his in defiance. He began feeling emotions he knew weren't his own. A peaceful mountain turned to a cacophonous avalanche. Raging fires, dying oceans, broken earth. Vin let out a yell in exertion. Pain popped along his body, skin splitting along his back, something wet streaked from his eyes; hopefully tears.

He felt pain, hopeless and endless pain as the world he loved was poisoned and abused. Angyo began yelling back, fear resonating in his voice. The whole battlefield was drowned in screams of every Weaver and their power. Until finally Vin's power snapped around Angyo, his human energy trapped. In this moment Vin understood everything Angyo felt, all his passions and pain. Vin too broke and fell, whether it was tears or blood he wept in earnest now. The elements, in that moment, no longer heeded Angyo's command and the full force of Amber, Matt and Magdalena ripped through him.

Chapter 39

V IN FELL INTO DARKNESS and silence took its place over the area. His ears finally heard the shuffling of feet and felt Amber reach down for him. His senses felt fried, singed, unable to reach out for Amber even if he tried. She grabbed his arm and boosted him.

"Can you walk?" she whispered kindly. Vin managed a nod, but still used her help as they hobbled over to Matt and Magdalena, who stood over Angyo. His corpse was hardly recognizable. His body was blackened, and mutilated. Vin looked away, horrified for more than one reason, and they left the area together in silence.

They made their way far enough from their little warzone, a couple of buildings over, and found a semi-empty parking lot save for a couple of parked cars. Amber lowered Vin to the ground, who grunted as pain flared along his back and arms. Magdalena walked on ahead, looking aimlessly around at the dark stores. She looked worse for wear as well but okay enough.

Amber sat down next to Vin; Matt continued standing.

"That was…incredible." Matt managed, then nodded toward his sister. "I gotta go talk to her." Vin managed a nod in return, and he left them to go talk to his sister.

Vin fell against Ambers arms; she slowly stroked his hair.

"It's really over," Vin whispered. "We're all alive, safe." He sighed. "We can finally go home, all of us."

Amber hummed peacefully, looking over at Matt and Magdalena talking. "Yeah, we can." She didn't sound like she believed the words, and Vin refused to admit he didn't either.

Matt came back over, but Magdalena continued to stay back. Vin finally stood, sore but able.

"She ok?" He asked Matt.

Matt smiled, "Yeah, we're good." He looked down and away, "We're gonna be fine."

Vin couldn't help but think to the future, the one they planned. College, together, beaches on the weekend, fighting over stupid things in their dorm rooms.

"She can't stay, you know that Vin. There's too much for her to figure out, to deal with, and that's not even if the police or someone worse is looking for her."

Vin's tears started before his brain came to the realization he refused to acknowledge. Amber's gripped tightened in comfort. Tears started in Matt's eyes as well, and Vin's thoughts of the future shattered all at once at the next words that came out of his mouth.

"I'm going with her."

Vin and Matt fell into a hug.

"I know, Matty. I guess I always knew."

Matt let out a halfhearted laugh. "But you hoped anyway." They pulled back Matt shaking his head. They wiped away their tears, Matt turned to Amber. She smiled sweetly even with tears stinging her own eyes. They hugged.

"Take care of him, won't you?"

"Of course, Matty." They released and Matt flashed a smile back to Vin.

"Don't lose this one. She'll keep you grounded; you need that."

Vin nodded, "I'll always keep hope, for both of you." He said nodding to Magdalena, who met his eyes. A silent exchange was made, with Magdalena finally turning and making her way to one of the vehicles.

The three stood holding hands, letting the rest of their goodbye remain silent. Magdalena drove up in one of the cars. Vin didn't know how she started it, but she assumed hot-wiring may have come natural to her. He added a second case of grand theft auto to their night. Matt gave one last long hug to Vin, nodding to Amber and walking around to the passenger side.

Magdalena looked at Vin through the open window. "I can never thank you enough for how much you cared for Mateo. The sibling I always wished I could have been if I had stayed."

Vin reached out and squeezed her hand, Magdalena returning it.

From her other hand she pulled something out, it looked like a necklace, with a small strange piece hanging on it.

"This was the only thing I found on Angyo's body. I'm not quite sure what it means. Any ideas?"

Vin took it in his hand and looked it over. A metal of some kind, it looked to be missing a piece, broken most likely in the attack. Vin shook his head,

"No idea." He said handing it back.

Magdalena nodded. Matt leaned forward in his seat to look at Amber and Vin. He looked sad, but hopeful. Vin couldn't think of a more bittersweet moment for him. Vin and Amber took a step back together, she wrapping a comforting arm around his.

"Be safe." Vin whispered.

Magdalena nodded then put it in gear and pulled out. Vin could barely make out Matt looking at them through the back window before they passed from the streetlights and back into darkness.

Vin and Amber followed them to the road and watched them drive away. Amber hugged a little tighter looking at him,

"We'll see them again Vin."

Vin smiled, earnestly. Using his abilities again to sense Matt's connection to him. It grew faint but Vin was sure when he wanted to, he'd be able to find it.

"I know we will."

Epilogue

NAP

Amber sat on her towel, toes dug into the cool sand.

Snap

She looked out along the beach, Vin stood on the shore's edge, water lapping against his feet. The moon was big and brilliant, he looked to have his eyes closed turned up toward the sky.

Snap

He left his vigil walking from the shore, bare chested with swimming trunks on, his hair wild in the wind. Like veins of silver the moonlight reflected his white scars on his chest and back, but Amber was more concerned with the scars within. He came back to her, leaning into a kiss before sitting down.

"I've been thinking," he said, rubbing a warm finger along her exposed arm. "I can feel something, a pull."

Amber nodded, "The Pilgrimage?"

"I think so. I'm not sure what else it could be."

"I feel it too. The elements calling me there."

Vin raised an eyebrow with a knowing smirk on his lips. "Elements?" he asked, emphasizing the plural.

Snap

Fire light ignited their eyes. Once again, she was lost in his leafy eyes, and he in hers, so full of life. The flickering flame danced on Amber's fingertips before them.

"Elements," she assured, tossing the flame to the side igniting their small bonfire they had laid out in front of their spot on the beach.

He reached up to caress her cheek. "You're amazing, you know that?"

She pressed her lips into his, "Then we make a matching pair," she said, pulling back.

They held each other, long into the night. Surrounded by the soft sand, warm fire, peaceful waves and gentle breeze.

Thanks for reading!

PLEASE ADD A REVIEW ON AMAZON AND LET ME KNOW WHAT YOU THOUGHT!

AMAZON REVIEWS ARE VERY HELPFUL FOR AUTHORS, THANK YOU FOR TAKING THE TIME TO SUPPORT ME AND MY WORK. DON'T FORGET TO SHARE YOUR REVIEW ON SOCIAL MEDIA WITH THE HASHTAG #WEAVERS AND ENCOURAGE OTHERS TO READ THE STORY TOO!

DON'T FORGET TO SIGN
UP FOR THE MONTHLY
NEWSLETTER

FOR SPECIAL OFFERS, GIVEAWAYS,
DISCOUNTS, BONUS CONTENT,
UPDATES FROM THE AUTHOR, INFO
ON NEW RELEASES AND MORE:

WWW.WALKERWRITESNOVELS.COM

Acknowledgments

Going on almost three decades strong I have almost always had a story in my head. Every car ride, every quiet moment, every uneventful class, I found myself lost in the stories I dreamed up. I am extremely proud and humbled I could finally put a story from my head onto the page and there are so many people to thank for that.

I want to first thank those whose stories inspired the ones in this book. If you found a little something of your life in these pages, I hope it was represented respectfully. I discussed some tough topics either directly or indirectly and it was never my intention to misuse traumas or life experiences for simple entertainment. So to those who feel the characters or moments in this book seem familiar, I want to thank you for your courage and hope you know you are not alone.

Specifically to this book I must thank all my beta-readers. Kelci Peterson, Vic, Samantha Secord, and Joram Van Vugt! I could not have come to this final version without their insight and time. As always, to YOU, my reader as well. It blows my mind that my stories could be in someone else's head now. Seriously, I appreciate you more than you could know, and I hope you return for any future stories I pull from this noggin.

I need to also thank my partner Andrew; whose technical know-how made a lot of the complicated aspects of publishing a book infinitely easier. His ever-present ear as I talked my stream of consciousness to him would not have allowed me to get my ideas out properly otherwise.

I of course need to thank my parents who were always excited for me to follow my passions. Even if those passions did not have the results I wanted, their encouragement let me know I could keep trying until I found what stuck.

Lastly, as an engrossing theme in this book would suggest, friendship is especially important to me. Many stories I have dreamed were inspired from friends that have come and gone in my life. Even if we do not communicate any more, wherever life takes us, they will always be in my heart and mind.

This is to all the bonds I made in my life, and to the ones that helped shape my first novel.

This is thanks to you:

NR, JE, FE, KP

John Walker is a Texas-based author of Fantasy and YA books. He attempted Art College at the University of North Texas. Though he decided it was not for him he did take his first study abroad trip to Italy which remains an inspiration and highlight for him to this day. After graduating with his Associate's of Art from Collin College he spent his years drifting from different jobs and enjoying his passion for art, video games, and even cooking. After settling down to his first 8-5 desk job he rekindled his passion for reading. Finally, in 2019, he was inspired by the NaNoWriMo challenge to write a novel in 30 days, and so was born his first written story. He continues to love drawing, reading, writing, his Partner and their two Huskie pups, Nova and Mira.

Connect with John on:
Website: www.walkerwritesnovels.com
Instagram: @walkerwrites7
Youtube: http://www.youtube.com/walkerwrites7

Printed in Great Britain
by Amazon